INCURABLE

ALSO BY JOHN MARSDEN

INCURABLE

THE ELLIE CHRONICLES

JOHN MARSDEN

SCHOLASTIC INC.

NEW YORK   TORONTO   LONDON   AUCKLAND   SYDNEY
MEXICO CITY   NEW DELHI   HONG KONG   BUENOS AIRES

Warm thanks for help in writing *Incurable* to, in no particular order, Sianon Daley, Sam and Lou Marsden, Susan Kirk, Warwick Kirk, Michelle Mitchell, Ronda Gawley, Grant Breadsell, Peter Richardson, Tom McCrabb, Annalyce O'Keefe.

ISBN-13: 978-0-439-78322-4
ISBN-10: 0-439-78322-4

Copyright © 2005 by Jomden Pty Ltd. All rights reserved.
Published by Scholastic Inc. SCHOLASTIC and associated logos
are trademarks and/or registered trademarks of Scholastic, Inc.

12 11 10 9 8 7 6 5 4 3 2 1   8 9 10 11 12 13/0

Printed in the U.S.A.   40

First printing, September 2008

TO PHILIP AND FAYE O'CARROLL,
AND TIM BERRYMAN...
"THE HIGHEST WISDOM IS KINDNESS."

CHAPTER 1

CHAPTER 1

WHEN THE COCKIES SPREAD THEIR WINGS AND FLOAT from one branch to another they hang for a moment, like they're caught in an eddy of air. Then they choose their landing pad and settle, with a squawk and a shrug of their shoulders. They go for a strut along the branch, their yellow crests flaring. If they had hands they'd beat their chests. They're pretty smug. You can chase them off a fruit tree or a barley crop or the back of a wheat truck but you never defeat them: they're the birds of defiance.

Against an overcast sky it's shocking to see how white they are. They're the whitest things in the world, not that there's ever been a World Cup for whiteness. Not as far as I know.

We were moving a mob of cattle along a dirt road in the bush, over the ford where the winter water flows, through the gum trees, underneath the cockatoos screeching the neighbourhood news.

It was a big mob, three hundred head, cows and steers, and there were some big beasts among them. But they were in no hurry. I had plenty of time to look up at the cockies.

On the left was Mr Farrar's place, where his fat black cattle grazed. I dribbled with love and envy every time I saw his main paddock. It was protected by lines of old manna gums, had a bit of a hill in the far corner, and the creek was its western boundary. I've never seen that creek dry up and I've never seen that paddock bare. The grass grew like it was showing off. You could run a hundred head in that paddock and not need to go near them from one year to the next, except to take their photographs for centrefolds in cattle magazines. In the whole district this was my favourite paddock.

Mr Farrar's bull waddled to the fence to check out the passing talent. He had a body the size of a furniture van and balls the size of truck tyres. All the cows in the mob wanted to have a chat. I could imagine the conversation. "Nice bit of rump steak on you, sweetheart." "Well, thank you. You doing anything tonight?" "Why wait till tonight? Just jump this barbed wire and I'm yours." "Oh yes, the barbed wire. We could have a problem with the barbed wire . . ."

Then this annoying human comes up on a noisy Suzuki and kicks out at the lady's attractive bum and yells something like, "Come on you old bag of hamburger meat . . ." and romance dies.

The annoying human was Alastair Young, helped by me banging my hand on the side of the ute or yelling or, in extreme cases, stopping the ute and getting out to flush a steer from a thicket of young trees and blackberries. The cattle belonged to Alastair's father, who was in his ute at the front of the mob. Keeping them moving was Alastair's sister, Shannon, on horseback, and Gavin, the little guy who lives with me. Gavin had our Yamaha. Mr Young had his dogs and I had Marmie, but I kept her in the cab of the ute most of the time.

The main thing was to stop the stock spreading out over too great a distance, but it wasn't difficult. They were pretty well-behaved. We'd have to work a bit when we got them to the main road, where there'd be traffic, but no-one used this road much. I could just poke along, sneaking up behind Alastair and bumping his bike with the ute when he was distracted by a noisy cow, chatting to Shannon for a minute when she came back to get a drink, waving to Gavin in the distance.

Gavin must have been in a good mood. He waved back and gave me a huge smile. Normally if I made any contact with him in public he looked at me like I was a demented stranger suffering from impaired vision. We were all skipping school, and for Gavin that was a good start to any day; besides, he had taken to life on the land like he was born wearing a Drizabone and an Akubra. For him this was better than a trip to Disneyland. Well, OK, maybe not a trip to Disneyland, but it was the kind of stuff he loved to do.

How strange his life had been already, and how unpredictable. From the little I'd learnt about him, he'd been brought up in a pretty crappy suburb in a pretty crappy family, no dad, just a stepdad who he'd mentioned once and then stopped with an expression like he'd bitten into an unripe olive.

Then he had survived a war, firstly by living like a rat in the ruins of Stratton, then by getting picked up by my friends and me and taken to a valley in the bush, and if that wasn't enough, gatecrashing our guerrilla campaign when he refused to catch a rescue helicopter to New

Zealand. After the war no trace of his family could be found, so he moved in with me and my parents.

And just when his life was starting to settle a bit, he and I were hit by an event so awful I couldn't even think about it that moist winter morning, as we moved the cattle from the Youngs' place to ours.

It's no good though. When you decide you won't think about something you can think of nothing else. It's like Tolstoy's brothers telling him that the secrets of the universe would be revealed if he stood in the corner of the room without thinking of a white horse. As I tried not to think about the death of my parents the mist moistened my face. The cockies suddenly sounded like they were a kilometre away and their squawks became desperate and savage.

Where does the salt in tears come from? Do we have little salt mines behind our eyes? Does the body somehow extract it from Vegemite and pump it from the mouthful of toast in your tummy, up to the head, storing it for future use? Tasting a tear as it trickled down my cheek I wondered about that. Fi had said to me just the other day, on the phone, "You seem to have a fit of sadness suddenly, and after a while it goes and you're back to normal until the next one."

"Is that strange? What do other people do?"

"I think they're probably depressed all the time for a while and then they gradually start to improve again."

"Oh, OK."

"What does that mean? Are you offended?"

"Oh no, not at all. I was just thinking about it and wondering if you were right."

But privately I thought I had both kinds of sadness.

I stopped the ute and went back for a cow I hadn't noticed, a little red scrubber who'd found a yummy patch of herbivorous matter in a dip beside a fence. I swatted at her and she took off with a clumsy stumble of the front legs, lurching up the slope.

We were using the Youngs' walkie-talkies and as I got back to the ute Mr Young called me up. It was a relief to hear his voice after the endless swearing of the truckies. No matter what channel you used on the walkie-talkies, you got the endless swearing of the truckies.

"We're just coming up to the pavement, Ellie. How are you going back there?"

"The last ones are . . ." I looked around for a landmark. I'd nearly said, "At the ute," which wouldn't have helped much. "Near that old windmill on the Farrar place."

"OK, that's pretty good. Shannon and Gavin and I'll hold them here till you bring them up. I don't like this moisture though. It'll make the road slippery, and some of these trucks are flying."

Alastair and I started to push a bit now, leaving the cockatoos behind. When we caught up with the others Mr Young gave me the signs to put out on the road. They were hand-painted, just two words, *Slow Stock*, a bit ambiguous I thought but I didn't think Mr Young would appreciate a lecture about punctuation.

As well as encouraging semitrailers not to plough into the mob at a hundred k's an hour, my other job was to shut the gates. Each driveway or paddock got its gate shut, to stop the cattle wandering into places they shouldn't go. You just hoped people didn't want to get out of their own driveways while we were going past.

There was plenty of feed here to keep the mob happy, and a rest would do them good. They'd already come eight kilometres.

When we started off again the atmosphere was totally different. Now we were out on the Wirrawee-Holloway Road, and we needed to move these beasts along. I went in front, still driving the ute, then came Shannon on her horse and Gavin on the Yamaha, keeping the stock off the road, then Alastair opening the gates again, and finally Mr Young bringing up the rear, driving like me, slow and flashing, hazard lights going with that monotonous, annoying, loud *tick-tock* that could give you a headache if you listened for long enough.

I didn't feel like having a headache though. It was too good a day, even if it was flavoured with sadness.

Alastair was using his dad's dogs. As well as opening the gates I'd closed, he and his gaggle of mongrels had the job of picking up any cows that fell back and were at risk of dropping behind the ute. Some of them were tough-looking dogs, so I kept Marmie with me, although it caused her a lot of grief. She made it obvious that I wouldn't be forgiven, until the next mealtime at least.

Probably the busiest out of all of us was Alastair, but that's only a guess, as I was too far ahead to know. I heard the occasional comment on the walkie-talkie though. "Get behind her, Alastair." "She's trying to get through the fence." "There's a couple of cars coming through." (That was me.) "Mr Nelson coming through in his Landrover." (That was Mr Young.) "Watch for that big ugly red girl, Alastair." "They're all ugly, Dad, hadn't you noticed?"

Alastair was shining with pride. Normally his big brother would be doing this job, but Sam was away at Brogan, the Ag College, checking it out for next year.

"Ellie, did you say the cattle-truck gate into the Perreiras' was open?"

"No. Leave it shut, Alastair."

There was a bit of fine mist for a while but not proper rain. The cows drifted along, grabbing at tufts of grass, trying to meander across the road occasionally and being given huge discouragement when they did.

Gavin rode past me with another grin and a wave then went back to his position, leaving me feeling good. Gavin had been so hot and cold lately, but mostly cold. I thought he'd be literally cold on the motorbike but he didn't seem too bothered. He looked a bit damp. Thank goodness I hadn't tried to make him go to school.

A grey car came towards me. I picked up the walkie-talkie. He was coming too fast and I flashed my high-beams. I realised a moment later who it was. Mr Rodd. Not my favourite person in the world. In fact on this side of the border he probably ranked dead last in my book, a little lower than Mr Sayle, the solicitor, and not much higher than the rats who got in the bathroom the other day and ate the last piece of my mother's favourite soap.

Bit by bit, piece of soap by peanut cookie, the memories of my parents were being nibbled away.

Mr Rodd's eyes met mine as his Audi got closer, but he immediately looked away again. And he didn't slow down. I grabbed the walkie-talkie. "Mr Rodd's coming through, way too fast." This was dangerous. Rodd was mad enough to smash into a cow deliberately, just to get revenge. Not to mention getting himself a brand-new car from someone else's insurance company. He probably thought they were my cows. It's a big problem with farming that you're responsible for any of your stock that are on the road. You just hope they aren't hit by a Rolls-Royce, or a busload of millionaires on a tour of the wineries. A couple of years back Mr Yannos had a steer that escaped one night and a car hit it. Mr and Mrs Yannos were the only ones home and they raced down there and luckily the people were OK. But the car was damaged and the steer was dead. While Mrs Yannos waited with the people for a tow truck Mr Yannos snuck home, got a knife, went back down and cut the ears off his dead beast, so no-one could say it was his. I don't think he'd like me telling that story, but it's true.

In my rear-vision mirror I saw the brake lights of the Audi come on, and the car slew a little to the right as Mr Rodd finally decided not to smash into a cow out of sheer bloody-mindedness. I heard the blast of the horn too, then Shannon in my walkie-talkie saying, "Jeez, what's he think he's doing?" and Mr Young saying, "Honestly, sometimes I wonder about that man."

That was extreme for Mr Young.

The car straightened up again and took off, still pretty fast. I shook my head. What was his problem? Wouldn't you think we'd all had enough violence to last us half-a-dozen lifetimes?

CHAPTER 2

WE DIVIDED THE CATTLE INTO THREE PADDOCKS. THE main thing with putting cattle in a new paddock is to take them on a tour of the boundaries and show them the water, and then you can leave them to get on with eating and drinking, sightseeing, relationships and romances. No doubt they'd find the water if you didn't do it, but it's meant to settle them in faster. I've always done it, so I don't know what would happen if I skipped it.

Afterwards Mr Young gave me a cheque for the first four weeks. Oh what a feeling. It was the first income from the farm since my parents died. Twelve thousand dollars. It was a thrill to hold it. Twelve thousand dollars of someone else's money was approximately eleven thousand eight hundred dollars more than I'd ever had in my hand before. I wanted to frame the cheque and keep it forever but I don't think that would have been a financially responsible thing to do.

It was only a few days since Mr Young had sat in my kitchen and mentioned the magic word "agistment."

The cheque felt like it was vibrating in my hand. I sat down that night with the notepad and calculator and spent more than ten thousand bucks in half an hour. It was quite exciting. Five thousand dollars to the people we were renting from. That covered the whole month, plus a thousand in back rent, so they'd know I wasn't trying to rip them off.

9

Three thousand, seven hundred and sixty dollars to the bank to cover a month's interest. Bills I hadn't paid yet, from Jack Edgecombe for stock transport, from the DMT for rego of the Toyota, from Larry Whelan for taking out a pine tree that was about to fall on the shearing shed. One thousand, four hundred and thirty-five dollars for those three jobs, and I knew damn well Larry had charged me charity rates. Basically only the rent of the cherry-picker, which wasn't his. Some blokes'd charge a thousand bucks just for looking at a tree as big as that. But Larry acted like it was a normal job so I swallowed my pride and didn't say anything.

I sat there looking at my calculator and notepad. Bingo. Almost all gone. Eighteen hundred bucks left. I'd hoped to reduce the overdraft but there wouldn't be much left of the eighteen hundred after a month. For Gavin and me merely to exist was incredibly expensive. I spent a moment wondering if it would be possible for anyone just to live, without having to spend money to do it. Why should we have to pay for the privilege of being alive?

I went back to the notepad. Gavin needed new everything, just about. He wouldn't stop growing, even though I banged him on the top of the head occasionally, to slow him down. There were a couple of odds and ends I wouldn't have minded for myself. Wirrawee was changing so fast with all the new people. Where we'd had one clothes shop, now there were four. Where there'd been zero coffee shops (unless you count the bakery, which I don't) now there were two. Mr Downs, who sold second-hand farm machinery, had been forced to move his yard out to Sherlock Road, and the new bloke who owned the chain-saw repair shop was moving in a few weeks because the rents in Barker Street were so high.

The new Wirrawee had shops like Main Drag in Barker Street. I'd seen this great top in there. It was pink, not usually my best colour, or my favourite, but I liked this one. It was eighty bucks. Before the war I'd have had every chance of talking Mum into getting it for me. Now? Could I talk myself into getting it for me? Which was more important, me having a new top or reducing the overdraft?

There was no time to make such big decisions though. Mr Young's cattle demanded attention from the moment they arrived. I've never known such pain-in-the-neck cattle. They had been so well-behaved as we drove them here that I thought they'd be the perfect guests. They'd just eat and put on weight and pay my bills. But I guess they thought that for three thousand dollars a week they were entitled to breakfast on a tray and a story read to them every night. When they didn't get that they kicked up a fuss. They just wouldn't settle. And on the fourth night we had a disaster.

I have to say that we were unlucky with the weather. The forecast was for scattered showers, local thunderstorms, clearing. Minimum 7, maximum 19. Not the kind of day you'd be planning a pool party or a BBQ, but nothing to get excited about. We were out early, Gavin and I, and checked them. I did think they were restless and I knew I really should stay home, but I just couldn't miss more school. I'd had Tuesday off already, to move these beasts, and Wednesday, to make sure they were OK, then I'd gone to school yesterday. The little man was sitting on my shoulder muttering into my ear: "Don't go, Ellie, leave your buns at home, girl, don't take your buns to town." I just shrugged him off and left him sprawled in the mud. We nearly missed the bus though, while I dithered around wondering what to do, and then when it was time for Gavin to get off he came down the back of the bus and said quietly to me, "Those cattle were a bit crazy this morning."

"Yeah, I thought so too," I said, wondering why we hadn't had this conversation back at home.

He waited for me to say something and all I could do was shrug and say, "Well, there's nothing we can do now."

The bus came to a halt, shuddering, and there was no more time for conversation. Gavin got off and I was left feeling nervous for the rest of the day. Not that I could necessarily have done anything if I had stayed home. I suppose it just would have been handy to know if trouble was brewing. Our paddocks are quite bushy and these beasts were used to flat and bare. I think they were shocked by things like rabbits and snakes and owls and young wattles that waved at you suddenly when the wind blew strong.

I could have called in some help, but I'd be a bit embarrassed to do that unless I was certain, and certainty is not a word in the cattle dictionary.

Anyway, I was keen to get home, and relieved as I cruised through the paddocks on the four-wheeler to see that nothing had happened. The weather was building though: the air was heavier, the grey stuff lower, and in the distance a dark patch of cloud was getting black and angry. This all added up to a storm, and I didn't think a storm was a good idea with these beasts so twitchy.

I went back to the house, got dinner and talked it over with Gavin. For all that Gavin could be a headache on the scale of a major migraine, it could be quite comforting to have someone to talk things over with. I don't know what I would have done without him. I don't think I would have stayed on the property. The loneliness was still pretty severe with Gavin there, because there were so many things we couldn't talk about. At first his deafness had been a big part of this, but as time had gone on, I'd gotten so used to him that I didn't notice it any more. The stuff we didn't talk about was more to do with his age and personality— and sex. Like, he just wasn't good to talk to when you were having mental struggles about whether you missed Lee so badly that you wanted to scream down the phone at him, "Come back, please Lee, I have to see you and feel your strong arms around me again." And the same when I was trying to figure out whether I liked Jess or whether she was too overpowering. And Gavin also didn't show a lot of interest in whether I should buy that pink top at Main Drag.

Cattle, they were a different matter. Gavin had hardly seen a cow till after the war ended but he was a natural cattleman. What he said about cattle was often pretty smart. He'd never seen a mob of cattle in riot mode—I hadn't seen it too often myself—but he knew something was wrong with these beasts. I mean I knew it too, but I just thought they were restless, toey. He seemed to know it was something more than that.

We were a good team, because he had more intuition but I was the one who knew what to do about it. I got the Yamaha and the four-wheeler out and checked the fuel and oil. Told Gavin to find some torches, put in fresh batteries and get us both some warm clothes. Did an extra delivery of hay, which was expensive, but I figured a well-fed steer was a happy steer. They still didn't feel right though. So I swallowed my pride and rang Homer's dad, Mr Yannos.

For once he didn't bother with the jokes and the questions about my health and life. "I'll send Homer over," he said briefly. "I'd come myself but someone has to look after the cattle here and George is away."

We waited out in the paddock for Homer. I stayed close to the worst offenders. It was dark now but I could pick out some of the ringleaders. They were the sulky ones, who wouldn't look at you and who poohed their great plops like it was personal. They pawed impatiently at the ground and tossed their heads. Him, with the perfect little white circle on his forehead. Him, with the piggy eyes and tough face. Her, with the roan coat, and her, who looked at you sideways. It was funny how quickly cattle took on their own personalities and funny how quickly you got to know them. I mean, it was deliberate on my part too. My dad had always taught me to notice those cattle in the mob you could use as pointers. Some cattle like to lead, some like to huddle in the middle, some like to dawdle behind, others prefer to be out on the flanks, going along with the crowd but keeping a bit apart. "I want to be in charge," "I don't want to be noticed," "I want my own space," "What's the rush—why is everyone always in such a hurry? And where are we going anyway?"

I felt more and more justified that I'd called Mr Yannos. Beasts were settling on the cold ground then getting up again a minute later and walking away to another position. I didn't like that.

But who knows what sets a mob off? Homer arrived with a list of stories he'd heard: a plastic bag blowing across a paddock; someone walking between a fire and the mob, so that their shadow looked like a giant looming out of the darkness. I added my stories: the clatter of a tank being rolled off the back of a ute; someone shaking out a tarp with a crack of the fabric; a kid screaming suddenly in the middle of hide'n'seek. And of course anything at night was a thousand times worse than anything in daytime. It was the same for humans. I often wondered about that. Why did night-time have that spooky atmosphere? How come it was the time for witches, hobgoblins, vampires, ghosts, cattle stampedes?

We held a committee meeting at the edge of the mob. Homer was being funny and wanting to pretend that it was like a meeting of Liberation or something. "So," he said, looking carefully at the closest cattle, who were only a couple of metres away, "if our friends decide to go for a picnic, and I think you know who I mean by our friends, and I think you know what I mean by a picnic, then what direction do we think they'll go?"

This just confused Gavin but once we'd sorted it out he pointed north and I pointed south.

"Well, that's very helpful," Homer said. "Personally I'd say east. Or maybe west."

"I think they'll go that way because it's all open once you get past those trees," Gavin said.

"I think they'll go south, because it's downhill, plus that's the way they came in," I said.

"I haven't got a clue," Homer confessed. "But Dad said to keep circling them so they're all together, and to do it all night. But if they calm down we can take it in turns."

Thunder growled from the other side of the ranges.

Maybe it was coming out of Hell. I had left Marmie in the dog run but I felt guilty because I knew how much she hated thunder.

"Won't it spook the cattle more having us go round and round them all night?" I asked.

"This brings me to the good bit. They won't be spooked because we'll be singing as we go round and round them all night."

"Excuse me?"

"The hills will be alive, Ellie, with the sound of music."

"They will?"

"I'm not singing," Gavin announced.

Homer turned serious, but only because he knew singing did not come naturally to Gavin and it would be a hard job to persuade him.

"You have to sing, mate. I don't really mean singing, like the national anthem or something. But you've got to make a noise, a steady noise, all the time you're going around the mob. Just a blah-blah-blah-blah-blah-blah is fine. The main thing is not to stop. It's so they know who you are and where you are. These guys are so twitchy that if you come out of the darkness at them with no warning they'll start running and they won't stop till they're in Wirrawee."

Gavin was—and I've been waiting to use this word ever since I learned it—nonplussed.

For a short time I felt like an idiot as we began our circuits. We stuck to the same route and the idea was not to catch up with the person in front or let the person behind catch up with you. I went first and it took me a few minutes to even think of a song. My mind had gone completely blank. But I heard Homer behind me calling quietly, "Come on, Ellie, can't hear you."

So in a voice that sounded like a windmill needing urgent maintenance I launched into "So Much Water." And if that wasn't sad enough I followed up with "Revelator," trying to sound like Gillian Welch. How would she feel, I wondered, if she knew her words were being sung in a paddock ten thousand or so k's from where she lived, to stop a mob of cattle from rioting?

Behind me Gavin's tuneless voice gradually grew in confidence, with a chant that had no connection with any song I'd ever heard, except that I'd heard Gavin chant like that before sometimes, when he was tired or unhappy and he didn't think I could hear him. And then behind him, fainter because he was further away, Homer launched into the kind of stuff Triple J was playing now that Triple J was back on the air.

In some situations it might have been quite nice doing this. And there were moments when I felt quite nice doing it. But too much had changed in my life. Since the attack on the house I didn't feel safe out here in the darkness. I didn't know if there might be another attack, and if there was, what would happen to me. I didn't want to die. It dawned on me gradually that the murder of my parents might have taught me something I didn't properly know about before. Oh of course I'd known about fear and felt fear, known what it was like to be scared. But it hadn't stopped me. Now I felt in my gut that maybe I had a new fear and it would stop me, it was already stopping me. I kept looking around, not at the cattle, but in the other direction, half expecting something to leap at me out of the shadows. And that something was death. I felt lonely so often nowadays, and being out here was like putting myself in the loneliest situation I could find. Like someone with claustrophobia locking herself into a tea-chest for a few hours.

The other problem that night was a bit more ordinary, a lot more ordinary, but in the end it kind of drove the first one away. And it was the good old problem that dominated our lives and had done since I was born and would keep doing so forever. Dad said to me once: "You've got the land and you've got the stock and you've got the weather, and that's all there is to farming."

I was too young to figure out what the point of this was so I just looked at him blankly and he said, "See, all you've got to do is know everything there is to know about those three things and you've got farming under control."

Then I understood that he was being funny—well, as funny as Dad ever got—and that if something can be reduced to one simple word, like "weather," it doesn't necessarily mean it is simple. A friend of mine had a saying, "If you don't talk about the weather, what else is there to talk about?" and that's hilariously amusing, ROFL too, but he was still making a serious point, that country people talk about the weather because it matters to them, it controls them, it is the be-all and end-all of their lives.

Well, the weather wasn't simple that night. The thunder rumbled again, and lightning wiggled across the sky in the distance, just a little bolt, but enough to have my skin prickling. The dark sky felt closer and heavier. We all had torches but I didn't want to waste the batteries so I tried to make do without mine most of the time. A scatter of rain fell across me, then stopped, then started again, this time with more dedication. We were so well organised that as well as torches we had rain jackets. I stopped and unrolled mine and put it on, trying hard not to let it wave around or make a noise in case it sparked the cattle. Looking back I caught a glimpse of Gavin in the light of his torch. He seemed to be doing the same as me.

The rain got quite enthusiastic. We were just doing personification in English the other day. This rain was having more fun as it went along, and soon it was having a party. I hunched up and kept going, singing louder to make up for the quiet drumming on the dead leaves and the bark of winter. Now I was onto "My dad picks the fruit that goes to Cottees . . ." Perhaps it should have made me sad about my dad but it didn't.

The thunder got louder, rolling and rolling. Ten-pin bowling by the Gods? That was Kevin's theory. I'd never been ten-pin bowling. Forget bowling and pay attention to the cattle, Ellie. All the beasts I could see were on their feet. I moved faster, to head off half-a-dozen who were peeling away for an unknown destination. It was hard to run and sing at the same time but I got to them and turned them. Then, just as they swung reluctantly around, a huge *crack* went off somewhere to my right, I saw a shower of blue sparks, the ground vibrated, the smell of lightning burnt into my nostrils, and the cattle were away.

My first thought was to sprint for the four-wheeler. I wasn't far from it and without it I'd be useless. But the cattle were surging towards me and they weren't going to stop. The white faces of the Hereford-crosses stood out but I saw the dark bodies too, and the earth quivered with the accelerating mass of the mob. They would run over me like they were gravel trucks and I was an empty drink carton in the middle of the road.

As they built up speed the ground and sky shook with their power. I sprinted for a tree on my right. It wasn't the closest but it would get me nearer to the four-wheeler. I knew if I tripped on a log or a bump in the ground I was dead. I had about two seconds to reach the safety of the white trunk. My God, the speed of a stampeding steer, the speed of a mob. They came at me, they were in my face, but they didn't see me. Their eyes were fierce and focused. I'd never seen cattle like this. All that breeding we'd done, that thousands of farmers had done over so many generations, all those carefully worked-out bloodlines, so we could get stock with good temperament, all that was gone, and in the primitive world of lightning and thunder the crack of one bolt had fused something ancient in their brains and bodies. They were still accelerating as I raced for the tree. One of them did actually see me and swerved slightly; the others never deviated for a moment, but I flung myself at the tree, feeling the hot breath of the mob wrapping itself around me, and smelling something that wasn't fear or rage or desperation, that was beyond fear, was something the English language is still trying to find a word for.

Wow. That was as close as I ever want to be to death, I told myself, panting like mad and for the first time in my life wanting to hug a tree.

The gap between the next tree and me was a shambles of bushes and bark and a broken branch. A cow was floundering around in it, but the rest of the mob had avoided it so I scrambled through without much danger except that my breathing was still crazy. I've never had asthma but I got an idea then of how it would feel, the chest heaving without my being able to control it, the lungs begging for air but not getting any, the white lights going off in my brain as I waited for the oxygen to arrive.

Unfortunately I didn't have time to wait for the oxygen. I ran to the next tree, dodging the last few cattle as I went. I thought I was home free but a young steer came charging at a different angle to the others. He came out of nowhere. I didn't see him till the last moment. I spun to try to get away but he caught me with his flank and knocked me sideways. I deliberately kept rolling as he thundered past. He wasn't interested in me, just in the mindless fury of the stampede. His back hoof caught me and the blow seemed to echo through my head. There was a dull shocked feeling. I thought the left side of my skull had been caved in. I got on my hands and knees and shook my head. It seemed to still be there, although I didn't shake too hard in case it flew off and I had to waste time looking for it in the under-growth. With no eyes it would take a long time.

I did think I heard my teeth rattle, and I certainly felt them. Trying to ignore the pain and the instant headache, I got up and went on towards the motorbike. For a few minutes I wasn't even sure why I was looking for it, but I knew it was something to do with cattle and by the time I'd found it my head was a bit clearer.

Really all this took only thirty seconds. Cattle were still blundering around on all sides but the main mob were well away. I could hear Gavin's motorbike, the farm Yamaha, but not Homer's Honda. The Yammie was going up towards the ridge. "Clever Gavin," I thought. "He's going to swing them back north."

If they ran into the fence I didn't know what would happen. A fence wouldn't stop a mob of stampeding cattle but it could cause a disaster. If the leaders went head-on into it and the fence wasn't immediately flattened, if there was a pile-up with the first twenty or so, then another hundred or two ramming them, we'd have an instant abattoir. It wasn't difficult to get a mental picture of a mob of cattle piled on top of each other, with broken legs, broken ribs, broken necks. Mr Young would be a little slow with the next agistment cheque if that happened.

My head still felt numb and strange as I got on the bike. I went flat-chat though. If Gavin could swing them to the north, I wanted to be in a position near the western fence so I could turn them again.

Riding through the night at high speed like that is pretty crazy. You can keep your Luna Parks and the Wild Mouse and the Shock Drop. I knew that sooner or later I'd be in the clear part of the paddock, where it'd be safer, but those first few minutes, going through scrub, making instant decisions every second, with a head that felt like an over-ripe pineapple, were on the wrong side of fun for me. There were no tracks but there was bracken, fallen branches, bark, a log here, a hole there, a wallaby trying to outgun the bike, a couple of bewildered-looking cattle suddenly looming up in the glare of the headlights. I never knew whether high-beam was a good idea or not on that bike, because with high-beam you can see further but you can't see the ground immediately in front of you. I kept switching from low to high and back again.

The rain started coming in hard. "Like we haven't got enough problems already," I thought. Tiny ferocious drops stung my face. More strange-looking cattle appeared. They looked strange to me because I wasn't used to cattle who'd turned their back on humans. And they looked at me strangely, as if they didn't seem to know who they were any more. I ignored them and raced on, squinting through the rain, trying to get into some clear space. I crossed a narrow bit of grass and suddenly nearly slammed into the mob. Above the *rat-a-tat-tat* of the motorbike I could hear the *thump-thump-thump* of their hooves on the earth, like there was a band playing at the Anlezarks' place and the beat of the bass guitar was travelling through the ground from five k's away.

The cattle were focused now. They must have been tired, although you wouldn't think it to look at them. But all their energy was going into the stampede. They didn't have the strength to bellow. They were rushing to nowhere but all their strength was needed for the race. Reminded me of some of the kids at school.

I had to trust Gavin to turn them. I waited till they had passed then gunned the bike up the hill. I was getting coldly wet. At the top of the hill I let the bike idle and tried to guess from the throbbing of the earth where they were going. The noise sharpened, seemed to rise a note, became louder. The throbbing of the bike and the ground were now synchronised. Gradually the beat of the cattle hooves got louder and stronger. I squared myself around a little on the bike, to face them, at the same time thinking how amazing it was that one average-size human could have the cheek to think she could have any influence on a mob of huge mad beasts coming straight at her.

Before I could think about that any more they were there, the leaders toiling up over the ridge, galumphing now instead of galloping. I strained to look at their eyes, hoping I'd see tiredness instead of madness, but they were still too far away and the rain made it impossible.

"Well Ellie," I said out loud to the wind and to the wild air blowing over the ridge and to the million miles of heaven above and beyond me, "this is where you get steam-rollered."

I revved up the bike and started forwards. Not too fast or I'd be in the middle of the mob in a second and the leaders would just go, "What was that?" and keep running. Not too slow or they'd go over the top of me and I'd be under their hooves and mashed into the mud. I flashed the headlights on and off. The four-wheeler doesn't have a horn but I yelled a lot. I zigzagged in big zigzags, shouting and waving my hat. A wave of heat hit me. It shocked me, that they could generate heat like that. They were almost up to me, the leaders rolling relentlessly on, and I could see their eyes now, and they were anxious and lost and wanting to stomp me into the earth so they could go somewhere, they still didn't know where.

CHAPTER 3

"Wake up, dear," the nurse said.

No, just kidding. I don't know what it was that had run so hard through the blood of this mob, whether it was rage or fear or a desire for freedom or a force that has no word. I suspect it was the last one. But whatever it was, the charge up to the ridge from where Gavin and Homer had turned them was enough to slow them just a little and calm them just a little more. And my yelling and zigzagging and flashing lights turned them again. They ran along the western boundary of the paddock and soon the stragglers were standing with sides heaving and heads down, ignoring us three; the leaders lost their drive then, with no followers, and they fizzled out and wandered off into the scrub, snatching at grass as they went. They almost looked embarrassed.

We were puffing harder than the cattle, but we still had a lot of work ahead. I divided the paddock into three and we split up and went looking for injured beasts. The rain kept going, not spectacularly, quite light most of the time, but it was soaking and cold and got you down a bit.

While the other two were still looking I nicked off home, mainly because I needed the rifle, but I grabbed a loaf of bread and a jar of apricot jam and three cans of Coke as well. I could hear Marmie yelping with excitement and anxiety and loneliness from her pen—whenever she heard one of the bikes she went off big-time—but I had to be hard-hearted and ignore her. This was not a dog party. I went back to the paddock and met up with the other two and we had a picnic, trying keep the bread dry under my Drizabone as I spread slice after slice and handed them around.

It was three-twenty a.m. The boys ate every slice I gave them. Gavin was shivering and Homer was too cold and tired to speak. I said to Gavin, "Have you done your homework yet?" but it took him four goes to get what I meant and then he just turned away as if I were demented. It wasn't much of a joke to begin with and by the fourth time around it had gone beyond lameness into permanent disability.

Gavin took me to a couple of steers who were injured. One was up, but with a leg hanging uselessly. I thought he had a chance but the other one had a leg fracture so severe that twenty centimetres of bone were sticking out, and I had to shoot him. I shot another one, a small beast with a funny face, all red and white squares. I'd noticed him before. But there was nothing funny about him now. He'd fallen off a bank, pushed by the rush of cattle I guess, and he'd impaled himself on a sharp old gum stump. Too many of his insides had become outsides for him to have any chance.

Homer had found a couple of others but they looked like they might get through with a bit of stitching and TLC. It would be a close thing though. Shock and blood loss and cold wet weather were three reasons they mightn't make it. Altogether we had four who looked like they'd qualify for disabled parking stickers.

I left Homer and Gavin to bring in the ones that could be moved while I went home to ring the vet. I had the after-hours number for Mr Keech but it rang out, so I rang the surgery, which was annoying because then I had to sit through all the "If your cat has a headache press 3" stuff. Finally I got an emergency number, which was different from Mr Keech's so I tried that. It rang and rang. At last a bloke answered. He said, "Hello," but he didn't sound like any of the vets I knew. I thought, "Oh no! I've rung some poor bloke at four in the morning and it's a wrong number."

I said, "Is that the vet?" and he said, "Yes," so we were making progress. I said, "It's Ellie Linton here, out at Mirrimbah. I've got four cattle who need looking at. The mob took off in the storm and quite a few got injured."

He said, "Oh damn."

I struggled to keep my temper, then lost the struggle. "So far you've said four words," I said, sounding as cold as the weather. "'Hello', 'yes,' and 'oh damn.' Are you coming out here or aren't you?"

He didn't sound the slightest bit bothered. "Oh yes. Where'd you say you were from?"

"Mirrimbah. It's on the . . ."

"Yeah, yeah, I know it."

The phone made that little *durrup* noise as he hung up.

As we waited for him we did a bit of cleaning up of the cattle that Homer and Gavin had brought lumbering in. We didn't bother to take them up to the new yards and put them in the press, just used the old wooden yard behind the house. They were in shock, shivering and shuffling around. It was like some of the boys at the B&S's, when they were supposedly dancing but they just moved their feet backwards and forwards, left and right, right and left, forwards and backwards. The cattle did their clumsy dance, grunting and rolling their eyes. We did a bit of cattle whispering, calming them down and shoving lucerne into their gobs. The lucerne probably helped more than the whispering. Three of them had big wounds, which would have sent a human straight to the floor, but even with their guts sticking out the cattle wanted to waltz.

They looked how I felt. My head seemed detached from my body. The jawbone wasn't connected to the neck bone. I wanted to put my head in a cupboard for a few days until it stopped throbbing.

Gavin and Homer were talking about the stampede and where they'd been and what they'd done and how smart and heroic they were. I didn't have the energy to listen. I think they probably had been heroic and smart but they were so good at telling each other about it that they didn't need me.

The vet arrived in a Falcon ute so splattered with mud that you couldn't see if it had number plates or not. I had to admit he'd got here in record time. And then he was so nice that all the angry speeches I'd been planning went out of my head. He was a young bloke named Seamus, and he went to his work so neatly and quickly that I watched in fascination. We were all so tired—including Seamus—that I don't know how we stayed awake. That heavy feeling behind my eyelids, the ache in my head . . . I did everything in slightly slow motion, and only the presence of my friends made it OK.

Homer stood holding the torch while I held the head of the beast who was being stitched, and Gavin was a general gofer, sitting on the step leading into the food shed when I didn't have a job for him. I thought he would fall asleep but each time I looked his eyes were still open. Most of the time I watched Seamus at work. He had good, strong, patient hands and he worked steadily, pulling the edges of the wound together, stitching away, swabbing occasionally. Homer watched too, and the light of the big Dolphin torch gave us both a good view of the bleeding flesh, the torn edges, the white muscle and severed veins.

Then it happened. Homer said to me quietly, "Can you hold the torch for a sec, El?"

"Sure."

As I took it he added, "I'm not feeling all that well."

With those words he slid straight to the ground and lay there unconscious under the big steer.

I yelped, which wasn't all that helpful. The beast was penned well enough but we hadn't allowed for a human coming at him from that direction. He shook his head and bellowed and started to step backwards. Homer was about to have a five hundred kilo–plus beast step on him. With cattle and horses the weight is all resting on those four thin legs and hard hooves. A steamroller running over you would have a totally different effect, but I wasn't sure which would be worse. I dropped the torch, which meant no-one could see anything, although I was aware of the light rolling over and over and pointing away towards the stars. Seamus and I dived simultaneously under the steer, cracked our heads and somehow got a grip on Homer and started dragging him out. For one terrible moment I realised we were pulling him in different directions, like a Christmas cracker. Then we seemed to be going the same way.

All of this would have been too late, with Homer cored like an apple, if not for one thing which is that the steer, having taken two steps back, and about to take a third step which would disembowel my best friend, suddenly shook his head, gave a low grunt, kicked a leg, and inexplicably took a step forwards. It saved Homer's life. All we'd needed was that extra second. We had Homer out of there just as he was starting to stir and give a grunt that sounded very like the steer. Come to think of it, he might have become a steer if he had been in there any longer.

I suppose this is another "amazing Gavin" story. When we got Homer out, Seamus handed me my torch and in its strong beam I saw Gavin coming calmly towards us. I suddenly got suspicious. I put the torch on my face and waved at him and asked, "Where did you go?"

He shrugged and pointed and said casually, "Round the back."

"What did you do?"

I realised how pleased he was looking, and excited, behind his calm and cool face.

He shrugged again. "Made him go forwards."

"You did?"

"He was going to step on Homer. Squish. Squash. Yuk." Gavin was beaming away like he was the face on Luna Park.

"So how did you make him go forwards?"

"Bit him."

30

"You what?"

"Bit him. Like a dog."

Homer was sitting up, holding his head. Seamus looked at me. "That's the fastest thing I've ever seen," he said. "You should rent him out." He asked Gavin, "Where exactly did you bite him?"

"Where the dogs do." Gavin demonstrated on the back of his own leg. "Not too hard," he added. "I didn't want him to go psycho."

"Give us your torch for a sec, Ellie," Seamus said. He took it over to the rear of the beast and, making sure he didn't cop a quick kick to the head, bent down and had a look just above the hoof. "You can see the teeth marks," he said to me. He shook his head. "How'd you miss the kick?" he asked Gavin.

"Uh?" Gavin looked at me for a translation. I demonstrated the steer's kick.

"Oh," said Gavin and mimed dropping flat.

"My God," said Seamus. "He is a cattle dog. We'd better test your beast for rabies."

It was fairly amazing. We hadn't had any working dogs since the war, but Gavin had seen them at the saleyards in town and at some of the neighbours' places, like the Youngs', where Dad had taken him. Because of course that's exactly what they do: bite just above the hoof, drop flat so they don't get kicked, then bite again.

Homer was standing, looking embarrassed. "Can't believe I did that," he said. "Never done that before."

"It can make you queasy," Seamus said. "Staring at it for so long. Happens quite often. You'd be surprised."

We went back to the steer to finish the job.

I didn't give Homer a hard time about fainting, although it was extremely tempting, and I hope he's grateful to me for the rest of his life for being so restrained. He did look at me very hard on the bus, when I started telling Shannon and Sam about the stampede. And I did take him close to the edge, when I told them about Seamus the vet, and stitching up the steers, ". . . and Homer was holding the torch." Homer shifted a little closer and glared at me. "And I tell you what, there were some pretty chunky wounds. It'd knock some people flat just to look at them. There was a faint . . ." I paused for a sec, just to annoy Homer some more. "A faint chance that one of them had internal bleeding, but he seems to be mending OK."

The weekend slipped away. I had to take Mr Young on a tour of the cattle and I had to repair a lot of fences, but the priority for all that stuff was in the reverse order to the way I've written it, because I didn't want Mr Young to see our fences when they were in anything other than great condition. And much as I was desperate for sleep I had to take care of the customer first, and Mr Young was our only customer. He coped pretty well with his cattle casualties. Some farmers seem to have an amazing sense of fairness, and he was like that.

Somehow we got to school on Monday. These days it felt like a TV show that you try to watch while you're cooking dinner. You're in and out of the room and then you're concentrating on the chicken stock and then you're in the pantry or asking Gavin to give you a hand with the onions, and suddenly the credits are rolling and you've missed two-thirds of the program. I was dropping into school and finding that they were talking about integration of polynominals in Maths and someone had changed the rules about who could use the computer room and Belinda Norris was now with Andy Farrar, not Ranald. . . .

It was the same on that Monday. I was lucky in a way to run straight into Jess, who always knew everything and was one of those natural-born-leader people who everyone turns to when they're confused. "Have you seen Ms Maxwell?" she asked. "She's looking for you. And Mr Addams said can you play soccer Thursday?"

"Soccer? God! Me! Any more messages?" But I smiled as I said it. I decided this was one of those days when I liked Jess.

In her best Telstra voice she said, "You have two new messages. Message received—yesterday—at two—thirty—four p.m. . . ."

"OK, I'm pressing the hash button. That does something, doesn't it?"

"I can see you haven't had a mobile for a long time. Actually there was only one other message. Jeremy Finley said to say hi."

"Oh really?"

She'd thrown me with that one. I knew she liked Jeremy, but so did I. He was a nice-looking guy with a great personality—you know, too good to be true, but he actually seemed fair dinkum. For better or worse he was the son of General Finley, whom I'd had a lot to do with during the war. Since Steve, my love life had been all to do with Lee and Homer, mainly Lee, with Homer running interference. Jeremy popping up in Stratton, and spending a good bit of time around Wirrawee, made a nice complication. I didn't know if he was interested in me or Jess or anyone else, but

I knew I tingled when I saw him. I also wanted to cross-examine Jess on exactly what Jeremy had said, the actual words, the look on his face, the tone of his voice, the way his hands had moved. Stuff like that means a lot to a girl. There's a big difference between saying, "Tell Ellie hi," and "Make sure you give Ellie a special hello from me." What if he'd said, "My life is stale bread and cold tea until I see Ellie again" or "Jess, if you die at the gates of the school, make sure that with your last breath you tell Ellie I'm thinking of her"?

But what if it had been, "Say hello to Homer and Shannon and Sam and Bronte and Alex and Eleanor and that other girl, what's her name"?

It was cruel getting this message second-hand and confusing getting it from someone who had her own feelings for him. But better than not getting it at all. I tried to figure out how I could get more info without letting Jess know I was interested.

"Oh really? Jeremy? So has he been around?" I tried to keep my voice casual. The trouble is that I had the feeling Jess was almost impossible to fool. No matter how much I tried to sound cool, that girl had special antennae. If she were a teacher you wouldn't even bother with the "Yeah, miss, I've done it, it's just that the guinea pig crapped on it." You wouldn't waste your time.

Still, I wasn't going to give in easily. It was a challenge to try.

"Around? God yes! Didn't you know?"

Owhh. Did she have to make this so hard? All I could do was grit my teeth and plough a straight furrow.

"Know what?"

"You haven't heard the big news?"

"So are you saying Jeremy's got some reason to be around Wirrawee more often?"

"God yeah."

"Jess, I'd love to stand here all day hearing about Jeremy Finley's movements, but why don't you just tell me. In fifty words or less. Seeing I do have a life."

"Well, he and his mum are moving here."

"Serious?" No good pretending now. She had me.

"Ellie, you really like him, don't you?"

"What? God no, not like that." I hoped I was doing OK with that "Jeremy Who?" voice, but I doubted it. The strange thing was that I didn't get any vibe from Jess that she had a personal interest any more. Maybe she'd moved on.

"Well, I believe you but I believed Mrs Barlow when she said the first convicts came out here on Qantas. Anyway, his mum's got a contract at the military base, putting in a new computer system that she's designed with some guy in Stratton. She's a pretty smart cookie I think."

"My dad always said that New Zealand women were the strongest women in the world."

"Well, that's fine except she's Australian. But she is strong. She told me that she wasn't going to let anyone get in the way of Jeremy making it to Vet at uni. I think she meant people who might distract him with invitations to wild parties. Or even long phone calls. She's kind of fierce with him."

I privately thought that Jeremy was the person most likely to be organising Homer and Lee and I didn't know who else into the Scarlet Pimples. Or Liberation, which was their official name, if you can have an official name for an unofficial organisation. I didn't see how that could help Jeremy with his school work. To be honest, I didn't see how any of my friends were going to pass anything much. I didn't know many people who were settling into regular school life, because we were still too stirred up and busy and crazy after the war.

I couldn't keep up with the social life of school let alone school work, but even though my uni ambitions were sinking slowly over the horizon, I didn't want to drop out. School was still my normal place, the place where I could pretend that I was just Ellie again. Rather than drop out, it was the place where I could drop in, and the place where life was closest to normal, as though there never had been a war. Even reading the noticeboard was reassuring. "Year 9 and 10 social on Friday night, come as a character from a James Bond movie," "Mrs Savvas wants to see students attending *Twelfth Night* at the staff room at one o'clock," "If you want to try out for a game of lacrosse against Stratton High School see Daniel Ciao NOW!" "LOST: one recorder, left in B3 on Monday afternoon, come on guys, please look out for it, I need it and I can't afford to buy another one." A lot of boring stuff about careers and uni and the school's policies on sexism and racism and bullying and the rights of students and trees and aluminum cans and retired lollipop ladies.

We never learnt anything much in school, it was just that by the time you stayed there enough years you'd somehow picked up quite a lot of information. The square of the hypotenuse of a right-angled triangle equals the sum of the square of the other two sides, Madrid is the capital of Spain, Charles Dickens wrote *David Copperfield*. At best I suppose you learnt useful information like how to treat snakebite and how to use PowerPoint. At worst you wasted a lot of time memorising the first twenty elements in the periodic table, the definition of personification, and the economic effects of the Gold Rush. It was like school was taking us on a road from ignorance to knowledge but there was another road from ignorance to somewhere else that school didn't take into account. What was that road called? The one from ignorance to wisdom, I suppose. The girl at the Wirrawee market who told me about Taoism knew about it but school didn't. If school had bothered with that road, if they'd even taken us to the start of it and shown us where it went, if they'd so much as lent us a map, I would say that school might have been worthwhile. I'm not saying it was a complete waste of time, but I think we could have picked up that info about snakebite and PowerPoint much faster and more efficiently somewhere else. So really what we were left with was school as a social club, and sometimes I thought the adults were happy with that: they secretly saw it as a place where they could park kids till we grew up and were useful to them. Giant child-care centres.

I liked the new-look Wirrawee High School though. Not everyone did. It was a lot more crowded, and the organisa-tion was a joke, and it didn't feel like our own place any more. We had to share it with so many people. The corri-dors were crowded and it was hard to get time alone with your old friends. The difference was that before the war it had been boring and now it had three times the action. The new kids brought a new energy. I mean, lacrosse against

Stratton High School? I didn't even know what lacrosse was but I was sure we wouldn't have been playing games of lacrosse in the old-style Wirrawee. School was noisier, it was messier, but it had more life. Now, with Jeremy Finley, it could get more interesting yet.

CHAPTER 4

SCHOOL TAUGHT ME PERSONIFICATION BUT THE WAR taught me suspicion. If it hadn't, the death of my parents would have done the job. I don't think I'm paranoid yet but I could easily end up there. I don't know why I wouldn't trust voices in my head. They'd have to be as reliable as some of the voices I hear from outside my head. Take Homer for instance. I know you'd only take Homer if you were desperate, but if you were, and you did take him, would you listen to him? Or believe anything he tells you? So when Homer and Lee and Jess all suddenly turn up at my place, and Homer tells me it's coincidence, I'm like, yeah, right, and people in France speak French, that's another amazing coincidence.

I didn't know Lee was coming until I got home from school, because the only warning he gave me was a message on the answering machine, and it seemed like no sooner had I played the message than he was there. Jess had given him a lift. And in the back seat was Lee's little sister, Pang, because she wanted to see me again and she wouldn't take no for an answer.

Hhhmm. "Wait a sec, it's my birthday and this is a surprise party, right?" I asked them. "Anyone else coming?"

But as soon as I got Homer alone I hissed at him, "This is about Liberation, isn't it?"

"Nah, just a fluke."

Since I'd knocked back the invitation to join the group I'd been left out of the information circuit. Disconnected from the bush telegraph.

"I don't want you guys doing stuff without my knowing about it. Don't go running off over the border again. It's too dangerous."

"Pang wanted to stay with you for a few days, that's why Lee's here."

"So will Lee be staying here too, with her? Or am I meant to look after her while you go off on another crazy raid? Am I the babysitter now?"

"No, of course not, he would have left her in town with the others, but she's mad keen to hang out with you."

"Well, you might have thought about Gavin before you planned all this. You're getting him all revved up."

I had to talk in a funny way, twisting up my face, so Gavin couldn't lip-read. He hovered around anxiously. Normally he'd have attached himself to Lee or Homer, as he was a big fan of both of them. I was pretty sure that Pang's arrival made him feel insecure.

I heard a loud *rap-rap-rap-rap* on the kitchen door and broke off the conversation with Homer to answer it. I nearly fell over to see Jeremy Finley. "OK, so it *is* a meeting of Liberation," I said to him straight away.

"Could just be a get-together of a few buddies," Homer said. He'd followed me into the kitchen.

"Thanks for organising it at my place without even telling me. Good one, guys." I let Jeremy in anyway. I didn't have much choice.

"It could be something so urgent that we didn't have

time to do it any other way," Jeremy said, looking straight at me. I was sure he was the Scarlet Pimple.

"Well, Lee must have known hours ago," I said. "You don't just blow in here from the city ten minutes after getting the phone call."

"It wasn't urgent last night, when I rang Lee," Jeremy said. "The rating changed about an hour ago. Lee was on his way already, but we were going to do it differently. By the time he got here we realised we needed a closer place to meet. I couldn't ring you because we can't talk about this stuff on the phone without using codes."

"And Pang did want to come and stay with you," Lee said with a small quick smile at me. "So did I."

I turned back to Jeremy. "You said 'closer.' Closer to what? The border?"

"Of course."

"Oh great." I felt quite sick. "So are you going to tell me what it's all about?"

There was a moment of indecision. I knew the Scarlet Pimple was one of them—well I thought so anyway—and I'd been so convinced that it was Jeremy. But now Jeremy was acting like it wasn't his decision. Jess was the one who, after a pause, looked around at the group and said, "Sure."

It was like the rest of the group weren't convinced though. Then Jeremy clinched it by saying, "Yeah, good idea. It's insurance for us."

"Are you all going?" I asked. I looked around the room at them. Homer, leaning against the doorframe, solid and reliable, leaving the planning to the others. Lee, watching through narrow eyes, scanning the room, assessing the situation. Jess, strong and sure but nervous too, I thought: probably the first time for her to go into this kind of stuff. And Jeremy, eyes alert and eager, face shining. He wanted to do this, whatever it was that had to be done, and he wanted it to work perfectly. He was taking after his father all right. I wondered if he and General Finley had a lot of contact, and if so what they talked about and what Jeremy thought of his father. That was a conversation we hadn't had, but then we hadn't had too many conversations full stop.

No-one put up their hand to say they were staying. So Jess and the three boys were going out there into danger. Together. Jealousy jumped in my stomach and made an angry noise. I mean literally, my tummy rumbled. Or maybe I was just hungry.

I didn't say anything after that though. It was up to them to organise themselves and get under way as fast as they could. What they didn't need was someone standing there giving helpful hints. "Wear sensible shoes." "Make sure you go to the toilet before you leave." "Have you enough ammo?"

At least Gavin wasn't around. I think the presence of Pang had scared him off to his bedroom, or some other safe hidey-hole, like Marmie's pen. Good thing too. With a bit of luck the group would be across the border before Gavin realised there was a raid happening and he'd been left behind.

As the meeting in my kitchen went on I started to get a sense of what was happening. There'd been intelligence—

a tip-off—that members of the same group which raided the Youngs' and did unspeakable things there were going to come across to our side of the border and raid another farmhouse. I already knew that Liberation was a group who got tip-offs from people in our Army, people who wanted stuff done that was illegal for the Army to do. By feeding info to Liberation these Army officers were guaranteeing that people from our side would cross the border and fight, but if they were caught, or if there were any protests, the government could say quite honestly that they knew nothing about it and they sure didn't authorise it.

It meant that Liberation had to be as careful on one side of the border as on the other. Everyone was out to get them. Still, I'd rather be caught on our side. Your life wouldn't be worth much if you got busted over there.

As far as I knew the Liberation group in our area was the only one run by teenagers, but I didn't know much. Just what I read in the paper. And some of that was about members of the group in other areas being caught and copping serious jail terms as the government tried to demonstrate that they were seriously trying to stop them. And then there were the stories about members of the group who went across the border and didn't come back. In one case just their heads had come back, five of them, in a bag dumped outside a railway station at Padapada. I felt sorry for the person who opened that bag. I felt sorry for the people whose heads were in the bag, too.

So, here were the four of them in my kitchen working out what to do about a group of thugs heading in our direction to rape or kill or burn or loot or, most likely, all of the above. Kitchens are meant to be the heart of a house but I'd have to cook a lot of comfort food to get this bad energy out of my kitchen.

It surprised me in a way but Lee was the one who was the least gung-ho. "Why don't we wait on our side of the border till they get here, then the Army can round them up legitimately?" he wanted to know. Then he answered his own question. "I suppose we don't know where they'll cross into our territory." He looked at Jeremy. "Is that right?"

"Apparently."

"But we know they'll be coming along Rawson Road at some point. Or what we used to call Rawson Road. So we could follow them till they're on our side and then use this fancy radio equipment to call in the Army and get them arrested."

"Yes. The trouble is it'll be at night and the chances of losing touch with them would be pretty high."

Lee lapsed into silence then. That was less surprising.

I could see the sense in Jeremy's arguments. They really only had two options. One was to catch these guys in their home base, before they set out. Time was against that, and so was the problem that people are in a strong position when they're at home. They know their way around pretty well. On the other hand, when you attack people at home you've got the advantage of surprise. I'd seen that from both sides, as the attacker and the attacked.

The other option was an ambush. That wasn't ideal either, but perfection never seems to be a goal in war situations. Only in school. And the ambush idea had a lot going for it.

"Under the coconut tree," said Jeremy.

I didn't know what that meant but before I could ask Lee said, "Well, if we're going to do it we'd better do it." Suddenly the kitchen was alive with movement. Then Jeremy asked the question that I'd amused myself with just a short time ago: "Have you got enough ammo?"

"Of course," Homer said, getting up from the kitchen chair that he'd been promising to fix for about three months now. Then he did that double-take thing like in the movies when the guy turns around and sees that it's a grizzly bear blowing on the back of his neck and not his girlfriend, but for a moment he thinks that it's his girlfriend and she just needs a shave. "Oh momma," he said. "It's still on the bench."

It turned out he was referring to the bench in their shed at home. So there was a short intermission as Jess and Homer raced back to his place to pick up the ammo.

I got the feeling that Homer might have quite a lot of Liberation stuff stashed at his place. I bet his parents didn't know about it. He probably had it hidden under his bed. As I never intended to get close to his bed I wouldn't find that out. But I had a mental picture of Homer sleeping on top of a pile of hand grenades and detonators and bombs.

Anyway, Jeremy didn't seem to need to do anything more to get ready. They had a ute I hadn't seen before, as well as Homer's, and they had a motorbike loaded on the back of each ute. So they were OK for transport.

Lee was outside. I stayed in the kitchen and got Jeremy a coffee. Pang appeared. She'd been down at the lagoon, talking to the ducks maybe. Knowing how quirky she was, she could have been running around the lagoon flapping her arms and quacking.

Gavin was still in hiding but she said she'd seen him in the big shed, fuelling the bikes. That'd be right. When a girl appears you go out to the shed and do a bit of work on the motorbikes.

I asked Jeremy how long he thought we'd need groups like Liberation. Suddenly he burst into this amazing speech about history. "You know, Ellie, when Churchill took over as prime minister of Britain in 1940 he realised one thing, which is that when you fight a war you have to fight it. You have to get out there. The Germans, the Nazis, knew that. They went through France at a hundred and twenty k's an hour. The French were dug in waiting for them. They had all these great fortifications and they sat behind the walls ready to defend France, you know, and what did the Germans do? They just went around them. They went through the Ardennes Forest. Everyone thought it was too thick for the Germans so they didn't put many defenders there, and the big panzer tanks ploughed straight through. They made their own roads. The French were still sitting behind the Maginot line waiting for the invasion, and by the time they woke up all they saw were the tail-lights of the tanks. France surrendered inside a couple of weeks. After that Hitler was sure Britain was finished too, it was just a formality. He'd knock them off in no time and that'd wrap up western Europe, pretty much.

"Then Churchill took over. The first thing he had the Poms do was attack the French fleet and wipe it out, so the Germans couldn't use the ships. It was like a declaration: 'This war is still alive. Don't write us off.' See what I mean? Churchill didn't just put up a lot of walls and get people to sit behind them and wait for an invasion. He went out and attacked in every way he could. Sink the *Bismarck*, go after the *Graf Spee*, bomb Berlin, go here, there and everywhere."

"And that's the way you think we should do it?"

"That's the only way to do it. Be tough neighbours. Have them scared of us instead of the other way round. Knock them around every time they think they've got an edge on us. Keep them off balance."

"I thought you were a calm and peaceful guy."

"I am. But it drives me crazy when people don't learn from history. I love history. It tells you the answer to everything if people only take the trouble to read it. Being weak is as bad as being a bully. Chamberlain was weak, Hitler was a bully, Churchill was a bully."

"Who was Chamberlain?"

"He was the British prime minister before Churchill. He wanted to believe Hitler wasn't a threat so he let Hitler have Czechoslovakia. He thought that'd keep him happy."

"How can you give away a country that you don't even own?"

"Well, I don't know the answer to that. I think he probably just said that he wouldn't help Czechoslovakia, and the Czechs couldn't beat Germany on their own, so they were pretty much rooted then."

I wasn't so sure about Jeremy's philosophy but I was impressed by how much he knew. There's something really attractive about people who know stuff. In a way it doesn't matter whether it's a science teacher or a chef on TV or an old shearer talking about the Tally Hi shearing pattern and why wide gear is no good.

Homer and Jess came back at high speed and then it was

action action action. Within four minutes they were gone, leaving Pang, Gavin and me by ourselves. Suddenly I felt very funny. It was like the women and children being left behind while the others went off to war. It didn't help that Jess was with them. Three guys and a girl. She shouldn't be one of the tough ones, the fighters, the ones who get out there and take the risks. She didn't have the experience. Officially she was going as a sort of back-up, because she didn't know much about guns. But I knew how quickly that would change if they got into any hot situations. How would she handle it? She might jeopardise the whole thing. If she did she would jeopardise the lives of three of my friends.

I couldn't decide how much of my emptiness was personal. Off went these three boys and maybe none of them would come back. Off went these three boys with Jess, one of the best looking girls at Wirrawee High School. I realised I was angry at being in a war situation again, mad at Homer and Lee for jumping into it, and furious at Jess for cutting across my tracks. I also realised that if it had not been for Gavin I probably would have signed up for Liberation and gone. Even allowing for Gavin maybe I should have gone. But the thought of Gavin without me was not good. I was all he had. If I got knocked off, Gavin's best chance then would be to move into the dog pen with Marmie. I needed Homer and Lee, and of course Jeremy, to stay alive for a very long time to come, but Gavin needed me to stay alive for at least ten years. Funny, by then he'd be older than I was now.

Speaking of Gavin, it was time to round him up and organise the evening before it got any darker. At least looking after him and Pang would keep my mind off the danger that the other four were approaching. I called Pang. But just as she answered from the spare room, where she'd be sleeping, the phone rang.

It shocked me, because I wasn't expecting it. I jumped, and then grabbed it, thinking, completely irrationally, that it might be Homer or Lee. It was Bronte, inviting herself to visit. She was only a couple of k's away and calling on her mobile. Her mum had said she'd drop her off at my place and she could get the bus back to school tomorrow.

To be honest, even though I liked Bronte a lot, I thought I had enough on my plate already, but I could hardly say no when she was so close.

Pang was waiting in the doorway. "Let's go find Gavin," I said. "There's a friend of mine coming over, so we'd better think about some dinner."

As we crossed the yard she took my hand. Funny how that little hand in mine made me feel all protective. Gavin wasn't really one for hand-holding. It made me think, not for the first time, that it would be nice to have a sister. To have had a sister. I could never have a sister now. I would always be an only child.

I know some people would say I was irresponsible in the way I looked after Gavin. I know there are people in the Wirrawee district who are saying it right now, although of course they are the ones who have the least idea of what we do and the way we live. The most ironic thing that had happened to me in the last twelve months was that I had been put under a court-appointed guardian after my parents died, but the legal system that did that to me completely ignored Gavin. That was fine by me, and

49

anyway, my guardians didn't interfere much with my life except to bring around casseroles and give advice on farming. When your guardians are Homer's parents and they've kind of been your guardians all your life, nothing has to change much. But it's a bit strange when you think about it.

So, just to give people who think I'm irresponsible a bit of evidence they can use, I'll say it straight out: I lost Gavin that evening. He wasn't in the big shed. He wasn't in any of the little sheds, not even the woodshed. He wasn't in the woolshed or in the dog pens or over with the chooks. None of this might have mattered too much on a normal day. I mean, we were meant to be red-hot on security these days and taking multiple precautions every time we brushed our teeth or went on a picnic, but of course the truth was that most days there were moments or minutes or even hours when we forgot or made a mistake or simply thought, "Stuff it, can't hide under the bed all day every day."

This day though was different. There was such an atmosphere of tension that I couldn't imagine even Gavin ignoring it and going off on his own into the paddocks. Not only that, but he wouldn't want to be away from the action. Where there was Homer and Lee, there would be Gavin. Sure Pang's arrival might have thrown him off balance, but not this far off balance. I cursed myself for not being more aware of him earlier, of thinking it was OK for Gavin to be missing when Homer and the other three set off.

I couldn't hide my anxiety from Pang as I walked faster, searching a wider and wider area. She became silent, trotting beside me to keep up. I appreciated that she didn't chatter any more. She seemed so different to Lee in every other way that I was almost surprised to find that she had the same sensitivity as her brother.

Running now, I went back to the big machinery shed. I looked more carefully. First thing I noticed was what I three-quarters expected to see. The motorbike was missing, the Yamaha that was Gavin's favourite. I remembered Pang telling me how she'd seen Gavin fuelling motorbikes and I asked her which bikes. Where was he doing it? Did he say anything? How was he looking?

"He didn't take any notice of me."

"Did he know you were there?"

"Oh yes, he glanced at me, but just looked away. He wasn't very friendly. It was like he didn't want me to be there. I thought, 'Well, if you don't want to be friends, that's OK,' so I left."

That didn't prove anything. Gavin probably would have treated Pang that way at any time. Standing in the area where he'd done the fuelling—the area where we normally service the bikes—I looked around quickly. And I did notice something. The door at the back of the shed was open. Only by a metre, at the most, which is why I didn't notice it before. I went over there. A cold breeze wafted through it. Pang slipped ahead of me and went outside as I looked at the gap. "Just enough room for a little kid on a Yammie," I thought.

"Look here, Ellie," Pang said. "That's from a motorbike, isn't it?"

She was pointing to the ground. In the mud were the tracks of bike wheels. Pang was onto it. For a Thai-Vietnamese-Australian she would have made a pretty good Aboriginal tracker.

I heard a car and guessed it would be Bronte. Before going back to the house to meet her I ran with Pang along the road at the back of the machinery shed. The motorbike tracks were clear enough in the winter mud and wet grass. They were heading straight for the gate that led to the paddock that led to the lagoon that led to the next paddock that led to another paddock that led to the track that if you followed it all the way led to the border. This didn't prove Gavin had set off for the border but it sure as hell suggested that he wasn't thinking about his homework or making a sandwich or watching TV.

Panting hard now, from fear more than physical effort, I ran back through the shed to the other side of the building. Between the shed and the house was Bronte. Her mother's car was already heading down the driveway. For a moment I thought of trying to call her mum back but then realised we had to deal with this on our own, for now anyway. I grabbed Bronte by the hand and tried to explain things to her. There was a problem though. I didn't know how much she knew. But she was a smart girl, Bronte. I had the feeling she'd always know more than I expected.

"Whoa, whoa, wait a sec, Ellie, surely he wouldn't go off like that. What do you think, that he wants to be with the others? To be with Homer?"

"No! Well, yes, but it's not just that. He thinks they're going off to have a look at the . . . well, to be honest, the other side of the border. And if Gavin thinks there's any fighting going on, he'll be there. He's mad about it. Has been ever since the war."

"But Ellie, he's only—"

"Oh forget that. You know how adults love saying they've got an inner child? Well, Gavin's got an inner adult."

"So tell me exactly what you think he might have done."

I had to pause and work that out. What was I exactly expecting?

Carefully I said, "I think he's most likely going to wait for them a long way down the track, and either join them there or, more likely, follow them right over the border and then pop up and say, 'Here I am,' at a point where there won't be anything they can do about it. If they see him too early they'll send him back. With Jess maybe. He's smart enough to figure that out."

"OK, so what are your options?"

I was impressed by Bronte, not for the first time. Even standing there I was thinking, "Gosh, she is just who I need at this moment." She didn't ask any unnecessary questions. In fact she didn't seem too surprised to hear what had been going on. I guess she was well aware how crazy people like Homer were, and she'd probably heard a few rumours. Not for the first time I wondered if she was a member of Liberation herself.

"Well, to follow him, I guess. Or to stay here and do nothing. I don't think that's much of an option. But I've also got Pang to look after."

"I don't need looking after," Pang said. "I look after the other kids all the time at home when Lee's out." She rolled her eyes. "When he's out chasing girls."

"Chasing girls?" I was distracted for a moment and had to shake my head to get my thoughts back together.

"I can look after Pang," Bronte said. "Or I can take her to Homer's. I'm sure she'd be fine there. They're your guardians, aren't they?"

"Yeah," I said. Already I was clearing my mind of the Pang Problem. I've noticed before how the brain doesn't keep what it doesn't need. If Bronte was going to take care of Pang I could erase Pang from my memory for now and concentrate on more important things. It sounds a bit brutal but I suppose it's the way the brain keeps you functioning efficiently. In year 9 I'd memorised heaps of stuff about the Myall Lakes Massacre and the Protector guy in Tasmania, but straight after the test all I could remember was the Protector's name. Robinson.

I ran back into the shed, started up the four-wheel Polaris and moved it to the bowser. "Can you fuel it?" I asked Bronte. She just nodded. I went back into the house and got some warm clothes, for both me and Gavin. I was pretty sure Gavin wouldn't have thought of practicalities like that in his mad rush towards the action. I grabbed a couple of bananas, three hard-boiled eggs and an apple, and filled my jacket pockets with biscuits. I shoved all the other bits and pieces into a backpack and then got the rifle and the ammo. My heart sank when I opened the gun safe, because one of the shotguns was missing. Bloody Gavin was way out of line. He had survived for so long that he thought he was invincible. I suppose the more people succeed, the more confident they become and the higher they stretch. But I knew something that Gavin was too young to understand. That the higher you stretch the closer you get to the crash. If you keep going higher forever you end up as a God. That's not an option for most people, including

Gavin and me. The time to take great risks is at the start, when you've got little to lose and you haven't used up your luck. The time to get super careful is when you've done brilliantly. Every success brings you nearer to the failure. For Gavin's sake I had to hope and pray he had one more success, one more crop of luck still to be harvested.

Bronte had fuelled the Polaris, checked the oil, cleaned the headlight glass and, most amazingly of all, tied a full water bottle to the luggage rack at the front. I thanked her, said goodbye to her and Pang, and blasted out of the yard at maximum revs, wondering if I'd ever see either of them again.

CHAPTER 5

BASICALLY I TOOK THE FASTEST ROUTE I KNEW TO RAWSON Road, or, like Lee said, what we used to call Rawson Road. I stopped three times, when I got into muddy sections of the track, to see if I could figure out what was going on. And the third time, about two k's past the border, I did get a beautifully clear picture of what had happened. It was like reading a story. The two utes were hidden behind a tree. In some places the track was better than the last time I'd come this way, but in most places it was starting to degenerate, and you could see where Homer and the others had swung off the road and parked. Up ahead was a rocky section that would have tested the utes beyond their limits. There was a whole chopped-up area behind the utes with footprints and motorbike tyre marks, where the four of them had obviously gotten on the bikes and ridden away. And although it took me three or four minutes, three or four minutes I couldn't afford, eventually I found the marks of a third motorbike. They were on the left-hand side, away from the other two, which went down the middle. The same as I'd seen back at the machinery shed with Pang: a chunky tread but with bigger spaces between the chunks than the other bikes. It had made a lighter impact in the mud, as though it had less weight on it, and like the others it was fresh.

I ran a couple of hundred metres back towards my place, looking for more evidence. I needed to know whether Gavin had joined up with them or not. Near a huge gum tree, in another long stretch of soft ground, I saw where his tracks had left the road. I followed them and lost them almost straight away, but when I went to the gum tree I found where he had hidden. There were a couple of oil spots and part of a Fruit Tingles wrapper. I reminded myself to have a look at the bike sometime in the impossible future to see how much oil it was losing. My guess was that he had hidden somewhere further back, waited for the utes to pass him, and then followed. While they abandoned the utes he waited behind this tree then continued to follow. He was too close to home to let them know he was there. If they realised he was dogging their steps they would still send him back.

I set off again. I knew I was a long way behind but there was nothing I could do about that. I rode into darkness. The daylight failed fast. At least it seemed to get a bit warmer as the wind dropped away. At the first crossroads I went left. I had a feeling this road was called Sutherland's but I wasn't certain. It didn't matter much, as I was pretty sure of my general direction.

I was trying to plan my strategy for when I got to Rawson Road. The whole idea of planning for something so out of my control was dumb but I suppose all planning is dumb in a way. Seeing you can't predict the future, and seeing you can't control other people, not to mention vehicles, animals, falling trees, the weather and your own self most of the time, planning has got to be . . . what? A kind of insurance policy. A way of trying to make yourself feel OK, because you can pretend you do have control of your life and the world around you. This is very reassuring when you're heading into dangerous and horrible situations.

That's what I thought about, riding along in the cold damp evening, trying not to use my lights. Generally I used a torch instead of headlights, which was not nearly as good of course. Safer in terms of attracting attention but violently dangerous when it came to road safety. I knew the others would be doing the same though, so at least I wasn't losing more time.

I'd thought I would find Rawson Road pretty easily, but something basic had changed. I don't want to sound too cosmic and psychic but because it wasn't our country any more it seemed almost impossibly different. How weird that was, to be in a foreign country where such a short time ago it had been a part of our everyday world. The dirt road I was going down now for instance: not much more than a year ago I could have driven or ridden or walked down here without much thought. Just another dirt road lined with gum trees, a fence that badly needed fixing, a concrete-lined ford across a dip, and in the distance a farmhouse with lights on and people at home. I should have felt at home myself. But a new spirit had spread across the land and I trembled as I pushed forwards, knowing that although it felt like my land it was not. It smelt different. The energy was not the same. I was in alien territory. Instead of getting onto a plane and flying for a zillion hours to get somewhere else, now we could do it by wandering down a track for four hours.

Soon enough though I had to think about stuff that was more down-to-earth. Like self-preservation. All those days back in Wirrawee, going to school, looking after the farm, managing the cattle, trying to manage Gavin: all of that suddenly slipped off me and once again I was the hunter and the hunted. I felt like I'd turned into an animal, a fox maybe, and without any effort I was focused on finding the prey without being shot. I'd seen foxes do terrible things but I'd also admired their cunning. They could grab a duck in broad daylight, when I was working less than fifty metres away. They could find the only hole in the wire; they could tunnel into a chook yard; they seemed to know when you were holding a rifle and when you were only holding a stick; and on the one night when you'd forgotten to lock the gate into the poultry yard, they somehow knew and came sneaking in and killed everything that moved.

Well, I had to be the fox, and somehow I put on the skin of a fox and became a fox on a four-wheel motorbike. You can make a bike go pretty quietly if you keep the revs down and sneak along. I thought my problem at this stage would be more to do with finding Rawson Road than with aggressive enemies. I was trying to picture a map in my head and I thought Rawson Road ran from north to south, from my right to my left, across the flat monotonous country that I was in now. I forced the pace as fast as I could, but the noise of the bike got too loud when I went above thirty or thirty-five. I wondered how the others had done it. Would they have abandoned their bikes and gone on foot? With two bikes—plus one they didn't know about—their noise problem would be more severe than mine of course.

Time was passing too fast and I felt under pressure to push on. Headlights travelling from right to left showed me I was coming to an intersection. It looked big and busy. Rawson Road? I waited for the headlights to pass, then had to wait for two more vehicles going the other way. Busy road. Maybe it was Rawson. I rode out onto the bitumen and looked around, feeling kind of bold. There was no way to tell what road it was. I rode cautiously down it, wondering how far I should go. If I'd got the wrong one this could be an expensive side trip. I suddenly remembered too that you're not meant to ride four-wheelers on made roads. Well, not my four-wheeler anyway. It was something to do with the tyres. They ploughed up the paddocks any time I went off the tracks. Around the front of the machinery shed where I rode in and out, you could see nothing but muddy tracks. The grass was worn away in no time flat. They were heavy-tread tyres and I don't know why they couldn't tolerate pavement but apparently they couldn't.

Well, tough luck. For tonight they had no choice.

I'd gone about a k and a half when I saw one of those green and white direction signs ahead. Thank goodness. I'd been lucky no more cars had come. If I was really lucky the sign would tell me I was on Rawson Road. If I was really really lucky Homer and Lee and the others would be waiting there with Gavin to say, "Hi Ellie, the whole thing turned out to be a false alarm and we can all go home."

I wasn't too lucky. The sign was not in English but the numbers were the same as ours, and it looked like they'd kept the road numbering system we'd used. I didn't know what number Rawson Road was meant to be but I knew it wasn't Highway 3 and apparently I was on Highway 3.

Swear swear swear. Swearwords can be satisfying sometimes. I wheeled the bike around then had to go straight off the road because there was a car coming. In fact it was a truck with a string of cars behind it so I had to lie low for about four minutes while they all trundled past. As soon as there was a break I revved the bike back to the intersection. I didn't have to worry about noise now, not out here on the highway.

I turned left and headed off the dirt again. The landscape looked exactly the same. Sometimes it gets so boring, the way it just goes on and on. Sometimes it's depressing. On TV ages ago they were talking about the Germans invading Russia during World War II, and how the landscape of Russia sent some of the soldiers crazy. It was to do with the way they woke up each morning and set out again and marched all day but nothing changed. Nothing ever changed! For day after day, month after month, they kept moving through a world where they felt like they weren't moving at all. Walking and walking and walking and the horizon never moved and it all stayed the same.

No, I remembered, I didn't see it on TV, I heard it on the car radio, and Mum was driving, because I remember her looking out at the bush and saying, "Yes, God, yes!" when she heard this.

I didn't agree with her—our landscape never had that effect on me—and I was worried by her saying it. For one thing I thought she was being disloyal. But still, I understood what she meant. At the same time if you knew the bit of bush you were in, or if you stopped and spent some time there, or if you opened your eyes and had a decent look around, you couldn't see it as monotonous. It was only when we were driving that the endless miles got slightly depressing sometimes.

I sort of knew Rawson Road when I came to it. I'm not sure what it was, but something gave me the vibe of "Yes,

I think this is it." It must have been three years since I'd come along here, and that was in the car, with my parents.

I turned left and rode fast on the gravel at the side, looking for another green and white sign. There wasn't one, but after a couple of k's I passed the entrance to a farm, and in paint on the front gate was the address, unaltered since before the war, *1274 Rawson Road*.

What a relief. I pressed on. My next problem was to find out whether I was going in the right direction. I figured I was now on the hypotenuse of the triangle. The other two sides were from my place to the start of Sutherland's, and Sutherland's itself. The hypotenuse didn't really lead back to my place, but it came out about eight k's away. Close enough.

I knew that the square of the hypotenuse would be equal to the sum of the square of the other two sides. Thank you Wirrawee High for that piece of knowledge. But it didn't seem much help right now. I needed something else. I needed the intuition and awareness of a fox. I remembered how foxes do this thing where they get a rooster to stick his head through the wire of the pen so the fox can bite it off. I didn't know how they did it but I'd seen it a couple of times myself and the Yannoses had it happen to their chooks too. I don't mean I actually saw it, but I saw the results. You go down to the chook pen in the morning and there's a decapitated rooster lying inside the wire. How is it possible? We have quite a big pen and yet somehow the fox was able to get the rooster to come all the way to the wire and obligingly stick his head through so the fox could have it for supper.

I needed to find the trick, to know how to do it. I suppose it's like using the energy in the ball and deflecting it to win a point. I vaguely remembered Robyn explaining something like this to me once when we were playing tennis. She understood sport in a way I never could. She said you don't try to hit the ball hard. You let the other player do that, and you just put your racquet in the way and let the ball go back with the speed the other player has already put on it.

If a fox can make the rooster come to the wire and put its head out to be bitten off, the fox doesn't have to do much work. I didn't want to start a war here; all I wanted was to bounce Gavin back to the other side of the border.

I kept going but I could see I was heading into a serious problem. Rawson Road was quickly turning into a suburb. There were houses ahead, and they were close together. Being in a rural environment had been fine by me, but there was no way I could ride through settled areas on a four-wheeler. It was one of those mid-moon nights, where you could see well enough, not like a full moon, as good as daylight, but light enough to put me in a dangerous situation.

I snuck past the first group of houses, took the curve, saw another even longer row of houses and slipped past them too, but I was running out of nerves and I knew I'd soon be running out of luck. I didn't want to wait until my last bit of luck actually fizzled out like foam on the sand. I pulled over onto a bit of broken ground and sat there trying desperately to think. I hated being in this position, where I had to make life and death decisions in a matter of seconds, with practically no information to go on. I like being in control. I was biting my bottom lip one minute and chewing on my knuckle the next. What to do? What to do? My mind threatened to break out and stampede, to knock down the fences and run wild, to go in a dozen directions at once.

"All right," I told myself, "at least work out what you want most of all. What are you doing here?" I knew the answer straight away. I was here with a mission and that was to find Gavin and keep him safe and get him home alive. It would be nice to help Homer and Lee and Jeremy and Jessica, and save innocent people from being attacked by a bunch of terrorists, and preferably to keep myself alive too, but this was a Gavin mission and it was as simple as that.

OK, so how was I going to do it?

No easy answer, just keep going and look everywhere and hope like hell or heaven I could find him.

I had to leave the bike though. I rolled it behind a tree. It wouldn't be safe for long but if this was the beginning of the suburbs I couldn't ride any further. I slung the rifle onto my back and trotted down the side of the road, keeping to the shadows, looking for something, anything, a clue, a prop, a guide.

Sometimes in life you do get what you want. In this case, though, I was quite a way past the sign before I recognised it.

It was another road sign, this one from pre-war days, a sort of mustard colour with a green logo. A tourist sign I think. There was no name on it, just a picture of a palm tree and *800 metres*.

I was so busy looking for a car to steal, some sort of transport, that I got a hundred metres past the sign before I started thinking about palm trees. By now I was well and truly in the land of the flats and the low-cost houses and the tar and cement. A set of traffic lights was ahead. I was getting really wary. Things were quiet, but there were cars occasionally and I saw a kid on a skateboard and a couple of people going in and out of their homes. It was weird. This didn't look like a war zone. I felt like I was the terrorist. I was the one with the rifle.

Palm tree. Wait a minute. Palm tree. Jeremy's voice. Ambush. "Under the coconut tree," that's what he'd said. What did he mean? An ambush under the coconut tree?

I started jogging. I had to take a long detour to get around the intersection. Luckily half the lights weren't working, so it wasn't as well lit as it would have been in the old days. The whole atmosphere was like that though, everything run-down, shabby. Potholes in the road, a drain blocked and water banked up in a big pond, a bus shelter with the roof missing. I ignored all that and hurried on. I covered maybe half a k and then saw the coconut tree. It was hard to work out what it was. On my left was an old house, like a historic place that was probably open to the public or something before the war, but on the right was a shopping centre. Out the front was a row of palm trees, all looking a bit old and trashed, and in the middle of the main entrance was a big neon palm with three-quarters of its lights out. Why on earth would anyone choose this as a place for an ambush? I could see an arcade or mall in the middle, a lot of individual shops, and a car park all around it. Down the far end was a supermarket, with big bins of fruit or vegetables out the front. Watermelons or potatoes or whatever. The lighting wasn't too great here either and I couldn't tell what half the shops were, let alone whether the bins held watermelons, or cans of dog food, or toothbrushes. Closest to me were a hairdresser's and a clothes shop. There were shoppers everywhere. These people had a serious commitment to late-night shopping.

The next thing that happened was that I saw Jeremy.

It was a shock. I was scanning the car park and everything was alien and unrecognisable and in the middle of it all was a face that was familiar and friendly and part of my life. I focused on him at the same time as a leap of wild excitement happened inside my chest. Although I had been looking for them for hours, I could hardly believe I was seeing him. He moved quickly from the far side of the car park and as I watched he went behind a row of dump bins that were at right angles to the supermarket. He'd been trying to walk naturally, like he belonged there, but he didn't look too natural to me. For one thing he walked a bit fast. That's what had attracted my attention I think.

There was no sign of the others. I stayed where I was, behind a small tree, and tried to figure it out. They were probably behind the dump bins with him. Or maybe they were in different points around the car park waiting to ambush the terrorists? It still seemed a strange place for that.

Another movement attracted my attention. This time it wasn't someone walking too quickly. It was someone moving too slowly. I gazed with a slowly building sense of horror. A man was creeping around the far side of the car park towards the dump bins, and it wasn't Homer or Lee. And a moment after I saw him—this is hard to describe—it was as though I now, almost immediately, plugged myself into a new network of seeing. Now I was no longer looking at the car park and the occasional shopper with a trolley and the family at the boot of their Daihatsu and the seagulls swooping around looking for scraps. Now I saw a different view: this man with an automatic weapon, and another man coming around from the other side, also armed, and three others following him, and at least three more advancing through the car park, dodging from car to car, and all of them holding their rifles and moving like professionals.

I didn't even have time to swear. I lost control of my legs for a moment, tried to move but just wobbled, then made myself set off across the road. "Why did the chicken cross the road?" I asked myself, in one of those stupid thoughts that come into my head in the worst and wildest situations. I didn't have an answer. "To get eaten by the fox, I suppose." I had no plan. I got control of my legs, though, and was suddenly in full war mode again. Keeping my head down and grabbing the rifle so tight I hurt my hand, I raced down the right-hand side of the car park, using the shadow of an overgrown hedge for cover.

With everyone's attention focused on the dump bins, it wasn't surprising that no-one noticed me but I wasn't thinking about that. Just hoping that for once in my life I could be invisible. Just praying no-one would look my way. Arriving at the next tree panting like I'd run three thousand metres in an Olympics final.

I had about four seconds to decide what to do. Go in behind the dump bins and join Jeremy and whoever else was there? Attack the hunters? Hardly. A fox wouldn't do that. Beyond the car park a rough old track ran uphill. There was a building site, probably an extension to the shopping centre, but it looked like no-one had done any building for a long time. What was that joke? Why do they still call it a building after it's finished? Why don't they call it a built? Well, this was definitely a building not a built, because they hadn't got far past the foundations. What to do? What to do? The question kept pounding at the walls of my brain. It was paralysing me. Go to the dump bins? No. I'd just be joining Jeremy and anyone else there so I could die with them.

Attack? No, instant suicide.

I had to create a diversion, draw those men with guns away. OK, run across the car park firing the rifle so they chased after me? That sounded horribly like suicide too. But lying here on the damp and cold ground wasn't going to save anyone and it wasn't going to get me any closer to finding Gavin. Remember the reason you're here, Ellie? Remember what you said to yourself just a few minutes ago? You can't leave it to future Ellie to deal with the situation. This is the situation.

No, there was only one way and one place where a diversion might work. I took a deep breath but still felt as though not a skerrick of oxygen reached my lungs. Didn't matter. I had to assume my body would take care of the breathing thing, like it had done fairly well up till now. I had to throw my life to the winds.

CHAPTER 6

THANK GOD I DIDN'T STOP TO THINK ABOUT IT ANY longer. If I had, there is no way in the world I would have moved from behind that tree. But those dumb old legs and arms work quite fast sometimes, and this was one of those times. I checked the safety on the rifle again, took a rough aim at the hairdresser's, and shot three rounds into its window, aiming high so I didn't kill anyone.

Then another two at the clothes shop.

All the lights went out in the hairdresser's straight away. Half-a-dozen people near the clothes shop scattered and went skidding away to the right and left. A bell started ringing, like the world's biggest alarm clock. My insides were suddenly cold and twisted, like a doctor with hypothermia had grabbed hold of my large intestine. I ran forwards, bending at the waist, straight towards the mall. People started pouring out of a side exit like a million ants who've just heard there's a jam spill at the factory up the road. Not very intelligent of them but who thinks clearly at times like these? I could see them pushing each other to try to get people to go faster. But for me the automatic doors at the front opened perfectly, inviting me in. There were people still moving normally at the far end, like it hadn't yet registered on them. I kept running. My insides felt wet and mushy now, no longer cold and twisted. I had a sudden memory of the men in the barracks at the airfield, the men

I'd shot, and how they'd looked like road kill. I definitely didn't want to kill anyone here. These people had just popped in to pick up their Sorbent and their Sanitarium and their Nappisan. I fired at the ceiling, four shots, as I ran straight ahead. Suddenly people were diving for cover. Bags of groceries lay all over the floor, in among the deserted trolleys. There were spilt coffee cups, dropped ice-creams, an overturned pram. I deliberately shot out the front glass in a chemist's shop, on the left, and then the same to another clothing store, on the right. The panes of glass slid down like water over a waterfall. It was almost calming to see the smooth rush of glass.

I was at the supermarket. Now I did have a plan. Not much of one, but a plan. I swung left and raced in there. I think they'd probably turned off the main lights but some kind of security lighting had cut in and everything was dull and dim but visible. I went straight through a checkout lane. No-one asked to inspect my bag. I could see movement all around. I wasn't stopping to do a survey, but there was a glimpse of an old man to the left, a shop assistant to the right, and a young woman behind a rack of bread. She wasn't too smart hiding behind bread. The dog food might have been better. The cans of fruit maybe. Boy, you'd get some dramatic ricochets if you started firing near the cans of fruit. I ran past the potato chips. Some foods in this place I didn't recognise but potato chips must look pretty much the same in any language.

A guy in a suit suddenly popped out at me as I passed a stack of bottled water. He'd been hiding behind it. He wanted to be a hero. He grabbed at me, at the same time turning his face away, like he didn't want to be hit. His eyes were almost closed. His arms were strong, though, and he got quite a good grip. I got such a shock that I nearly dropped the rifle. But it was like he didn't quite know what to do. If he did fight me he risked being killed. He was like a softball player who's stolen a couple of bases but is too scared to run home on a hit. But just as I realised he wasn't totally committed, he realised I was a girl. He'd stolen a look at me and his eyes widened and he got a stronger grip. He had me around the waist in a face-to-face hug and I knew I had to break his grip or I was done for.

How funny that after everything I'd been through it could all end here, suddenly, in a moment, in this dingy supermarket, among the bottled water and the bags of rice, killed by a man with a forgettable face, a man in a suit and a boring blue-grey tie.

He was trying to pull me over. We struggled wildly. I still had the rifle and the first thing I did was get a finger to the trigger and squeeze off a shot. I knew it was pointing upwards, so it wasn't going to kill anyone, but I also knew it'd give him a helluva fright and that might give me the advantage for a moment. I was used to the noise but he wasn't and it really was loud, especially in this place with a low roof. When it went off the man gave a jerk so violent that for a moment I thought I really had hit him. He did loosen his grip on me, and I shoved hard and sharply, hop-ing to send him off balance. He went backwards, letting go of me, his arms flailing like a player in netball trying to stop you passing. I moved in fast and pushed him again, deliberately aiming him at a stand of cans of something, I don't know what they were. Tomatoes maybe? He went into them with his back and his bum and the whole thing

71

kind of exploded around him. I picked up a can as it rolled towards me, threw it at him, missed, grabbed another one and threw it hard into his head. I saw red stuff fly. It was like it was a can of tomatoes and it had burst open and the tomatoes were splattering everywhere. But the can hadn't burst open. It was the other red stuff I was looking at. He put his hands to his face and turned sideways. I didn't know if he was still conscious but I had to assume he wouldn't be a threat for the next few minutes at least.

I raced towards the back door, the one into the storage area. Glancing behind me I saw a few people putting their heads up from their hiding places. They looked undecided. Will we chase her or what? She's only a girl. And there's only one of her. But she's got a gun.

It was a double door, a heavy thing made of rubber and/ or plastic or something. It was partly transparent. As soon as I burst through it I entered another world. No more fancy displays or canned music or ladies handing out little samples of tofu, like we get in Wirrawee. This was even darker than the dim supermarket; the floor was concrete, hundreds of boxes were in big stacks everywhere. It smelt different too, but nice, like biscuits at the very first moment when you open the pack.

I saw one guy, a young employee who looked about my age. He was paralysed by fear, I think, backed up against a big refrigeration unit, staring at me. Nothing but his eyes moved. I thought it was probably safe to ignore him, so I kept running.

Further out the back were the loading docks. There were no deliveries happening—too late in the day, I guess—so it was all closed up and very dark indeed. I jumped off the dock and ran to the big roller door. There had to be a way to open this mongrel thing. I glanced around frantically. A whole length of new chain lay on the ground, along with tools and a big tin of grease. Looked like they were about to fix or replace the doors. I hoped they were still working. On the side was a big red button with a dirty old notice in English, on a bit of cardboard, saying *Press twice to open*. I pressed twice. The door started to clank up, slow and heavy and noisy. Jesus, it would take half an hour. Panting, I looked behind me. Had they organised themselves yet? As the door ratcheted up I heard rifle shots, close. Seemed like I was opening the door onto a shooting gallery. The door was up to my waist. I ducked under and stayed low, looking around madly. Where was the danger? Which direction? Quick quick, find it before it finds you. Then, thank God, I saw Homer and Jeremy. They were behind the dump bins, like I suspected, both turned slightly away from me and lying low, like me. As I saw them they both fired, almost simultaneously. I couldn't see the others but I saw flashes of flame which made me think they were further to the right. I hoped it was them anyway.

Also to my right, but down on the road were four vehicles, three of them utes and the other a small truck with an open back. There seemed to be people on the road, using them and the rocks and trees as cover. I hissed to myself as I realised how bad it was. Although these guys had the disadvantage of being downhill, there were more of them and they looked pretty well-protected.

To the left, around the perimeter of the car park, the news seemed better. I started to pick out soldiers again, maybe the guys I'd seen before, but now they had swung their point of attack to the front of the mall, like I'd meant them to. I thought that it probably gave us half a minute or so of relatively clear ground, both ahead and to the left.

In the darkness the weapons were like little flamethrowers, with the constant leaps of hot orange-yellow-white from the barrels. It made it easy to see where people were, but the problem was to work out *who* those people were. I realised for example that at least two people were shooting from inside the fruit shop, which was now in total darkness. I assumed these were not people who were there to pick up avocadoes.

Crouched low, I started running to Homer and Jeremy. As I closed in on them I couldn't resist calling, "Hi guys."

It was the second nearest I'd come to being shot. The nearest was when I was shot. You can't get much nearer than that. Jeremy swung around and lifted the rifle to his shoulder. His expression was that of a guy who is so hypnotised you could ask him to be a chook and he'd immediately lay an egg or stick his head through the wire. I realised he wasn't going to see me in time but even so I screamed out, "Jeremy!" and raised my hand to cover my face from the shot, not that my hand would have done much good. I owed my life to Homer. He didn't have time to say anything, just took one look, lunged and pushed the rifle away as the shot went off. The bullet howled past me like a banshee, except that I don't know what a banshee is, let alone what sound it would make. But something about the word "banshee" makes me think that a screaming bullet wouldn't be far wrong.

Jeremy went white when he realised it was me. He looked like he'd seen a ghost and he looked like he'd become a ghost. He just stood there staring. Homer, on the other hand, was as calm as ever. His natural brown skin didn't lose any colour. He shook his head and said, "Seen any shops you like?"

"It's clear to the left, for a couple of minutes maybe," I said. "I think it's your only chance."

Homer didn't hesitate. "I'll get the others. You two cover me. Wake up, Jeremy."

He slid away to the right. I was panting like a horse with wind. I peered anxiously, trying to see Homer, trying to tell what was happening. The firing down there seemed to have increased by about ten times. It was nearly continuous now. That meant they were either attacking or getting ready to attack. Whoever was down there, Lee and Jessica perhaps, and maybe even Gavin, might be overwhelmed before Homer reached them. The constant banging of the guns was getting to me. They seemed louder and louder, but I wasn't sure if they were getting any closer. The shots drove out every other noise and every other sensation. I wished they would stop. It was like operating a jackhammer and having a migraine at the same time.

In among all that I tried to think. At least the four of them had achieved part of what they wanted: whatever raid the soldiers were planning, it wouldn't go ahead now. Not tonight anyway. A smart retreat was the only way for us to go, but the odds were heavily against it. Would Homer and the others have planned for a retreat? Maybe Jess, say, was back at the bikes, ready to take off in a hurry? Gavin even? Gavin would have been good for a job like that. Getaway driver.

Did they know Gavin was around? Was Gavin around?

I got a glimpse of Homer and fired a couple of rounds into the darkness above him. He was almost at the other bins. That was a pretty good effort, but I felt we could only have seconds left before the soldiers who'd run into the mall came spilling out again.

I was in a tug of war, and it was all happening inside me. They say a watched kettle never boils. Knowing that, I didn't want to keep staring at the other dump bins, using all the power in my mind and body, willing Homer and the others to reappear. Nor did I want to stare to the left, willing that area to stay clear of the enemy. Superstitiously, I thought I would make more soldiers appear if I did. The stresses on my mind and body were terrible. Jeremy still looked white-faced and had not said a word. I think we were both in post-traumatic shock, but the trauma wasn't post yet. Then I suddenly remembered and yelled at Jeremy, "Have you got Gavin?" He took a long second to work out who Gavin was—I think he was still working out who I was—and then he suddenly said, "No. Why should we?"

I groaned. Things couldn't have got any worse, and now suddenly they had. At least Jeremy's voice sounded stronger than I'd expected. He asked me again, "Why should we?" But there was no time to answer. The shots from all around the perimeter, on our right-hand side, had eased up a bit and were now just random pops. I didn't know whether that was good news or not, but I figured it probably was, as it meant that they couldn't have caught everyone yet, and they probably weren't getting good targets. But suddenly the shots took off again, like an extremely revved-up car accelerating down the main road of Stratton. I could see two soldiers coming out of the entrance to the mall. I jerked my head around to the right. What was all the excitement? Then I saw Jess do a neat zigzag from one dump bin to the next. "If only these dump bins had wheels," I thought. Actually, engines as well would be nice. I wondered how safe we'd be inside a dump bin, whether the bullets would penetrate it or bounce off. Maybe they'd ricochet and kill the people attacking us. But it would be nice to drive along in a dump bin, like a tank, feeling secure.

$A + B + C = D$. That's algebra. Algebra imitates life. Algebra is life. Or maybe life imitates algebra. A was the dump bin. B was the Toyota Landcruiser about fifteen metres to my left, with the driver's door opened, where somebody had abandoned it in the early heat of the battle. Presumably. It was crammed with stuff. Big cardboard boxes that filled the rear section, as well as the back seat and even the front passenger seat.

D represented a possibility, a hope, a faint chance.

And just maybe, C was the length of chain back at the roller door.

As a bonus, the Toyota had a tow bar.

You have to understand that in this situation there was simply nothing else, and once I put the three objects together they burnt so brightly in my mind that I couldn't think of anything else. We were completely cut off on the right, the mall was behind us and probably now full of enemy troops, and we would never get across the vast desert of the car park to the left without being cut off and killed. So in that situation, the Toyota, the dump bin and the chain were like a dying guy in the outback seeing a drink machine, a power point and a pile of dollar coins. The combination the three objects made in my mind was suddenly irresistible.

If everything goes in threes, I also knew that there were at least three major problems. And they were major major major. On the Richter scale they would have rated a nine. I knew from talking to the bloke who emptied our dump bin at home that they weigh six hundred kilos. Of course I had no idea what else was in the dump bin. It could have been full of concrete blocks that some bloke had chucked out from the building site. So, first problem, the bin might be too heavy.

On the other hand, Toyota claimed that these vehicles could pull anything. Elephants up Everest.

I also knew that bullets might penetrate the steel wall, in which case the people inside would be dead, dead, a thousand times over. And the third thing: I knew that the person stupid enough to do the driving was extremely vulnerable.

On another hand, one person in the car was a much better risk than five people in the car. I didn't know what was in those boxes, the ones that filled the Toyota. If they contained inflated balloons for a party, they were not going to be much help. But if they had pillows or china plates or TVs they might just act as bullet-resistant barriers. The best thing of all would be books. Oh how I hoped they were books. I've always liked reading, but at this moment I felt an attraction for books more powerful than ever before. I hoped that whoever owned the four-wheel drive was equally keen on them.

At the same time, my sitting at the wheel of the Toyota was going to leave me highly exposed. I wouldn't be much of a challenge to a marksman. Or a markswoman. Or a markschild. Even a marksbaby.

D, in my equation, represented what? Beyond a faint chance, beyond hope, it represented escape, safety, getting out of here. D would need a lot more than A, B and C. It would also need roads we could use, roads free of traps and ambushes and flying bullets. But that would have to wait. This was all about short-term solutions. This was about the here and now. I've never been any good at games like chess, where people can think five or ten moves ahead. On yet another hand, in farming, you do that all the time, so maybe I'm selling myself short. Anyway, there was nothing I could do about the long-term while I was in the car park at that mall. I yelled at Jeremy, "Cover Homer, I'll be back," and took off for the roller door.

Chain is terrible stuff to carry. This one was heavy. These weren't the roller doors they put in suburban garages; this one was serious. But it wasn't only the weight of the chain that caused me problems. Chain is like picking up a boa constrictor. It slithers and slides and gets away from you and tries to escape, and just when you get a grip on one section another part manages to run off.

I grabbed armfuls, as much as I could manage, and set about dragging it all backwards, to the dump bin. I was sweating like a very anxious pig. In twenty or thirty seconds I was almost clear of the roller door, having made an excellent five metres of progress. Great! I should be back at the Toyota by Christmas.

Feeling desperate, I looked up and nearly dropped the chain again. Three soldiers had simultaneously appeared on the loading dock. They were in a line across the dock. Weirdly, they were like dancers in a theatre. Their movements seemed to be so synchronised. And these guys wore uniforms. Somehow Homer and Lee and Jeremy and Jess had stumbled into half an army.

At that moment I was dead. At the next moment a series of shots roared behind me, bullets no doubt whistled past me, but I was too deafened from the explosions to hear them. One of the soldiers went flying backwards into the storeroom as though he had been king-hit by the heavyweight champion of the world. The other two bolted back into the darkness.

I turned around. Lee. He was kneeling. He had evidently dropped to one knee as he had fired. Before he could get up again I said, "That's the way I like to see you."

He got up quickly when I said that, although I doubt if he heard me—I couldn't hear myself after the noise of those bullets. He grabbed half of the chain I was trying to hold, without even asking why I needed it. Trust Lee. In fact, Lee was all about trust, except when he was with girls. With two people the boa constrictor gave up its fight, and we were back at the dump bin in seconds.

At least everyone was there. Everyone bar Gavin. Jeremy, Jess, Homer. That was an improvement in the situation. They were all pale. We tried to smile at each other. But it was pretty much impossible. I'd noticed before how when things get really frightening and dangerous I lose the ability to smile. It's because of the tension in my face. The whole face locks up, and I have the feeling that if I look into a mirror I'll see shiny pink skin, like someone who is recovering from burns. It gets too stretched for smiles. The others seemed to be the same. The smiles were in the eyes.

Nothing else improved. In fact it got significantly worse. The car park to the left was now full of visible danger again. I could see four guys with rifles, all advancing, running from car to car. They had spread out too, so that they were almost impossible targets. I didn't even bother to look to the right, because I knew what I would see. I left the others to do the shooting, and instead carried an end of chain to the loophole at the base of the dump bin.

There was only one hole, at the left-hand end. As I fed the chain through it, I nodded to Lee and then to the tow bar of the Toyota. He got the idea straight away and started wrapping the chain around it. I figured the shorter the chain the better, up to a point, as that would reduce sway. Whatever, the people in the dump bin were in for a bad time.

I wasn't sure if Lee had worked out exactly what I was suggesting. He sure hesitated when I yelled at them, "Get in! Get in!"

Certainly Homer and Jess and Jeremy looked at me like I was mad. "Bullets won't go through it!" I screamed at them, running around to the driver's door. It was a big statement to make, but if I was wrong, I would never have to see their accusing faces or hear their accusing voices, for the rest of my life, although I would see them and hear them in my nightmares sure enough.

I realised I had forgotten my rifle, and hesitated, wondering whether to get it, and wondering whether they needed more incentive to get in the dump bin. Then I saw

Lee pick up my rifle. At the same time I saw Homer scrambling up the side of the bin. It was going to be fun getting in there. But that was their problem.

I jumped in the cab. When I saw the keys I realised that there had been at least one factor I'd forgotten in my equation. I should have had another letter, E, to represent the keys of the Landcruiser. If the driver had taken the keys with him, we would have been totally rooted. I can't hotwire a car, and I don't think any of the others could either. One of those little jewels of knowledge they didn't teach at Wirrawee High School.

I started the engine. Looking back, I could only see Jeremy and Lee. This was good news, as it suggested that Homer and Jess were already inside. Normally I wouldn't have been too keen on the idea of Jess being in a confined, darkish space with either Homer or Lee, but I was guessing that whatever was in the dump bin, if it wasn't concrete blocks, was likely to be rotting fruit and vegetables, or the contents of the mall's rubbish bins, or the out-of-date sausages from the butcher in the supermarket.

Anyway, they would have other things on their minds. As did I. I saw Jeremy sliding over the top into the dump bin. It looked like he went in headfirst. Then Homer's head and shoulders popped up. He must have found something to stand on, possibly Jess, and he dragged Lee, as Lee's feet scrabbled at the sides, trying to find a foothold.

Well, now to test C in the equation. Would the Landcruiser tow the dump bin?

Elements A and B were also about to be tested, and tested to their absolute limits. Algebra doesn't allow any room for doubt or ambiguities. Either X represents 1.7852801, or it doesn't. It was the same here in the car park. Either the dump bin resisted bullets, or the people inside it were dead. Either the driver of the Landcruiser would escape getting shot, or else everyone was dead. Either the Landcruiser would tow the dump bin, or else we were all dead.

Not much doubt or ambiguity there.

I shoved it into four-wheel drive, low range, low gear, low everything. If there'd been an "activate bullock train" button, I would have pressed that. It was an automatic, so there wasn't much more I could do except to go easy on the take-off. I started easing down the accelerator with my right foot.

CHAPTER 7

I STILL COULDN'T HEAR TOO MUCH, BUT I FELT THE PRESsure as the chain tightened. I could picture it, stretching and straining, starting to quiver, either unravelling at the tow bar, or at the dump bin, or tearing off the side of the dump bin. Or snapping. My mind started to race ahead, trying to work out other possibilities if the chain didn't hold. I couldn't think of a single thing.

There was a sort of shift, almost a grunt, from the dump bin. I heard that all right. I had a feeling that I was going to move it a few centimetres at least. If I could only get some momentum up! Tugs can tow ocean liners, can't they? Those little tractors at the airport that pull the jumbo jets around, they had to be good role models for the Landcruiser, didn't they? Oh God, why did you invent wheels and not put them on every dump bin?

We were inching forwards. Lucky we were, because a bullet hit the right rear window of the Landcruiser. I decided I never again wanted to be in a car where a window is shattered by a bullet. It's terrifying. You feel like there's been an explosion in the car, as though someone's tossed in a bomb. There was enough space between the boxes and the window for the noise to expand. Whatever was in the boxes must have slowed it down though, because it didn't hit the other window. I found that mildly comforting. But really, my focus was on the dump bin, and whether

I could shift it. Gradually it started to move, and there was that magic moment when you're towing anything successfully and you realise you have momentum, you have lift-off.

However, it wasn't that easy. I soon realised there was going to be no such thing as momentum. I could hear the car engine really grunting, and wondered again what else was in the bin. Say the car was packed with books and the dump bin with concrete blocks. We'd run out of fuel before we got to the end of the car park. But I started to realise that it wasn't just the weight of the thing, it was the bitumen as well. If this was the middle of a hot day I'd have had no chance. We'd have been in bitumen soup. I had the horrible feeling that the dump bin was actually lifting and pushing the bitumen, like when you're chiselling a long curly shaving from a block of wood. I could picture the bitumen piling up, getting bigger and gluggier, until it brought us to a halt.

All of these thoughts were going through my head in the space of seconds, and at the same time the bullets were storming against the car. It was *thang thang thang*, like hail on a galvanised-iron roof, but about twenty times louder. Like popcorn popping against the lid of a saucepan, but a thousand times louder. We were getting up a little bit of speed, but I wondered how long the clutch would last. Grunt, strain, squeeze, *thang thang thang*, push, groan, *thang thang*, lurch. Every fibre in my body seemed to be strained like piano wire. If someone had strummed me I would have given off quite a note.

Yet one thing was changing. There weren't so many bullets hitting the car. I had time to wonder why. Maybe

Homer and the others were taking pot shots at them, sticking their heads up in the dump bin. I hoped not, but I also knew they might have to do that for us to survive. The trouble was that I couldn't see in the rear-vision mirror, because of the boxes in the vehicle, and I couldn't see the dump bin in the wing mirrors. For all I knew the dump bin was now riddled with bullets and my friends were all dead.

Perhaps we should have surrendered. Funny, that thought had never entered my head.

But perhaps the soldiers were just running out of ammunition. They must have used thousands of rounds. God knows, we couldn't have many left either. Up till now I'd been gazing at the steering wheel, the gear stick, the accelerator and brake. I guess I thought it might work a kind of magic and make the vehicle do what I wanted. Now I looked out and around, as much as I could. Amazingly, we were going faster than a man could run, although the creaking and banging and rattling of the chain and the dump bin suggested we wouldn't get much further. I could see soldiers in the distance, but only to the left, and I think we had put a little space between the others and us.

There was only one place I could aim for and that was the dirt track I had seen before, the one that led up to the building site. I had no idea where the boys' motorbikes were, but the dirt road looked like it might lead to wildness of some kind. The official roads offered nothing but a suburban death, a journey that sooner or later would be halted by a roadblock or an army vehicle or a sniper. I had to go dirt.

By now I'd actually got up to a speed of between forty and fifty. We were humming along.

Wisps of white smoke drifting out of the engine put a stop to my optimism. I've always been one of those people who prefer not to look at something bad in case it turns out to be bad. My father always preferred to look because, he said, "It's better to know! If you look and it's good, you can stop worrying. If you look and it's bad, you can figure out what to do about it."

Well, I wasn't about to stop, get out and look under the bonnet. The way I see it, smoke is always bad. But I did force myself to look at the gauges, and immediately wished I hadn't. I've never seen a temperature gauge in the red before. I'd certainly never seen one at the max, with the needle practically bowed, like it was about to release an arrow. For all the terrible things I'd done to our vehicles at home over the years, I'd never cooked an engine. My mother did once, but I never had.

The wisps of smoke were strong now, getting more like a solid column. I hoped the owner of the car had insurance. The engine started coughing and heaving, like it was going to vomit. That's how I felt too. I was pressing down harder on the accelerator but we were losing speed. It was exactly like that movie with the guy being chased by the truck and he's trying to get up the hill but his engine's giving him nothing any more. The only difference was that in the movie it took about ten minutes. In the car park it took about forty-five seconds. Suddenly the car was panting and dying.

Still, we were nearly at the edge of the park. But at that point I gave up. It was a question of whether we would get a few more metres with the Toyota or whether we would be better off on foot again. Assuming there was anyone else left alive to be on foot. I think that was one of the reasons I stopped where I did. I couldn't stand the not knowing any longer. I had to see whether they were still alive. I had to see whether my idea and my decision had killed them or saved them or somewhere in between. This was one situation where it was better to look.

Here's a bit of historical trivia. When the United States Army invaded and won the Japanese island of Okinawa in World War II, they suffered nearly forty thousand casualties. But they also had more than twenty-six thousand men evacuated because of mental breakdowns. When General Finley told me that, in New Zealand during the war, it really shocked me. But as the war went on, it didn't shock me much any more.

When Homer and Lee and Jeremy and Jess came crawling out of the dump bin I thought, "My God, what have I done to them?"

Their hair was frazzled like they'd had electric shocks, their faces were tight, but it was their eyes I noticed. I wondered how much longer they'd be members of Liberation. Would they be any good to the Scarlet Pimple after this? Their eyes reminded me of the cow I'd pulled from the dam. She was stuck so fast and was so worn out by her struggles that I'd given her a handful of illegal pills to get her moving. By the time she got onto the bank, her pupils were as big as frisbees.

Even more disturbing was that I couldn't work out whether these four looked like the traumatised cow before

I gave her the ecstasy, or the crazed cow tripping after I shoved the pills down her throat.

I shouldn't try to be funny about it because there was nothing amusing in it for them, and I'm sure I would have looked worse if I'd shared the ride with them. But I saw at a glance that the sides of the dump bin were intact. Dented and marked, almost every flake of paint gone, but no holes. I felt a little surge of jubilation in my chest.

At least they hit the ground running. Homer looked around briefly to orientate himself. "Quick, go!" he gasped. He started stumbling towards the dirt track.

"Where are we going?" I screamed at him as we took off.

He looked around at me with a surprised expression. "I thought Jeremy must have told you."

"So I was heading the right way?" I asked, pleased again.

He didn't bother to answer.

At least I was reunited with my rifle. For a few moments the position of the Toyota and the dump bin had protected us from the firing. But as we got free from that cover, it started again. I'd already been pulling out any last rounds I could find in my pockets and cramming them into the magazine. The trouble is that when you do it too quickly you get in a mess and the rounds jam up with each other. "Patience in small things," my father used to say. I hardly had any bullets left anyway. It's a feeling of lightness and relief when you take the last of them out of your pockets, because they weigh so much. It's also a horrible feeling of panic, because once they're used, you're truly on your own.

CHAPTER 8

WE WERE LUCKY THAT EVERYBODY WAS ABLE TO RUN. I'm not sure what the American troops on Okinawa did when they collapsed mentally. I'm guessing they fell down in little heaps and wept and could not move or speak any more. Or maybe they threw away their weapons and ran screaming at the enemy. Or maybe they dived in blind panic into the ocean, desperate to swim to Australia or Hawaii or California.

We were lucky that none of us was in that condition.

I realised when we were in the shadow of the first new wall that we were heading for a twin-cab ute. Somehow they'd stolen it and put it here ready for use. It had drums in the back that looked like fuel, which could be a bonus with the price of petrol these days. Homer grabbed the keys from off the front tyre and threw them to me, then went around to the other side. I took the driver's seat. Jess and Lee both got in the back, from my side. When I noticed how badly they trembled I could only hope that dump bin syndrome didn't last long.

Jeremy was in the front, shaking so much that he bounced on the seats. Homer didn't seem much better.

I took off with a skidding slide that sent dust and gravel flying behind me. I was trembling pretty badly myself, but hanging on to the steering wheel helped. From the back seat Jess yelled at both of us, "Put your safety belts on," which was good advice, and a relief, because it showed she hadn't completely shut down. I put mine on with one hand as I accelerated over the crest.

Accelerating over a crest is probably always a bad idea. Many a story I'd heard at Wirrawee B&S's about people being wiped out in head-on collisions as they flew over crests. There were so many stories that I didn't know if they could all be true. But as a general principle, I did see that accelerating over crests was in no-one's best interest.

On this occasion I thought that it was in our best interest, but I wasn't expecting to find a bulldozer. This building site was a mess, with materials and vehicles everywhere, so maybe it shouldn't have been a surprise to find a bulldozer casually parked in the middle of the road. It was just a regular-sized bulldozer but to me it looked like a mechanical T-Rex. Jess screamed, and Jeremy made a noise that's as close to a scream as a boy can get, and I spun the wheel. We went into a massive slide that made the first one look like a delicate piece of ballroom dancing. At every moment I fully expected the ute to roll. Somehow it didn't. If Jeremy had been trembling a bit before, now he was registering a force-ten gale.

We took off again.

The track faded fast, as we got away from the building site. We were heading towards a paddock, which looked like it was being marked out for a housing estate. There were no gates, so at least we didn't have that problem. We did have a lot of other problems though. In the middle of all of them I managed to remember the biggest one. "Have any of you seen Gavin?" I yelled.

Nothing but the thrum of the engine and the rushing of the wind through the windows. I felt despair. "No-one?"

"There's a couple of motorbikes coming after us," Lee said. I hated him when he was like this. At the same time I had to process the information. Motorbikes. They were more difficult to deal with than cars. They were so mobile, so hard to stop. It was like swatting mosquitoes. They could get into much more difficult country, use different tracks.

"Did Gavin follow us?" Jess asked. I loved her for this, as much as I hated Lee for his cold-heartedness.

"How many bikes?" I asked Lee. "Yes," I said to Jess.

"Three," Lee said.

"That's terrible," Jess said. I loved her even more. Then I realised she was talking about the motorbikes.

"How far behind are they?" I asked.

"Not far enough," said Homer.

"About a hundred metres," said Lee.

I glanced at the wing mirror, and saw one of them. Objects may be closer than they appear, but this guy looked pretty close. Closer than a hundred metres. I groaned, but only to myself. Outwardly I just swore. Life these days seemed to be nothing but problems, and a lot of the time there seemed to be only one solution. Death. I had the horrible feeling that someone was going to die here. How else could we stop the mosquitoes on motorbikes? I gritted my teeth, put aside my doubts and memories, and decided that if there had to be fatalities it wasn't going to be me or my friends.

But how to stop them? I couldn't think and drive at the same time. If you think and drive you're a bloody idiot.

92

No, that wasn't right. But already my brain was at maximum output. If they could breathalyse my brain for concentration I'd blow .15. Here I was, at night, headlights on, weaving and dodging around rocks and ruts and fallen timber and ditches. The track was getting worse. Then I noticed we had a good lead suddenly. We'd opened up a break. It even looked like they'd stopped completely. Could we get that lucky? No, because soon they started to move again. But we had a good lead now. It wouldn't last for long, but it was a welcome relief because it gave us a few more moments to be alive, and when you're facing death moments become important. Like, if you were down to your last dollar, I guess you'd value every cent.

I nearly lost the track and had to swing sharply left hoping that the faint line I'd seen out of the corner of my eye was a road. Those bush tracks are so deceptive. They'll run along like a regular road while you listen to the music and enjoy the view, and then for no obvious reason they start to degenerate, and before you know it there's not much more than a choice of paths, decorated with kangaroo droppings and rabbit holes, and you can't be sure they've got anything to do with humans even. They look more like animal routes to the tastier patches of grass. And then you can't pick up any radio stations and you think, "OK, what happened to civilisation?"

Still, I thought I was on a man-made track. It seemed to be heading back towards a highway I could see in the distance, with regular traffic. We started going across the crest of a hill, but then the path turned again and went down the back of the hill. That's when Lee called out, "Are those rocks up there?"

"Yeah I think so."

"Hit the brakes when we get there. And stay ready. Don't get out."

He and Homer had been talking in the back seat from time to time, but I hadn't heard what they were saying and I hadn't tried. Too busy keeping us alive. But I knew from our experience in the war that when someone like Lee tells you to do something, if it's a time of real danger, you'd better do what he says. Every other time you can ignore him, and you're probably better off if you do.

As soon as we reached the rocks I stopped with a lurch. I knew now why he wanted to stop. It was because the motorbikes were out of sight for a minute. The three boys piled out. The vehicle rocked as someone got up on the tray. I heard the scraping of a drum across the metal floor.

"What are they doing?" Jess asked nervously.

I glanced back at her but didn't answer. At least she'd stopped trembling, more or less. How should I know what they were doing? It involved the spare drums of fuel, that's all I knew. The ute lurched again as the boys jumped off the back. It felt lighter now, somehow.

Lee's face appeared at the window. "Get going," he said. "Stop up there somewhere after we've set it off."

Set what off? Lee turned to the other two boys and said, "You two spread it and I'll light it. That way I won't get any on my clothes." By the end of his sentence we were gone.

We rocked and bumped on, going up a rise now. It was tough stuff. Smart of Lee to think of that detail. Otherwise he could have become a human torch. We turned right, still following a track. The motorbikes appeared again, coming pretty fast, making up the time and space they'd lost. I couldn't see the boys. From one of the bikes came a familiar flash of flame. It was the mark of a gunshot. So they were still keen to kill us. And of course there could be no other outcome really. They couldn't take us prisoner. They'd be too scared to try that in the middle of the night when we'd already proved how dangerous we were.

I didn't really understand how Lee would stop them with a small petrol fire. After all, the bikes could be manoeuvred around that. No big deal really. The three boys hadn't even taken their guns, so it wasn't like they were going to shoot the riders while they were distracted by the flames. Then I realised and I cried out.

"What?" Jess asked, looking scared.

I stopped the ute and looked back down the hill. I wasn't sure how good a view Jess had. Mine was pretty good. Of course Lee had volunteered to be the one who'd light the match. He was the only one who could do this. I couldn't have done it.

Like a pack, the bikes came on. There were three, not two. I saw at least one pillion passanger. Maybe they'd paused when they did to pick up reinforcements. Now they probably had time to register that the car had stopped, up on the rise. They were in a bunch bunched together. Lee had chosen the spot well, considering he'd had so little time. The gradient on either side of the track meant they were forced together and the rocks caused them to slow down.

I wondered if they smelt the petrol and had time to think about it for a moment. They lit up slowly, or that's what it seemed like. Of course it must have all happened in a second. When I replay it in my head it seems like slow motion. I didn't see the match. The first thing I saw was a glow that was almost phosphorescent. It rose like a dancer who was getting to her feet to start the performance. Funny how something so terrible can be so beautiful. It spread across some grass and almost instantly came to the first motorbike. It paused there. Everything seemed to hang. This bike, and one of the others, had a rider and a passenger. The rider threw up his hands as though he suddenly didn't care about the bike; he was just going to let it fall, let him and his passenger be thrown into the flames. Suddenly all three bikes, all five men, became blazing statues. Lee's timing had been as perfect as his choice of location.

I turned away, sickened, unable to watch any more. Even above the engine of the ute I could hear screams. "Revenge for Shannon," I thought, trying to give it meaning, make it bearable. I put the car into reverse to get the three boys. I only had to back up about thirty metres before they arrived. This time they had the sense to use different doors, Jeremy and Homer on one side, Lee on the other. They reeked of petrol. I think the horror and enormity of what they'd done had sent them into supershock. But they had given us a chance to get out of here. I put my foot to the floor. We went on to the top of the rise. The track now took on a more definite direction again. In the distance I could see the highway again, with quite a few cars going along it. How strange, that normal life was going on over there, while behind us men were staggering around trying to put themselves out. Well, maybe sometimes we all had to be foxes and feel nothing for our victims. For some minutes my main concern was the petrol fumes in the car. It was terrible, even with the windows down and me driving as fast as I dared. I even used the word "terrible" when I was yelling at Jeremy to wind down the window, which says something about me or about language or about both, because there was only one thing that was terrible during that time.

We got to the highway through a couple of gates. Jess got out and opened them. I thought it was a good sign when she did that but a bad sign when she started closing the first one again. God, what a waste of time, although maybe she thought she'd slow down anyone else who was following. I think we all screamed simultaneously at her. We'd be on the highway before any more chasers appeared. "Always leave gates as you find them," yes, and it went against the grain to leave these open, but what did we care about their stock? They'd probably stolen them from us anyway.

Getting away always seems lighter somehow. Of course it's logical it would feel that way, but almost every time we'd had to escape during the war it worked out to be easier and quicker. Maybe the relief gave wings to our feet, a richer mixture to the fuel in our carburettors. When there were no cars in sight I slipped onto the highway—it wasn't really a highway, just a busy main road—then took the first turn to the left. It was a long straight road, heading vaguely in the direction we wanted. I pulled over to the side, opened the door and got out, saying to them as I did so, "Well, have a nice ride home, people. I'm going back to find Gavin."

CHAPTER 9

THE THING I MOST DON'T LIKE ABOUT JESS IS THAT SHE
wants life to be a huge drama with her as the star and so
she kind of organises people that way. Not to an extreme,
like I've seen worse, but at the end of the day it's always
about her. Steve can be a bit like that too, which is one reason we broke up, but Jess is worse than Steve.

The reason I can say that about her is that sometimes I
do it too, which may explain why there are times when Jess
really irritates me.

I have to admit that the way I got out of the car that
night was a good example. I knew I had to find Gavin, so
it wasn't a bullshit situation, but to do it that way, OK,
yeah, I knew there would be a certain impact on the others. To be honest, it was more like a scene out of a movie
than real life. I guess the others knew that. Lee covered his
face with one hand and groaned, Jeremy said, "You must
be joking," and Homer just looked straight at me and said,
"Here's a suggestion—why don't you tell us what's going
on." To my surprise, Jess opened her door and came around
to where I was standing. I'm not sure what she had in mind,
I don't think she was planning on coming with me, but she
sure wasn't running away.

I realised I hadn't been fair to them. I made a bit of a
face, and said, "Sorry." It took me a minute to think of
how to explain it all. So much had happened that I could

hardly remember Gavin, let alone what he had done. In forcing my mind to go back a few hours I felt like I was taking a thousand-kilometre journey. It was actually tiring, and I didn't need it, on top of the exhaustion that was leaving me limp and feeble. But somehow I got back the full thousand kilometres and remembered, and said, "Before you went Gavin had already left. He hijacked a motorbike, waited somewhere down the paddock and followed you. I lost his tracks near the border. But he took a shotgun."

"You don't think he went shooting rabbits or something?" Jess asked.

I shook my head.

"He could be home again," said Jeremy.

"If you knew Gavin," Homer said to him, "well, put it this way, you remember that Japanese soldier they found in the jungle forty years after the Second World War? Still fighting on?"

I didn't, but I got the general drift. Nobody said anything else for a few moments. But the trouble with the kind of situation we were in is that you can't sit around having a group discussion. Finally I did something which I don't remember doing too often. I said to Lee: "What do you think I should do?"

He raised his eyebrows slightly, which for Lee was the equivalent of laughing hysterically. It was probably the first time I'd asked him directly for advice about something personal. And this felt personal to me.

"I don't see what you can do," he said. "He could be anywhere. I mean, we're talking about an area of maybe a thousand square kilometres. It's like looking for one particular grain of sand on the beach. Like Jeremy said, he could be back home. I think you'll have to start again from there. If he's still missing, we can try to get information through the Scarlet Pimple or Liberation."

He was clever, Lee. He'd thought of a reason to get me back home. Two reasons even. Gavin could be there, and if he wasn't, I might have a better chance of finding him from my place than by zigzagging aimlessly about the countryside.

I got back in the ute. Jess got in too.

Somehow, as we took off again, I felt quite fearless. Considering all we had been through, and the danger we were still in, that seems a bit ridiculous, but my mind was on Gavin, and that stopped me getting too scared. I think also that after surviving the Battle of the Coconut Tree I felt a bit invincible. By getting ourselves out of that almost impossible situation it seemed like God wouldn't be so cruel as to have us caught by an off-duty gardener with a whipper-snapper.

We had a bit more to contend with than off-duty gardeners though. We'd been stupid to stop for so long and have a conversation. Well, I'd been stupid, but the others were nice enough not to point that out. To be honest, I was probably underestimating the opposition too. Just like those netball games when Robyn was captain. Wirrawee was quite a netball powerhouse, and it wasn't unusual for us to win games by forty points. One season, when we were in Year 5, we won every game by a minimum twenty-five points. But by Years 6 and 7 we drifted into bad habits. In particular, in almost every game, we would lead by a big margin at half-time and either lose the second half or play really scratchily. It cost us a few games. It nearly cost Robyn her sanity. Oh, those half-time speeches! Oh, those full-time accusations!

We could have done with Robyn in the car that night. We could have done with Robyn any time. But in particular that night, because it would have helped to be reminded of the netball games and the importance of not getting too casual, of maintaining the intensity.

About a kilometre down the road we started to climb a bit and Homer, looking back, said, "You know, it's really buzzing over there."

"My God," said Jeremy, "you're not wrong."

"What's happening?" I asked, thinking that I had better keep my eyes on the road.

"Helicopters," Homer said.

I had been driving with headlights on, thinking that we would look like any other car on the road, but now Lee said, "I think you better turn the lights off." I did so, straight away, and almost straight away Homer said quietly, "That might have been a mistake."

I didn't trust Homer when he spoke so quietly. I was slowing down as fast as I could without using the brakes, because I knew how bright brake lights are. I'd been pulling over to the left, but I jumped when he said that, and applied a bit of handbrake and got even further left, looking for shelter in the few straggly trees that lined the road. Suddenly Homer yelled from the back seat, so loudly that I jumped like a firecracker had gone off in my bum. "Get going!"

I hit the accelerator. We took off with gravel and dust flying and the tail of the ute swinging madly from side to side. During the war I'd quite often had to drive at night without headlights, in fact without any lights. It was terrifying, but luckily I'd often had good moon. The moon had been medium strength this night, but now it was pretty much obliterated by cloud, and of course I'd had no time to let my eyes adjust. If you've got plenty of time to get used to it, there's a chance you can do it and not kill yourself in the first hundred metres. But here I was in severe darkness, with my eyes still thinking "headlights," not even knowing what I was escaping from, but with the dreaded word "helicopter" echoing in my ears.

Jess started to scream, thought better of it, gurgled instead, and said, "Oh my God." Then she did scream.

With a rush and a roar the helicopter was on us.

There's nothing more savage than a helicopter on the hunt. This seemed like a small one but that just made it more agile. It swooped low over us like a magpie and more dust swirled and more gravel flew. I was on the pavement but with no idea of where the pavement went, and the lights of the helicopter blinded me all over again. Then he switched on a spotlight, which for a moment lit the road ahead, and I saw we were heading for the trees. The road seemed to go left, and it looked like a long curve. I spun the wheel and we angled left, but almost too late, we were on gravel again and a low branch whipped the windscreen. The spotlight came onto us and settled on us for a moment. As far as my seeing where I was going, I didn't know whether it was a good thing or a bad thing, because although it gave me some light it was way too blinding. As far as our safety went it was definitely a bad thing.

A voice yelled at us through some kind of speaker from the helicopter.

"Oh my God it's God," Homer yelled from the back seat. He actually sounded quite cheerful but I don't think even Homer's that stupid.

"How come he doesn't speak English?" Jeremy asked.

They were doing a comedy routine! If they thought they were helping they were wrong but there wasn't time to tell them that. The spotlight was bobbing and weaving because whoever was holding it had to match up with both the pilot and me, so there were times when I had a glimpse of the road ahead and times when I didn't. When it shone right on us it was like a physical creature, not just a light but something real, a blinding white dragon that attacked from out of the dark. I was driving fast when I could see a straight patch of road and then clamping on the brakes when I got to the end of the bit that I'd seen—or where I thought the end was. It was a rough ride for the passengers. Lucky Marmie wasn't on the tray, like she would be if we were going around the paddocks at home. She'd have been thrown off in the first fifty metres.

The voice was shouting a whole string of stuff but we didn't understand a word of it except "Stop," which the person repeated about six times as we were taking a sharp bend. Then the spotlight went out. My God that was a moment. My stomach lurched so hard I nearly threw up. I had to hit the brakes: there was nothing else to do. I hit them pretty hard too because I had no idea of where we were in relation to the road. If we'd had time to take a vote I think the seatbelts would have come in for a unanimous big *thank you*. I flicked on our headlights. We were facing a solid row of gum trees. I reversed, spun the wheel and got a look at the road. It was tricky, looked like more curves ahead, but maybe those and the trees were forcing the chopper up away from us a bit. I wondered why they'd turned off the spotlight. Had they figured it was helping us too much?

We raced up through the next two corners, me driving pretty much solely from memory, Jess giving a sharp cry as a branch hit her side of the car with a hard bang. I turned the lights back on. A straight stretch. Good. Put the foot down. Racing insanely along in darkness, the wind rushing through the car, a sense of complete madness as though we were driving straight at the edge of a cliff at a hundred k's an hour. Not that we were really doing a hundred. Maybe eighty. Maybe even ninety.

I've seen a rabbit bolting across a flat, bare bit of land when it realises a hawk is after it. It comes down to a simple contest of speed. Can the rabbit get to the edge of the bush before the hawk reaches it? The rabbit flat to the ground, ears pinned back, the hawk pouring on the power as it drives hard across the open paddock. It's a right-angled triangle and the hawk follows the hypotenuse.

A helicopter has an advantage though. It doesn't need to reach you and grab you in its sharp, cruel beak. It has bullets that fly through the space between you. As it roared in behind us it started to fire almost straight away. I saw its lights in my mirrors, not the spotlight, just its navigation lights, and I saw the spit of light and colour and flame. "They're shooting," I yelled. Not that anyone could do anything about it.

I held my line. I knew from the war, if not from shooting rabbits, that we were safe enough for the first moments. It is too hard to hit a target like us from a helicopter that's rocking and rolling and trying to find its target. But maybe this guy had new equipment or maybe he was a brilliant shot or maybe he was just plain lucky. Bullet holes tore through the ute like a huge metal-punch was suddenly and roughly slamming a simultaneous line of them from our rear to our front. The ironic thing was the guy was such a perfect shot that he missed everyone. The line was straight down the middle, and Lee and Jess were squashed together on one side, Jess trying to support Lee's rifle so he could get a few shots in, and Homer hanging out the other side hoping to get a shot away himself. The holes were like a row of stitches. If he'd been off his line by about half a metre he would have scored at least two hits. How unlucky is that? For him I mean. We were lucky twice over because not only did he miss us all but he must have missed everything vital in the engine. It didn't even hiccup.

For a moment I thought he'd somehow even managed to miss the windscreens but then the back one caved in with a terrible crack and a second later the front one went in sympathy. It was way different to the window in the Landcruiser. I'm sure the front one hadn't been hit; it might have been something to do with the different air pressure in the cab when the back one went out. Windscreens O'Brien would have loved me if they had a branch on this side of the border. I'd promised myself I wasn't going to let anyone shoot my car windows out again. That promise hadn't lasted long.

Maybe the only good thing about the war is that it taught us not to panic if we can possibly help it, but I gotta admit this was testing the limits. I'm not sure about that theory anyway, because Jeremy and Jess had a fairly comfortable time during the war and they weren't panicking now, no more than the rest of us. All I could think was, "I'll panic later, but for now we need to get out of here." I yelled back over my left shoulder, "OK, if I hit the brakes, you guys roll out, you might get a shot at him as he goes over."

"OK," I thought I heard Homer answer, although a second later I realised it could have been, "No way." There was so much noise that my hearing was suffering. I had to hope it was "OK" so I yelled "Hang on," and slammed the brakes with everything, and I mean everything. Not only the foot brake, but the hand brake as well, and then for good measure dropped the gearstick down to low. The ute practically stood on its nose. "Hhmm, nice brakes," I thought, "must remember to write to Toyota." I wouldn't have been surprised if we'd done a forward roll. I think the boys already had their doors open but we stopped so hard that they fell out instead of doing a graceful exit. Lucky their rifles didn't go off in the process.

In one way it worked beautifully, because a few moments later the helicopter went right over the top of us at about zero altitude. If we'd had the radio on I reckon he'd have taken out the aerial. OK, slight exaggeration, but he was extremely low. If I hadn't stopped when I did, I think we would have been dead meat, so that was the way it worked beautifully. In another way it didn't work at all, because although I think Homer and Lee both managed to fire a few rounds they were too off balance and it had no effect on the chopper.

They piled back into the car and I accelerated gently away. The helicopter was now throwing enough light again for me to see the next bit of road. It was fairly straight, bit of a curve to the right a few hundred metres ahead. The helicopter was doing a tight circle so he could come back for the next round. I'd bought us a bit of time, if nothing else. I tried to go faster but we were driving in crazy swerving patterns, half the time because I didn't know where the road went and half the time because I knew where it went but I didn't want us to be shot.

"Where is he?" I yelled back over my shoulder at Homer.

"Starting another run at us. Straight behind."

"Got any ideas?"

"Not right off the top of my head, no."

This all sounds like a calm intelligent conversation but it was done in jerks and bits and pieces as I slowed and accelerated and swerved and nearly stopped and zigzagged. I don't know why we weren't all carsick.

"Here he comes," Jess yelled. "God this is exciting isn't it?"

I looked at her in disbelief. Well, I didn't actually look at her but in my head I did. I was running out of strategies. I didn't plan to do this but at the last second my foot did it for me; I must have instinctively felt that it was a good idea. My foot went down on the accelerator, the ute hesitated for a long second, then took off. I guess twincabs don't exactly have the power lift-off of a Porsche but this thing did get going at quite a rate. And that meant we were suddenly going flat out at a wall of darkness. It took me a second to remember I had headlights, another second to decide whether it was wise to use them, and another second to find the switch. I suppose it then took another quarter of a second for them to come on.

If I'm going to be strictly mathematical about this I'd have to add a few more units of time to register the fence coming up and then some more for my reflexes to start operating. When you panic, the reflexes are not as quick because they're paralysed. By this time we were well and truly off the road, off the ground too I suspect, and although I finally got around to turning the wheel it was way too late. Jess let out a scream like Courtney when she got her first period. So much for her finding it all exciting. We hit the fence. "We don't need the helicopter to kill us," I thought, "I'll take care of the job all by myself." An image of Chris appeared strongly in my mind.

The fence was not a great one, but it wasn't too bad. I hate to think what might have happened if it had been freshly strung with hard lines of steel barbed wire. But this farmer knew his fence had a good few years in it yet and he wasn't ready to update. So we thundered into it almost headfirst, as I hadn't got far with turning the steering wheel, and we burst through into the paddock, dragging quantities of wire and droppers and a fence post or two.

We were bouncing hard in a fairly rough paddock. I snapped the headlights off but I'd seen that the paddock was quite open and seemed to go a long way. Now I had some room to manoeuvre, but if the paddock had the usual quota of cattle, logs, drink troughs, rabbit warrens and other hazards, I was fairly sure that I could find lots of ways yet to get into trouble. The helicopter's light picked us up and I swerved violently to the left then back to the right. I flicked on the lights again, to get a glimpse of our future, but also to distract him. As I turned them off I thought I saw something. Well of course I saw something. Grass for example. But something else. I had a moment's agony of indecision. I felt I couldn't risk turning them on again. I had to trust my judgement and assume that I'd seen what I thought I saw.

CHAPTER 10

A SPATTER OF BULLETS CUT ACROSS THE CAR. IN THE DARK I couldn't see them properly but I heard them above all the noise. The car shuddered and there were a couple of bangs on the roof. I hunched up and accelerated again. Someone swore in the back seat and I heard Jeremy say anxiously, "Did they get you?" and Homer said, "No, don't know how they missed."

I was still thinking about what I'd seen in the far distance in the headlights. Just that glimpse. The huge pylons they use for high-tension wires, the ones that march across the country like giant soldiers. If it hadn't been an illusion, and if the pilot hadn't seen them, if I could somehow guide them into them . . . well, put it this way, if I couldn't, we had no hope.

I had to reverse our roles. I had to become the fox, making the chook do what I wanted. Somehow I had to get him turning, and watching me, so that he didn't notice the wires. And that's still assuming the wires were there. I had serious doubts about that. You can see anything at night, and maybe I'd been looking at a big gum tree. Or a giant kangaroo.

I couldn't turn my headlights on again, because if the pylon was there, I would just illuminate it for him. Based on my glimpse, I figured it was about two hundred and fifty metres ahead, but since then we'd probably halved that distance. So we were getting pretty close.

The helicopter had banked sharply and was coming in from my right. I started to veer left, and at the same time called to Homer in the backseat, "When I stop, can you and Lee both jump out and run back the way we've been coming?" I wanted to distract the pilot, give him lots to think about. I expected that he would still follow the car, but would keep an eye on the boys, wondering what was going on, trying to see where they were heading, and that would keep him glancing to the left.

I braked pretty hard. As the car doors opened the helicopter came throbbing overhead. It was so close and so loud and so menacing that I felt deafened. The car rocked in the down draught. I heard more firing, but I think he missed completely, probably because he wasn't expecting me to stop.

I only gave the boys a second, and then took off again. I had to let him know that the car was still moving, that we hadn't abandoned it, so we would be his first target. I started to do a big circle, hoping I hadn't underestimated the distance. If the pylons were another hundred or more metres away, this wasn't going to work. And I wouldn't get another chance.

In fact, I'd done the opposite, and a pylon loomed up so suddenly that Jess and I both screamed. It looked like a huge robot, standing in the field. A visitor from another place, from out in the far distant universe. I had to pull the wheel back the other way to miss it, and at about that same moment the helicopter hit the wires. If we'd hit the pylon we might have been electrocuted.

And there in that dark and lonely paddock, we had Guy Fawkes night, the Fourth of July, Commemoration Day, and the opening and closing of the Olympics, all in one. The helicopter turned into flowers of light, scorching my eyeballs. I saw at least half-a-dozen fireballs, going off quite slowly, each in different directions. So many sparks came out of the wires that it was like a Niagara Falls of fire. The helicopter lit up inside, and for a moment I could see everyone and everything. Three men, each sitting in their different positions, glowing bright with fire and electricity.

It dropped the short distance to the ground. We were about eighty metres away, and by then it was on my right again, because of the turn I'd done, so I saw it explode. And I heard it, and I felt the ground rock, and the car being buffeted by a huge wind and rockets of fire shooting at me, and the next thing, I'm getting picked up and tipped over like a giant hand has grabbed the car, and I'm suddenly looking down on Jeremy, feeling as though I'm at a great height above him.

Of course I wasn't at a great height, just the usual distance, but you don't expect to be in that position. Once again the good old safety belts helped. It took me a long moment to realise that the car had been turned on its side. I didn't have much of a view any more, but there were still streaks of fire going past the ute, and I could see grass burning about twenty metres away.

I spared a thought for Homer and Lee. I had no idea that I was dropping them into an inferno, and I hoped they had survived. I wondered how anyone could. There were whooshing and zinging noises, which I realised were pieces of metal from the helicopter flying past us like rockets.

By the time the three of us crawled out of the ute, most of it was over. Four different grass fires were spreading, in different parts of the paddock, and the helicopter was burning brightly, with black smoke coming from it. I guess it had a lot of plastic and toxic parts. There was no use looking for survivors in that. They'd had no chance. And just as I was wondering about survivors, Homer and Lee came running towards us.

They were both a bit hysterical. They were kind of laughing and babbling, but not in a normal way. I wondered if I should slap them in the face, which is something I've often wanted to do, but even while they were in this condition I thought it might be a bit dangerous. I realised I was a bit hysterical myself, when I heard myself babbling back at them. Basically we were all trembling and terrified. All I wanted to do was get the hell out of that place before any rescue parties arrived.

I looked at the ute and wondered if we could get it back on its four wheels. I couldn't see how, without ropes or chain. Homer started yelling, "Let's go, let's get out of here," so I guess he felt it wasn't worth bothering with the ute any more. I assumed he knew what he was talking about, and that fuel had probably tipped out of the carburettor or something (that's about the extent of my mechanical knowledge), and besides, all those bullet holes might have affected its performance by now. So I followed him, and the five of us ran towards the road, turned left and continued to run, in a line behind Homer, on the right-hand side, for what felt like fifty kilometres, but was probably only one.

When we couldn't go any further, we gathered under a big gum tree. It was very dark now, and there was still no sign of traffic. The running was good in a way, because although it brought me to the end of my physical endurance, it calmed me down, and I think it had the same effect on the others.

"God, Ellie, did you know about those wires?" was the first thing Jeremy said.

"I thought I saw them, but I wasn't a hundred percent sure."

But I knew there was no use having a conversation about that.

"What are we going to do?" Homer asked. "We need a vehicle, but it's pretty quiet around here."

"All we can do is keep going as fast as we can until we find something," Lee said. "If everyone's feeling as stuffed as me, we mightn't get very far, but the further away from here the better."

No-one had a better suggestion, so we kept walking and jogging, talking a bit as we went. Jess said to me, "This is amazing. I never thought I'd be in anything like this. I can't believe it. It's so weird and wild and terrifying."

I laughed. But I wasn't feeling very funny. "Hey, welcome to my world," I said.

We passed a house about two kilometres further on, but there was no sign of life. I assumed they were out, or else they'd slept through the whole thing. A dog started barking wildly as soon as we got near, so we didn't look for a car or a motorbike, just hurried on.

I was tired and really hurting. I was starting to pant and gasp for breath, and left the talking to the others as I had no energy for conversation.

We passed three more houses before we came to someone nice and messy. There are times when I love messy people, and this was one of them. There was a tennis court, but the wire in the fence was badly torn; they had half a truck on the front lawn with bits of engine all around it; and they had kids who didn't put their toys away. We couldn't do much with the truck, as the idea of assembling it, fuelling it and then driving it away didn't seem too practical. But between us, as we tiptoed around in the dark, we collected two bicycles and a pair of rollerblades. It wasn't much, but we didn't dare go closer to the house to look for a car. Anyway, they were more likely to notice the loss of a car straight away. The chances were that the owners of the bikes and skates wouldn't realise till a good while after breakfast.

In the distance I could hear another helicopter, so I figured they'd started looking for us. It seemed a good time to go, even if we didn't have much to go with.

Homer and Lee got to do the pedalling, and Jeremy seemed attracted to the skates, so that left Jess and me to be dinked. There was an awkward moment when I was an equal distance between Homer's bike and Lee's and both of them were looking at me, expecting me to get on behind them. I chose Homer. Lee just turned his head away.

For a while I think we weren't going much faster than if we'd been walking. Both of the boys were pretty rusty on their bike skills, and having a passenger didn't make it easy. Jeremy got quite a way ahead, but once Homer and Lee settled into a rhythm they began to catch up, and soon we were together again. It was not the kind of glamorous getaway that people make in Hollywood movies, but it was all we had, and it worked fairly well. Three times we had to dive into bushes as headlights showed cars coming towards us, but we could see the headlights from a long way off, so we had time.

At about three in the morning we hit the road that I'd taken earlier. A simple right turn took us back to the border. By then the pedalling was pretty slow again, and clumsy, and we had to take a couple of rest breaks. We reached the border a bit after four.

At about five o'clock we were trudging up a hill, Lee pushing one bike and me the other. Jeremy had chucked the skates into a patch of scrub quite a bit earlier. He was a few hundred metres behind. Our heads were down and we were making very slow progress.

Things were so desperate that Homer had taken to telling bad jokes to keep us awake and moving. He'd just told us one about three girls telling their mother where they are going that night, and the first one is going out with Pete to eat, and her sister's going out with Vance to dance, and when the next sister says she wants to go out with Chuck, the mother stops her. Jess laughed, I groaned, Lee didn't react. Jeremy was the lucky one: he didn't hear it.

At that moment a single bullet came shooting towards us, splitting the darkness and our group apart. It went right between Homer and me, like a knife cutting the night into two worlds. A knife made of flame. The noise was like a single stroke of thunder.

I nearly ruptured myself. I sort of jumped up and twisted around at the same time. I couldn't help making a screaming sound as I dived to the right. I couldn't see which direction the others were diving in, but I hoped that they were all right.

Then the next thing a little voice called out, "Sorry," except that the r's sounded more like l's.

I rolled over and sat up again. I'd grazed the right side of my face on a rock, and a stick had poked into my knee. I stood up and went forwards, ready to throttle the owner of the voice. I didn't throttle him, although I probably should have. When I saw him I just shook my head and said, "Where have you been?"

Gavin, being deaf, couldn't hear that, but he was pleased to see me. He threw himself at me, and hung on, tight hands digging into my back. He wasn't even crying, just hanging on. Well, no wonder. He knew he had done the wrong thing in following the utes. He'd lost contact with the motorbikes, punctured both tyres on the yammy, and spent the night on his own. He was probably lost, although he didn't actually admit to that, not after the terrible consequences of his being lost in the bush last time. And then firing at these vague human shapes coming towards him in the darkness, and realising an instant later that it was us, had been a bit much even for Gavin.

There was nothing for me to do except let myself be held, and to stroke his back and pat his head and put aside thoughts of strangulation. I couldn't let myself admit the obvious, that as glad as he was to see me, I was that and more to see him. I did have the horrible thought that even though the bullet had missed us three it might have got Jeremy, coming along behind, but he came trotting up a few moments later, without any holes through him.

Everyone patted Gavin for a while, without making remarks about checking your target before you pull the trigger. That would have to wait for another day. In the meantime, we still had a long walk home.

We dumped the bikes, taking them well into the bracken and hiding them behind fallen logs. We hadn't yet sat down to figure out the trouble we'd be in if the shoot-up at the mall was traced to us, but as long as we went out and got the utes and the Yamaha back, it was unlikely we'd be connected with it. We'd be just as likely to cop the blame for global warming or tasteless strawberries or World War II.

After covering up the bikes it was trudge, trudge, trudge, the familiar part of war, which I'd almost forgotten about but which seemed to form the majority of my experiences during the time of the invasion. Plod plod plod. Slog slog slog. Gavin kept so close to me that he kept getting his feet tangled up with mine, but I bit my tongue and reminded myself of what an awful night he'd had. Even if it was his own fault.

Plod plod plod. I kept thinking about home. Home is where you go and they have to let you in. Home is whoever loves you. There's no place like home. All of that seemed true enough, but there was no-one at my home to let me in, and there was no-one there to love me any more. It seemed so empty with my parents gone. The house was too big now, and Gavin and I rattled around in there like a couple of grains of wheat in a silo. When I walked the corridors I heard echoes. There had never been echoes before.

When we did get within sight of the farm I was quite shocked to see lights on in the house. Like, someone's broken in? This is the revenge attack already? But the others kept walking, and then I remembered Bronte and Pang.

Pang had ignored the spare room and was asleep in my bed but Bronte had kept awake somehow. She came to the door. It was strange, I was being welcomed into my own home by someone I still didn't know all that well.

She ushered us in and with no fuss got us organised with Milo and noodles and toast. I don't know what it is about toast. It's the most comforting smell in the world. Even if you're not feeling hungry, once you get a whiff of someone else's bread in the toaster, you find yourself hypnotically drawn towards the loaf, and before you know it you're pulling out a couple of slices and dropping them in. That liquorice smell that hangs around Darrell Lee's, which someone told me they get by burning liquorice oil in an aromatherapy thing, that has a strong effect on me too, and so do chooks cooking in supermarkets, but nothing beats toast. I reckon home is where the toast is.

Anyway, even though I could hardly keep my eyes and lips open, it was incredibly comforting to sit around the table and talk. If anyone's going to keep a secret, it'd be Bronte. She has such calmness and strength that you know you can trust her with the name of your newest boyfriend, the password for your emails and the Riddle of the Dead Sea Scrolls. If we were going to stop news of our activities spreading around Wirrawee, we didn't have to worry about it coming from Bronte. All that aside, I was still worried about how much we could tell her, because of it being Liberation business, but the others didn't hold back at all. So I went along with their judgement.

Homer did most of the talking, but this time he had a bit of competition from Jess. "The intelligence was pretty good," Homer said. "We found them approximately where we were supposed to find them. They had three houses, right next to the shopping centre, and at least four vehicles. We watched for about forty-five minutes, and there were a heap of them, getting themselves organised. They were obviously planning a major raid. But we're good boys and girls, and we did like the Scarlet Pimple said, and we didn't attack, just watched."

"We counted eighteen guys," Jess said. "They were pretty open about what they were doing. Carrying rifles around and loading ammunition into the car. Anyone who was wandering past could have stopped and taken a look."

"Yeah, like we did, more or less," Homer said. "Anyway, we decided to move on to phase three, and head down the highway a few hundred metres and wait for them there. We'd seen a good spot. But at that point things went horribly wrong. We'd borrowed a couple of utes, so we piled into one and left the other as a back-up. Our quickest way out was through the supermarket car park, and we figured that it was dark enough to be safe. So off we went, but unfortunately we didn't get very far."

"I'd better interrupt at this point," Lee said. "Because otherwise Homer will take half an hour to get this out, but the fact is I ran over a woman in the car park."

I did stop eating my toast when he said that. I sat there with the slice halfway to my mouth, staring at Lee.

"It's okay," Lee added. "I didn't mash her into a pizza shape. She bounced right up again. But you know how it is, you can't just drive on, although if I had my time again I would have. But I was so shocked, I stopped the car and I opened the door. The woman was standing right in front of us, looking pretty wild, which is fair enough, and I didn't think I should run over her a second time."

"Then," Jess said, "before we knew it her husband or someone appeared jabbering away, getting all excited, and we were in the middle of a diarrhoea epidemic."

I did laugh at that. But now I understood how things had gone so badly wrong.

"To cut a long story short," Homer said, "we had to abandon the vehicle. We had a couple of cars up our arse, which was pretty uncomfortable, as you can imagine, but it also meant we couldn't reverse. Lee jumped back in and did this amazing manoeuvre to the corner of the car park and then we piled out and ran for it. We hid about a hundred metres down the road and waited till we thought the excitement would have died down. Then we tiptoed delicately back, feeling very happy that it seemed so quiet."

"Too quiet," Jess said.

"Seems like they were waiting for us," Jeremy said.

"And then," Homer continued, "Ellie arrived."

Lee made a trumpet noise.

"She practices doing this," Homer said to Bronte and Jess.

I had the feeling that Homer and Lee were getting a bit sick of me saving them, or worse, me getting credit. Well, I was happy to stop any time.

Jess stuck up for me though. "God, it was amazing," she said. "Ellie, you are an amazing hunk of womanhood. You sure came at the right time, and you had so many smart ideas. I swear, if you hadn't turned up, we'd be in the dump masters, and not because we were making an escape either. We'd be on our way to the tip, in little pieces."

"Oh, shucks," I said. "You know the trouble with the world nowadays? There's no telephone booths for superheroes to get changed. Everyone's got mobiles. I had a serious problem with that."

"What happened?" Bronte asked me.

"Well, I'd tracked them to this coconut tree place," I said, "because I remembered these guys mentioning it before they left. They were in a slightly complicated situation when I found them, but there was a four-wheel drive with keys in it and the door open. So I suggested they get in the dump master, because I figured the steel sides would keep bullets out, and then I got a bit of chain and used the four-wheel drive to tow them across the car park. When I think back, it seems like a crazy idea, but it worked. Then we just piled in a ute they'd laid on, and drove home. Except that we lost the ute along the way."

"It's been the most amazing twenty-four hours of my life," Jess told Bronte. "You wouldn't believe what we've been through. We were being followed by these guys on motorbikes, and we ambushed them, with petrol. It was terrible. But Ellie . . ."

I could see that the next little while was going to be uncomfortable. I wasn't just being modest, like "Oh no, really, I'm not that great," it was a bit more than that. I felt that if they all had to sit there telling Bronte how good a job I'd done (because I knew I had done a good job) it would make them uncomfortable and they'd even get a bit jealous. No matter how much you like someone, or admire something they've done, there's a limit to how long you can sit around praising them to other people, especially in front of their face. So I went to the bathroom.

By the time I'd got back, Gavin was asleep in the old brown armchair and the others were staggering around like zombies. I put Gavin to bed, then crawled in beside Pang, leaving the older kids to their own devices. They were big enough to find beds for themselves, and they knew where the spare blankets and pillows were stored.

CHAPTER 11

IT'S AMAZING HOW ADAPTABLE HUMANS ARE. I GUESS IT'S not just humans. Cows can adjust from one paddock to the next, from thunderstorms to sunshine and back to thunderstorms, from eating lucerne to eating clover, from being on a truck to not being on a truck.

At school one day I'd been walking behind a Year 10 kid who was going down the long corridor from Block A to Block B. It struck me, because I didn't have anything else to think about, how flexible she was at reacting to so many different things just in that short time. She smiled and gave a huge "Hi" to a Year 11 guy, she picked up a book for a Year 7 kid who was having trouble balancing all his stuff, she said, "Good morning Mrs Barlow," very politely as Mrs Barlow headed past, she yelled, "Love the eyebrows, Daphne," to another Year 10 girl, she said, "Why don't you stand in the middle of the frigging corridor and stop everybody getting past?" to a group of Year 8's who were standing in the middle of the frigging corridor and not letting anybody get past. She jogged ahead of me to catch up with a friend, put her arm around her friend's shoulders, and said, "Hi, Laura," as they turned left together into the classroom.

Only stupid little stuff, and we do it all the time, but that's the point. As well as doing that, she'd probably swatted at a fly, taken a piece of gum out of her pocket and put it in her mouth, adjusted her hair, flicked a look out the windows to see what was going on, and so on. I just think it's seriously impressive that humans can do all that, and maybe we can do it more than cows.

So anyway, the night after we got back from the Battle at the Coconut Tree, I was sitting in the office doing accounts.

It was quite a change of pace and I found it hard to concentrate. So much had happened, not just the night before, but even during the day. Jeremy, Gavin and I went and got the utes and found the Yamaha. Homer had homed, so to speak. He was no doubt in the middle of a very very long explanation to his parents as to how he had managed to lose a motorbike. I had no idea what he would tell them. Knowing how shrewd Mr and Mrs Yannos were, I guessed they would have a fair idea of some of the stuff Homer was up to, but that didn't necessarily make them happy to contribute an expensive motorbike to the cause. I could imagine Homer's conversation with them might last for a few days.

For that matter I had lost the Polaris. As much as I felt for Mr and Mrs Yannos, the loss of the Polaris was a disaster for me. In many ways it was the most useful vehicle on the farm, and not only because it was quick and convenient. The other motorbikes were quick and convenient too. But being a quad meant that I could tow stuff in the little red trailer, and tow it easily. All you had to do was lift it onto the tow bar, pull up the sealing bit and drop it down again, and you were ready to roll with a load of kindling, a couple of bales of hay, some bags of chook food or whatever.

Of course that would apply to any quad bike, but having a Polaris was a bit of a bonus. They are so powerful. Dad's policy was always to buy the best, even if it meant more money, and the Polaris was bloody expensive, but it could go anywhere, and it could tow big weights. It even towed me when I was younger. I loved riding in the trailer, hanging on to both sides while Dad bounced me over every bump he could find. Its only disadvantage was that it was heavy to steer in four-wheel drive, and the big wide wheels chopped up the lawns.

To replace it, the way prices of vehicles were going, I figured would cost fifteen thousand dollars minimum, although I was only guessing. They could have gone up to twenty thousand dollars since the war ended. I definitely didn't have that kind of money, but I definitely needed a quad bike.

So there I was, going through the accounts yet again, worried sick about losing the Polaris, trying to shut out the noises of Lee and Pang, Gavin, and Jess and Jeremy, who were meant to be getting a meal ready but sounded like they were banging on saucepans with every implement they could find, like toddlers with wooden spoons, and at the same time wondering why there was no noise from Bronte, who I hadn't seen all afternoon.

I guessed she was asleep, but looking for any excuse to get away from the books, I thought I'd go and check on her.

I didn't know who'd slept in which bed, but I found Bronte in the little spare room up the far end of the veranda, the one that no-one ever used. I opened the door. It was dim in there, with the curtains drawn, but I felt her presence, and also felt that she was awake. I'm not saying I was psychic, I think it was just that I didn't hear her breathing the way people do when they're asleep.

"Are you okay?" I asked.

There was no answer, so I went over to the bed. She was awake all right, lying on her back gazing at the ceiling. But as my eyes adjusted to the dim light I could see the tear trails on her cheeks.

"What's wrong?" I asked.

"Nothing," she said, and then added, "God, that's a terrible answer, isn't it?"

"I guess it's the reflex answer," I said.

To be totally honest I wasn't very much into the idea of having this conversation. Not only was I wrecked in every possible way from the stuff that had happened the night before, but I think since my parents were killed I needed all my emotional energy for myself, with any surplus going to Gavin. And believe me, there wasn't much surplus. But I liked Bronte a lot, and the same as anyone, I hate to see people upset, and after all, she was in my house and there was no-one else around to do this.

Anyway, she didn't say anything for quite a long time, just continued to lie there looking at the ceiling. Then, like a robot, she said, "I sat and listened to their description of the helicopter flying into the powerlines . . ."

Suddenly I remembered, and realised.

". . . and how it exploded, and I listened to the way they celebrated it and were so relieved and excited . . ."

"Yes, I know now," I said. It had been such a short time since our conversation about her little brother getting killed when a helicopter hit powerlines, but so much had happened in the meantime that it had gone from my mind. Afterwards though I did wonder whether my noticing the powerlines and realising I could trap the helicopter in them might have come from my unconscious memory of that conversation.

She continued to lie there. I took her hand. Even now that I understood why she was so upset, I still didn't have the energy or intelligence or imagination to think of a whole lot of comforting and inspiring things to say. After about ten minutes she said, "Well, back to duty," and started getting up. I still couldn't think of anything. "War is hell"? "I wish I could bring him back for you"? "You must feel awful"? It was vaguely like a time when I was about six and we were shopping in Stratton and my mother had bought all the stuff we needed, all the boring stuff, and I'd been nagging her in every shop for something for me: sweets, toys, dolls, ice-creams, anything. Finally, to shut me up, she said, "You can have whatever money's left over in my purse after I get the ammo." We went into the gun shop, and she bought fifty or a hundred rounds or whatever, and paid for it, and then gave me the purse. I was quivering with excitement, because I thought her purse always contained quite a lot of money. I opened it and found fifteen cents.

With Bronte, I wanted to open my own purse and give her everything inside it, but it was empty. I'd spent it. I stood back and let her leave the room, then followed her down the veranda, watching her back, feeling guilty and ashamed and inadequate.

Anyway, it was hard to concentrate on invoices and bank statements and cheque butts while all that was running so powerfully through my mind. But I wondered if it might be possible to buy a second-hand quaddy. I never thought that at my young age I'd already be sitting around with my friends saying, "Ah yes, I can remember in the good old days, when you could buy a Paddle Pop for . . ." But we were having those conversations all the time. Prices had inflated to levels that were insane, but you didn't get much choice: you either paid them or starved. The good news was that the price of cattle was going up just as fast, if not faster. To be honest we had overvalued our stock when we used them as security to get loans from the bank, but already it looked like our overvaluations weren't so over.

After tea I went back to the office and sat at the desk staring at the big sheet of paper where I'd done my calculations. Mr Yannos had been at me to do a budget and I thought I'd better get on with it, but it was difficult because every day came something I hadn't thought of or hadn't expected. Like the quaddy. But there was always something. One day the pump would break down, the next I'd have to get a drum of Roundup, then a falling branch wiped out the TV aerial and cracked a few tiles. Luckily the aerial saved the roof from worse damage.

I knew a lot of the figures off by heart. With the new loan from the bank I was now paying $3760 a month in interest. The leases were a $1000 a week, or $4333 a calendar month. That was eight grand a month going out the door without me getting up from the desk. I hoped interest rates would stay on hold for a while, as the bank had already mugged me with one rise. Well, I had no control over that.

I still owed about $5000 in rent to the people we'd leased

bits of the farm from. I'd paid the funeral directors ten grand, using the eight thousand my parents had in their account, plus two thousand from the bank. So I still owed the funeral guys about two and a half, and was getting nervous every time I went to the mailbox in case they sent me a letter threatening to dig everyone up again.

The only way I could buy a bike was to sell some cattle. The steers Dad had bought way back were in good nick. If I sold ten I could buy a new bike, pay the back rent and square up for the funerals. But it also meant that if the income from the agistment suddenly stopped—and face it, Mr Young could decide to move, or to sell his cattle any time, especially after the stampede—I'd have ten fewer of my own cattle to carry us through.

I sighed and pushed away the papers. I'd have to ask Mr Yannos. What on earth was Homer going to tell them? He had already come home minus one of their bikes such a short time ago when we'd rescued that Nick guy. Now he had another lost motorbike to explain away. Losing one motorbike is bad luck; losing two is a bit sloppy. How was I going to ring Mr Yannos, or drop in for a Sunday roast, and casually mention that I'd misplaced the four-wheeler?

I couldn't stay awake. But as my head started to fall forwards I heard a cough—just that throat-clearing noise—from behind me. And it was Jeremy. I was a bit surprised, as he had been half asleep over the dinner table. I smiled at him and he came in behind me and started massaging the back of my neck.

I got a bit of a shock. But right away I realised what was happening. All the previous guys I'd had relationships with, all two of them, had done a lot of talking. Steve and Lee had both launched into it with a lot of "Is this going to work? Is this a good idea?" although, to be fair to Lee, he was more forceful than me in the early days. I was the one with lots of reservations—well, I was the one who expressed them anyway.

Jeremy had a confidence that even Steve didn't have. He just took it for granted that I was going to like what he was doing, and that I liked him. For a moment I tingled like I didn't want to be touched. But his firm fingers and strong arms . . . soon they felt too good to push away. To be honest, I think anyone with those hands and arms would have done OK with me when I was so tired mentally and physically. I let myself lean back and enjoy the calm pressure. I even closed my eyes, which I don't do with most guys. The thought, the memory, of the boy in New Zealand who had practically raped me at the party came back for a moment but I blocked it. I knew Jeremy had a good heart. His hands were good too, and his body was even better.

I can't describe people very well so I normally don't bother. But I'll have a go with Jeremy. He was one of those people who've got all their parts in the right proportion to each other, if you know what I mean. Well, I don't mean all their parts, but his legs and arms were the right length for the rest of him, and his head was right too. He wasn't tall or short, just average I suppose, which sounds awful, but he was a very nice average. He looked like one of those boys who'd be good at every sport that came along—he had the balance, the co-ordination. I remember him saying once that he'd played fly half when he lived in New Zealand, and one of the boys who was listening and who knew a lot about rugby laughed and said, "Yes, you're such a fly half," and I said, "What do you mean?" and he said, "Fly halves are like dancers, plus they can kick with left foot or right foot."

I liked the sound of that.

Jeremy had a real shine in his eyes, which his father had too, even in the middle of a war. You knew he was alive when you looked into his eyes. He was growing a bit of a goatee, which didn't exactly work, but I don't know, on a lot of boys it looks so bad, and I used to think if a boy with a beard wanted to go with me the first thing I'd say to him was, "The beard comes off." But on Jeremy there was something kind of cute about it. Like it seemed really sincere, or it made him look like a really sincere person, which I know makes no sense at all.

Oh yeah, and he had brown hair and brown eyes and a bit of that acne that comes with scars and his feet were size nine, and that's about the longest description of anyone I've ever tried to do since I started writing about the war, so long ago.

So there I was with the fly half giving me a neck massage and he hadn't said a word. His hands worked their way across my shoulders and down my back. I leant back a bit more and purred. In a way there was nothing sexual about it and in another way it was one of the sexiest things I've ever had a boy do. The only tension I felt was the tension of hoping he wouldn't stop, that I could lie there forever, and that somehow he'd never get tired of massaging me and he'd never want me to do anything in return.

That's the really annoying thing in relationships: you have to actually do something for the other person once in a while, instead of lying back and waiting for them to peel another grape and drop it in your mouth. Maybe robots would be better.

The funny thing was that Jeremy left again, about twenty minutes later, and in all that time we didn't exchange a word, but when he left there was a new vibe between us. I went to bed excited for the first time in ages, and realised, lying there in the dark, that I didn't feel that way about Lee any more, or rather, that Lee didn't make me feel that way any more, which may be the same thing. I hadn't planned on complicating my life any further, but love, I guess it strikes like lightning and suddenly there's a stampede. What am I talking about? That's not just love, that's life in general.

Oh, Jeremy. I was so tired but I couldn't sleep. I ran through all his beautiful qualities, over and over. His warm eyes, his firm hands, the pleasing way he stood and sat and walked, his sense of humour, his intelligence, the way he knew so much about history and was so strong and passionate when he talked about it. I love people to be passionate about something. I'd rather they were passionate about football than about nothing. I'd rather they were passionate about tractors or pigshooting or Dalmatian dogs or making marmalade. About the only exception is computer games. I don't find passionate computer nerds all that sexy.

Jeremy was calm as well as strong. He was a bit like his father in that way. He was kind and gentle and nice to everyone. I don't think he was too like his father in that way though. I got the feeling in New Zealand that Colonel, sorry, General Finley was pretty tough on anyone who wasn't doing what General Finley wanted. I wondered if that included his son. He would be a pretty strict father,

I think. He had Jeremy's shining eyes without the humour. And if Jeremy was the Scarlet Pimple, well, that would be impressive. I would like that. He would have to be a real leader to do that. He'd have to be someone who could take charge and make stuff happen. He'd be respected by everyone.

Oh, if my hands could only be his hands. I drifted off to sleep a while later, smiling for the first time in a long time.

CHAPTER 12

I DON'T KNOW WHETHER THIS IS ANYTHING TO DO WITH love but over the next few days I made a fool of myself a zillion times, except that luckily most of the time no-one was there to notice. Maybe it was just total exhaustion, but I managed to spray the griller with eucalyptus instead of cooking oil, then I left nearly a dozen eggs on top of the stove when I was doing a roast, which didn't do much for their freshness. The eucalyptus spray had been standing around in the kitchen for as long as I could remember. We used it for pretty much everything, like spraying around the room after I'd made a sardine sandwich (Mum hated the smell of sardines), spraying on burns, spraying on beds to get rid of dust mites, spraying on Gavin when he was being a nuisance.

Lee and Pang left and I missed Pang's bright friendly chatter but I didn't miss Lee much. I was scared of the way he looked at me, those dark brooding eyes, sombre and impenetrable. I didn't know what he expected of me any more, but whatever it was, I was fairly certain that I couldn't provide it.

I didn't hear from Homer but I assumed he was chained to the bed and banned from leaving the house again until 2050. Then he rang and said he'd had to tell his parents a bit about Liberation, and they weren't happy, and Liberation wasn't happy, but the Scarlet Pimple was trying to get him a new motorbike and he'd asked for a four-wheeler for me.

Jess rang twice and Bronte twice a day. Bronte and I talked a lot. I told her about Jeremy but needless to say I didn't tell Jess.

I didn't see Jeremy, or hear from him. In a way that didn't matter to me. I felt a kind of security, knowing that he was out there. I felt like now we had an understanding and it wouldn't go away in a hurry. I was in a strange mood. I felt a great tiredness after escaping from the shopping centre and the helicopter. Suddenly I was eighty years old. I'd been tired plenty of times during the war, but never like this. This was in my bones. I wandered the house, looking after Gavin but not after myself. I travelled the paddocks dreaming of life with Jeremy. I didn't know if I was in love or just distracted for a short time by his warm hands and strong presence. The thing I found strange was that most of the time I felt not happy but sad. Is that love? Or was it just the sadness of living my life?

Sometimes a river of sadness flowed through me. Not depression, not grief, not despair, just sadness. I moved heavily and I was clumsy, I couldn't think, and I couldn't laugh very much. I wanted my parents back. I wanted them so badly that nothing else mattered. And all the time, shadowing my sadness, was a terrible fear, the fear that I would never recover. If only someone could have assured me that one day the sadness would go, that one day I would charge up the hills running and puffing and laughing, one day I would roll down the hills giggling and wheezing and hurting myself on rocks and thorns. I wanted to see a hill that was warm and bright in the full open light of the sun. I knew I couldn't be on that hill yet, but I wanted someone to tell me, "Ellie, you will play there one day. It is your hill and you will be there."

I think the worst thing is to know that you will be sad forever. When parents lose a child, isn't that what they know from the moment the policeman opens his mouth? When a sister loses a brother, isn't that the truth that fills them in an instant? There is no cure for that kind of sadness.

Laughter and carefree love, all the bright things, it seemed like they gleamed and glistened for other people.

I think I was starting to understand one of the great paradoxes. I love paradoxes. I think they contain all the truth in the world. The only trouble is that I can't understand them. "The more things change, the more things stay the same." "The greater your knowledge, the less you know." "Most people aren't brave enough to be cowards." "Every exit is an entry to somewhere." "Less is more." I mean, I understand those, but I have to work at it. I remember during the war Homer saying to me, "I'm an atheist," and then adding, "Thank God."

The paradox about love is that it hurts and it heals. It makes you feel better, only to make you feel worse. You go into it knowing it will betray you but you go into it anyway. And another paradox is that you go into it as an individual, because you as an individual are in love with someone, but from the start you lose so much of your individuality. I was starting to fall seriously in love with Jeremy, so right away, what happens? I start worrying about what Jeremy thinks of me, trying to guess what he likes and doesn't like about me, thinking about ways of changing myself so that he will like me even more. It's pretty dumb when you think that I'm the person he seemed to like, not the me I was contemplating changing myself into.

I'd always had this image of myself standing on top of Tailor's Stitch singing "The Sound of Music." Not really. But I did go to the hills when my heart was lonely. If people are either mountain people or ocean people then I'm a mountain person. I love the ocean, the few times I get a chance to see it, but I'm a mountain girl. When the weekend rolled around and Gavin got a rare invitation for a sleepover, from Mark, even though Mark was born standing up and talking back, even though Mark would choke a chook that clucked the wrong way, I thought, "This is my chance," and pushed Gavin out the door with his bag packed.

As soon as he'd gone, I took the long walk up the spur. It's a bit strange, I suppose, but I hadn't connected that spur with the deaths of my parents and Mrs Mackenzie. I mean, it's not like they were killed there, but I was climbing it when I heard the shots that ended their lives and ended my world. As I got close to that place again I started to feel quite weird. My legs got heavy and didn't want to do what they were paid for; my arms tingled; my throat blocked up and starting saying no to oxygen.

Melissa Carpenter, who lived about three k's from us and got the same bus, was one of those mad horse people, along with her parents. Everyone knows the thing about how you gotta get back on the horse after you fall off. When Melissa was twelve she fell off big-time. Her favourite horse bucked at a snake and threw her. She knew right away she'd done some serious damage, and in fact it turned out she'd broken three bones in her back. She's been lucky—at one stage they thought she was heading for life in a wheelchair. So anyway, she's lying on the ground, waiting for the ambulance and wondering if she's ever going to walk again, and her father kneels beside her and whispers, "Honey, I know you're in a bit of pain but do you think you could manage to get back on Barney for a minute, just so you don't lose your confidence?"

I thought about that as I stood a hundred metres from that place on the spur and sweated with memories and fear. It was kind of funny the way Mr Carpenter had been so determined to get Melissa back onto Barney, because even though we all laughed when we heard the story (and once we knew Melissa was going to be OK), in a way Mr Carpenter was right, because from that day on Melissa never got on Barney or any other horse again.

Now here I stood gazing at the spur, suddenly awash with memories and wondering if I would ever be able to get up on Tailor's Stitch again. Because I couldn't get past that spot where I'd been when I heard the shots. I was dumbfounded. I hadn't known this was going to happen. The violence of my life was threatening to close the mountains to me. The war and the fighting and the killing were blocking the promise of good things in the future. I needed to get up that rocky slope and walk the high ridge.

I took a few more steps but my legs wouldn't move any further. I knew I couldn't do it. I hadn't been beaten by many things over the last eighteen months but I could not make this simple climb. The air wouldn't give way for me, the paralysis was too powerful.

I was lonely and I wanted to go to the hills and hear the

songs I had heard before. I wanted my heart to be filled with the sound of music. I felt that if my future were to include love I'd have to find a way to get past that spot on the spur. But it wasn't going to happen today. It mightn't ever happen again.

Seemed like it hadn't been a very successful sleepover either. Gavin was already home, which wasn't in the script. I didn't realise for a while. Normally I could tell where he was, as he often didn't know when he was making a noise. He'd figured out of course that certain sounds attract attention and certain sounds were louder than others, but he forgot.

When I heard a thump from his bedroom I thought we were being attacked. I grabbed the rifle, which nowadays I kept close at hand. It was behind the kitchen door. I broke out in a sweat, wondering whether to head for the bush or check out the bedroom. Marmie was asleep on the kitchen floor, which was a good sign, so I hesitated. I loaded half-a-dozen rounds into the magazine and slid one into the barrel, all of which was difficult to do quietly. But it did make me feel more confident. Another thump from the direction of Gavin's room. Marmie opened one eye and yawned. She wasn't the greatest watchdog in the world but she should do better than this.

I stole out of the kitchen into the corridor, only a metre, and swung open the door of the linen press so I could hide behind it. Standing there put me into a totally different theatre of sounds. Now the vibration of the fridge motor, Marmie's breathing, the buzzing of the early blowie, the flapping of the fly strips in the doorway...all of these were in the background and instead I could hear a magpie in the distance, beyond the end of the house, a moth flapping against the lead-light window in the door that led onto the little lawn, and the drone of a light plane.

Thump. What the hell was going on? If it was an invasion of the house they'd be doing more than hanging around Gavin's room kicking the furniture. I decided to take one more step. This could be extremely dumb, but I was getting more and more convinced that the biggest problem in Gavin's room could just be Gavin. OK, he wasn't due home until tomorrow, but he was a kid who made his own rules, and besides that, a sleepover at Mark's was as likely to last one hour as it was the whole weekend.

I took the one step, and as I did heard Gavin's distinctive voice yelling one of the most powerful swearwords in his vocabulary, and trust me, when it comes to swearing, Gavin has been hanging around Homer too long. I assumed that he was not talking to a terrorist who had climbed through his bedroom window. I sighed, flicked the safety catch forwards, unbolted it and let the bullet in the barrel slide out. I really didn't feel like a big discussion with Gavin about why on earth he was home when he was meant to be having a good time at Mark's. But a whole lot of thumping was going on and I couldn't walk away from that.

I put the rounds into my pocket, propped the rifle against the wall so that Gavin wouldn't think I was going to shoot him, and went into the room. Where Gavin was concerned there wasn't much point knocking. He was standing with his head in the corner, like he'd sent himself there already, like he was one jump ahead of the teacher. As if that wasn't bad enough, he was rocking up and down. As I stood there, he drew back, then snapped his head forward into the wall.

Now I knew what those thumps had been. I couldn't hear any Metallica, and neither could he, so it wasn't their fault. I picked up a cushion and chucked it at him. He spun around and glared at me. If looks could have killed I might as well have lain down then and there and got ready for the autopsy.

I was in the mood to be compassionate, forgiving and understanding.

"Gavin, what the hell did you do this time?"

He hurled the cushion back, following it with a volley of Lemony Snickets. All hardbacks unfortunately. "Ow! Gavin! You little rat! That hurt."

The ringing of the phone saved innocent blood from being shed. I'm just not sure whose blood it would have been.

"Ellie! I've been trying to get you all afternoon. I left three messages."

Mark's mother. I felt like I'd suddenly put on three or four kilos and it was all around the heart. She was definitely not ringing to tell me about Gavin's lovely manners.

"Yes, sorry, I was out in the paddocks."

"I had to leave Gavin at the house. He said you wouldn't be far away. Did you find him all right?"

"Yes, no problem. He's in his room. I haven't talked to him though. I thought he wasn't coming back till tomorrow?"

"Yes, well, that's what I'm ringing about."

I sighed and sat on the little leather stool next to the phone. I could almost hear her lips pressing tighter and tighter together.

"Ellie, I don't know what that boy's problem is, but I think he needs help, and the sooner the better. I've never seen anything like what he and Mark got up to today. I know he hasn't had an easy life, but I'm afraid I can't have him here again."

I didn't know Mark's mother too well, but I had the impression she was always a bit confused, trying to do six things at once and not finishing any of them. I'd never really thought about it before but it struck me then that one of the things she never quite finished was looking after Mark.

Feeling tired, too tired to be bothered asking her what crimes the boys had committed, I sat in silence, doodling crosses with a blunt pencil.

"Are you there?" she asked.

"Yes."

"I wish there was someone I could talk to about him, Ellie. I really don't know how it is that you're looking after him."

I understood that she meant I was not "someone." I was "no-one," because of my age. I wondered at what age I'd become someone. I felt I was slipping into a sulk, my lips pressing into each other too, and I wanted to be rude and rebellious.

"Well, I'd better tell you, I suppose. I've always been worried about Gavin's influence on Mark, so up till now I've said to Mark that he can play with him but not to sit next to him in class. But I'm afraid Mark is too easily led sometimes. And of course you've got to feel sorry for Gavin."

Grrr. My doodles were turning into sharp pointy things. The pencil was reaching that horrible state where there was so little lead that the wooden ends were scratching the paper, which is almost as bad as fingernails down the blackboard. I didn't feel sorry for Gavin. Didn't have the time or the energy for it. I don't think he felt sorry for himself either, although he did feel angry, which is a bit different.

"So what did they do?"

"Oh! I can hardly . . . my neighbours are the Chaus. They're very nice and we've never had any trouble with them and they've been so good to Mark. And they had this lovely cat, a little grey thing about three years old, called Missy."

My heart was heavy now. I knew how these stories always ended, these stories started with, "We had this new car, we'd only had it a fortnight," or, "My mum had this Royal Doulton vase that her grandmother gave her and it was sitting on top of a bookcase . . ."

"They had this lovely cat." I formed a great fear for the cat as Mark's mum continued.

"And the boys, I don't know what came over them, but they somehow got hold of this poor little cat and Gavin tied it on the ground . . . this is awful, Ellie, I don't know how I can tell you the next bit."

I didn't know how I was going to be able to hear it. I was starting to hate Gavin.

"And Mark's got this jump for his bike, and it seems like Gavin aimed the bike off the jump, aimed for the cat . . ."

"Did he kill it?" I asked. My voice was husky, hoarse.

"Oh yes. It's hard to get the full story of course, because of his disability, but I think he landed on it quite a few times."

His disability. Stuff disability. If Gavin wanted to communicate something, he'd communicate it. He didn't have
any disability.

"I'll call you back," I said to Mark's mum, and hit the
off button on the phone.

CHAPTER 13

THIS IS MY MORNING ROUTINE. I GET UP AT SIX, AND IF I'm not awake already the moo clock wakes me. The moo clock was a present from Fi. It's an alarm in the shape of a cow, black and white, and instead of ringing it moos. Moos, yes, let's move on. Sometime in the next five to fifteen minutes I slither out of bed, providing it's Marmie asleep in the middle of my doona. I don't understand how a small dog can occupy three-quarters of a double bed, but she manages it. If it's Gavin asleep in the middle of my bed I'm less subtle. I just jump out. I've tried to persuade Marmie to sleep with Gavin in Gavin's bed, mainly because the more they bond the better I think it is for Gavin, but they both seem to prefer my bed.

If Gavin's in his own bed I stop by on my way to the shower and give him the first of what will be a number of prods or shakes or pushes. The one sure way to get him out of bed is to kiss him, but I'm reluctant to use that tactic too often in case it loses its power.

The bathroom, yeah, well, it's not too good at the moment because of the rats. It would be nice not to have rats, not now not ever, but it's a part of our life that I suppose will never change. People from the city think we must live in filth and slime if we have rats but it's not like that at all. I'm quite tidy and Gavin's not bad and Mum was always pretty neat. Every year we get waves of mice and/or rats, and they arrive with no warning. Each time we wage war against them and eventually they're gone, either because we've defeated them, or because the owls and feral cats and magpies have wiped them out, or because they've heard rumours of a great new chocolate factory down the road. Whatever, they go, and sometimes it'll be twelve months before the new lot check in.

But it is really disgusting to wander into the bathroom half asleep and find rat droppings all over the floor and the soap half chewed and a roll of toilet paper that they've dragged to their hole and eaten away so they can make a nice soft nest with it. You wouldn't want to wipe your bum with that paper.

So this particular morning I picked up the droppings using a tissue and dropped them into our loo and flushed them away, because I knew I wouldn't have time to clean the floor properly till this afternoon or tonight, then I chucked out the soap and the loo paper. We had friends from the city years ago who'd never seen rat droppings and didn't know what they were, and when they found a half chewed apple in the fruit bowl, surrounded by these little black pellets, they thought someone had eaten part of the apple and put the rest back, so they cut it up and gave it to their little daughter. God, I practically vomited when I realised.

I put some Ratsak right down the hole, but they don't seem to be eating it at the moment. Then I blocked the hole with steel wool, which sometimes works and sometimes doesn't. Not far away was a perfect little star on the floor, a daddy long-legs, with a solid circular black body. I'd never seen one quite like him, so neat and precise. When I counted, he had only seven legs, poor thing. I thought he was dead but I wasn't sure so I touched him really fast and he didn't move but I still suspected him and flicked him again and then a third time and he suddenly came to life and went scurrying away on his seven good legs.

My last encounter with a spider had been just a few weeks ago when I'd been getting a bag off the top of my wardrobe. I'd pulled it down and taken it into the dining room to pack it with stuff for school. As I started chucking in the books I felt a tickling across my scalp. "Dear God," I prayed, "please let it not be a spider." I thought, "I'll go to the mirror, look calmly into it, and if there's a spider crawling through my hair I am not going to panic."

I went to the mirror, looked calmly into it, saw the biggest huntsman of all time crawling through my hair, and panicked. I scrabbled madly at my hair but I couldn't dislodge the spider. Now I'd made it mad. I imagined it going into attack mode and filling my brain with venom. Amazingly, it didn't do this, and I was able to have a second go, which was more successful. I swear, he was the size of my ear, and that's not counting his legs.

Yes, between rats and spiders, not to mention fights to the death with armed enemy soldiers, life was never dull.

Anyway, I took my shower. I'm a long-shower person, because I find it the best place to think. We have a pretty good supply of water at the moment, so I can indulge myself. My favourite shampoo is the citrus with a touch of ginseng, Sunsilk I think. I have no idea whether it is any good for my hair, but it smells so good I have to stop myself from drinking it.

On the way back I generally chuck another load in the washing machine, or unload it from the night before. I pay a second visit to Gavin, then get to my bedroom, pick out which of my wardrobe of dazzling Wirrawee High School uniforms I'm going to wear, get dressed, call on Gavin's room to deliver the very last final you'd-better-move-right-now-buddy warning, and then tackle the kitchen. It's fairly embarrassing how many times I have to start by cleaning up from dinner the night before, and no, that's not the reason we have rats, but once that's done I can think about breakfast and lunch.

Neither Gavin nor I are big on breakfasts, especially since the money got so tight we can't afford Coco Pops or Crunchy Nut Cornflakes. If I've got time and I'm in a good mood I'll make porridge, which Gavin quite likes but which I'm not mad about. I just have the boring Weet-Bix with as little sugar as I can manage or some bread and jam. If the bread's fresh I just eat bread, but if it's stale I toast it. If the day ever comes when I get sick of bread I'll starve to death.

By the time I've started eating, Gavin is probably stumbling down the corridor to the bathroom, or, on a good day, he might even be coming back showered and clean. Then he's likely to lean against me and let me feed him pieces of bread or toast, like he's a little bird in a nest. He seems to need this to give him the energy to go all the way to his bedroom and do the dressing thing.

As I'm eating, as well as feeding Gavin I'm also starting on the lunches. He likes the good old sandwiches with the conventional fillings, like cheese and Vegemite, chicken, or last weekend's roast lamb with sliced tomato. He'll still be leaning into me as I pop another square of toast into his greedy little mouth, and at the same time he has the cheek to complain about everything I'm doing with his sandwiches. "Err! Err! No more pepper!"

I prefer something a bit more exotic for lunch, which I'll usually do the night before. I tried making sushi once but that was a disaster. When I say exotic, I don't normally mean as exotic as sushi, but something like quiche or curried lamb shanks or vege kebabs.

By now the pace is starting to pick up. There might be time for coffee or there might not but there's usually time for juice at least. I chuck a bit of fruit or a few cookies in the lunch boxes and close them up. I flick plates and cutlery at the dishwasher. I persuade Gavin to go back to his room to get dressed and I achieve this in a variety of ways depending on the mood I'm in and the mood he's in. It could be putting him over my shoulder and running down there with him, or yelling at him to get a move on, or flicking at him with the fly swat.

I leave him to it and do a quick burn outside. I let the chooks and ducks out and scatter three tins of seed for them. Most of the seed goes to the rosellas, who've learnt that the Lintons' is the place to be at around six forty-five a.m. I swear, they email each other to let everyone know there's a free feed. As well as the rosellas, who are pretty, there's the currawongs, who aren't, and who steal the eggs; the magpies, who make a beautiful noise in the mornings and who are really cheeky; and the crows, who sound like death every day. We're still investigating which bird tore the last lot of ducklings apart. When the mother ducks hatch their clutch of eggs—and they can do big numbers, like eighteen if they put in the effort—we leave them locked in the yard for weeks, until the little ones are old enough to look after themselves. But with the last lot we had a disaster. Under one of the doors was a gap just big enough for a duckling. Eight out of the flock of eleven squeezed under it and found themselves in the great outdoors. That was the end of their little lives. Something attacked them and pecked them to death one by one. I got home from school and found these tiny bodies, each one with terrible wounds, and a couple of them flattened as though they'd been stood on as well.

You never never get used to death on a farm. What really upset me about this was that the mother duck must have seen the whole thing. My old enemy, the imagination, kept playing it over and over, the mother totally distraught, running backwards and forwards, the last three ducklings equally distraught but not knowing why, running backwards and forwards after her, the mother squealing and grunting her distress and agony as she watched her kids pecked into pieces while she was unable to do a damn thing about it.

Anyway, now we have a bit of four-by-two at the bottom of the door and so I guess it won't happen again. Shutting the chook shed door after the ducklings have bolted.

I still want to know, though, which bird did it? The magpies, with their big and savage beaks, so out of proportion to the rest of them, stalking around like they own the place? The currawongs, hiding in the trees, peeping down like Japanese snipers in World War II? The crows, black angels, or rather, black ghosts, spirits of people who led bad lives and now can't rest? I think it was probably the crows.

But I wouldn't rule out the kookaburras. We have a lot of kookaburras, don't know why. I don't mind, as I like them, and I think they probably keep the snakes down. I saw a kookaburra eating a small snake last spring. It took him a while but he got it down. Dad told me kookaburras are "the true communists," because they work together for the good of all. He said if one pair hatch some young, the other adults put aside what they're doing and help fetch food for the new chicks. I must admit I've never seen this happen, although I've watched for it often enough.

Kookaburras are pretty—they drop the most beautiful feathers, with lovely soft brown and blue colours—but they also have beaks which to a worm or a moth or a duckling must look like an Exocet missile with a pair of eyes.

When I let the ducks out and they've shovelled up enough seed they head down to a small dam that we put in to provide water for the turkeys and which was a project that never got off the ground (like the turkeys actually). (In fact it was a turkey.) (And I suppose you don't really want a dam to get off the ground.)

The turkey dam is one of the ducks' favourite places. They love to put their food through water, dragging stale hard bread crusts under to soften them and break them up. There's not many days when I can rush off without taking at least a minute to enjoy watching the ducks. Sure, when you watch them closely for a while you can see how they get up to some pretty ugly stuff. Drakes raping other drakes, drakes raping ducks that are too young, ducks killing their own ducklings. Somehow, though, as they launch themselves into the dam with satisfied clucks, like middle-aged ladies descending on the jam exhibit at the Wirrawee Show, you forget all that. "From troubles of the world I turn to ducks." I think that's the first line of a poem.

It only takes the ugly caw of a crow or a bellow from Gavin or a stick falling from high in a gum tree to break the spell the ducks put on me. Suddenly I'm rushing again to check on an ailing cow or to get an LPG bottle that I want refilled or to pick up a rubber mallet I promised to lend Mr Yannos. In the meantime Gavin's meant to be doing his jobs: making his bed, feeding Marmie and putting her in her yard, locking the house (something we never had to worry about in the past), fuelling the ute and getting it out of the shed and warming it up. Some days we take the bikes, but in winter it's usually the ute. Time's so tight on a school morning that I hit the ute running, like a Formula 1 driver, and take off for the front gate with a squeal of tyres. Traditionally, as we pass the shearing shed, Gavin asks me, "What you forgot?" I could never teach him any other way of asking the question. He was so eager to catch me out that he didn't care about grammar. And there is always something. It might be trivial, like taking the clothes out of the washing machine; it might be personal, like cleaning my teeth; it might be major, like leaving the lunches on the kitchen table or forgetting to cancel the Monsanto guy who is coming out to talk about sorghum.

We herb down the driveway, spraying mud or blowing clouds of grit and dust, depending on the time of year, me driving and checking out the cattle on the right, Gavin checking them out on the left. It's not a proper inspection of course—it's many hundred acres short of a proper inspection—but a couple of times we've seen things that have suddenly terminated any plans to go to school that day. That doesn't cause Gavin the least distress but it causes me enough for both of us.

Early in the trip we pass the skeleton of the Datsun 120Y that I used to have for these drives to the gate. It had been my personal paddock basher. Like all Datsun 120Y's it was yellow. I think it was compulsory for them to be yellow. They were born yellow. This one was still yellow, or at least those parts that had any paint left were yellow. The rest was rusty red. Something had happened to it during the war. If its skeleton could talk, it would have told a tale of suffering and tragedy and death. However, the chances were that I would never hear its story. When I got back after the war, my beloved little Datsun was already a wreck.

The trip to the Providence Gully Road gate is exactly four kilometres, or a bit over, depending on which speedo you use. Most days it tends to be a race between us and the bus. Occasionally the bus has gone; quite often it's waiting for us; most often it's in sight and waiting for us by the time we hide the ute, grab our stuff and lock the car. These days we're never quite sure who'll be driving, out of Mr Gruber, who used to be our nearest neighbour but who retired after the war and is now living in Wirrawee and is really nice; Mrs Nelson, who lives a few k's down the road and is really pretty horrible; and Jerry, who's about twenty-five and is no Otto, but is a thousand light years closer to Otto than the other two.

Mr Gruber and Jerry wait for a few minutes, even if they can't see us, but Mrs Nelson only waits if she can see the cloud of dust, and then she scowls at us as we get on. I mean, fair enough, it's up to us to get there on time, and most days we do, even though I've made it sound like we're hopelessly disorganised, but we do live in slightly difficult circumstances, and most of the days we're late because of "unforeseen circumstances," like someone else's cow wandering up the driveway, or a fallen branch blocking the road, or a koala injured by a fox or a dog.

You can't control nature and you can't control your neighbours, as my father used to say.

And I couldn't control Gavin. Sitting on the bus, the morning after the conversation with Mark's mum, I watched the back of his head and wondered what on earth I could do with him. These days the paper was full of stories about post-traumatic stress. There was a post-traumatic stress advice column, there were articles by doctors about post-traumatic stress, there were post-traumatic stress support groups. It seemed to me that Gavin was a post-traumatic stress kid in a post-traumatic stress world.

He was digging around in the seat, aggravating the boy next to him, chipping at the rubber lining of the window with his fingernails. Then he did something to the girl in the seat in front, a Year 6 from the primary school. She suddenly turned around and knelt up and yelled over the top of her seat, "Stop it, you little faggot."

My problem with Gavin was simple enough. Was he just a typical naughty kid or was he deeply disturbed and needing a lot of help? I knew one thing: I was deeply disturbed about him and I needed a lot of help.

CHAPTER 14

GAVIN NEARLY DISINTEGRATED WHEN HE REALISED I WAS getting off the bus with him. His eyes rolled around like they weren't attached to anything any more, and suddenly he was too weak to pick up his bag. I hadn't said anything to him the night before about his being sent home early, or about the cat, but when I got up and headed down the aisle towards the door he knew that this was D-Day, this was the hour of power, and he was about to be nailed to the wall like the fox skins pegged out in the barn.

For a moment it seemed like he was going to stay on board, but then he realised he couldn't do that, so he followed me off. But as soon as we were standing on the grass he ran up to me, turned me around and tried to push me back onto the bus. I wouldn't let myself be pushed.

Instead, I set off for the school gate. He darted around and got between me and the gate, dropped his bag and, with both hands, grabbed me by the elbows.

Again he tried to push me back.

"Gavin," I said into his furious eyes, "I have to talk to your teacher."

I wasn't trying to be smart by doing it this way. But if I'd told Gavin the night before, or at breakfast, he would never have got on the bus. Now, with so many kids streaming past, he was in a tough spot. He couldn't throw too spectacular a tantrum without embarrassing himself big-time. Even so, he threw a very intense small one. His hands dropped down and grabbed my forearms, and he held and squeezed them so tight that I had bruises for four days afterwards. He tried to outstare me but I knew I couldn't let myself be outstared so we locked eyes and, trying not to blink, I said, "I've got to find out what's going on with you."

He shook me then shook his head. Again he tried to push me away, this time down the street towards the high school, but other kids started to notice and stop and look. That didn't stop him but it did slow him down a bit and make him more self-conscious. I felt sorry for him, but I felt sorry for the cat too. I said, "Listen, kid, I've been bullied by experts," and I pushed him off and walked into the school.

It's a bit strange going back to your old primary school. For one thing, they look like the same kids you were at school with and you have a weird feeling that you've jumped back a few years and they really are the same kids—that's Fi over there with her back to you, Homer running past, Kevin hunched over a Game Boy with another kid who didn't look like anyone I knew. But the ones who did look a bit like Fi and Homer and Kevin, when I saw their faces, it was quite disconcerting.

For another thing, you feel like a giant. Everything's smaller, including the students of course, and you get a sense of just how much you have grown in the last few years. The doorways are smaller, the classrooms are smaller, the lockers are smaller, and how I ever managed to sit in those chairs is beyond the freakiest imagination.

The third thing is that you do get mobbed a bit, which might look quite glamorous when you see it happen to superstars on TV but is a bloody nuisance when you're in a hurry and in a bad mood, and it does seem like the girls who most want to mob you are often the obnoxious ones. I'm talking about the ones I knew from the swimming pool or I knew their sisters or brothers or parents, or they were on my bus and their main reason in coming up to me seemed to be to show off to their friends that they knew me. Most of them could talk to me just about any time, so I don't know why they suddenly had to make a big deal about it. This is pretty horrible to the nice ones, because of course there were plenty of those, but I was too stressed to notice them.

So I was motoring across the yard like a car through floodwater, throwing up a wake that consisted of Year 4 and 5 girls saying, "Hi Ellie, what are you here for, Ellie, you here to see Gavin's teacher, are you coming to Brendan's eighteenth, Ellie?" and it was all I could do not to turn around and screech at them, "Bugger off, the lot of you."

I knew her name was Mrs Rosedale, and of course I'd seen her plenty of times, but we'd never talked for more than a minute. And even then it was only about basic things like, "We could do with some rain," "Did Gavin give you his excursion money?" "Sorry he was away yesterday but we had a couple of trees down after the storm," "Thanks for finding his library book."

You'd think someone with a name like Mrs Rosedale would be really nice. I mean, it's like that book where the kid stays with Aunt Bridget Wonkham-Strong, and then at the end he goes off to live with Aunt Bundlejoy Cosysweet, and you figure he's got to be better off. Like, it wasn't as if she was Mrs Grumpywitch or Mrs Sourtits. Gavin seemed to like her well enough. He never said much about her really, but then he never said much about school. She seemed nice enough from what I'd had to do with her, just one of those straight-down-the-line, you-know-what-you're-getting, middle-of-the-road primary school teachers.

I didn't even know what I wanted to say to her, just, more than anything I think, to talk to an adult who knew Gavin well and could give me some idea of how to deal with him. That nice dream of us all living together as a family, and Gavin being the brother I never had, was disintegrating fast, now that I had to be his mother and father as well as his sister.

I was actually a bit pissed off at my parents for leaving me with this problem, conveniently forgetting that I was the one who had lumbered them with "this problem" in the first place.

Mrs Rosedale was in the library and she didn't give me the brush-off, like I expected. I thought I'd have to make an appointment and come back later. "Sure, the kids have got Music," she said. "I'll just be five minutes."

While I was waiting I wandered along the shelves having a little nostalgic meander. The library had survived the war almost untouched: I remembered one of the teachers telling Mum that although people had obviously borrowed books, they'd returned them too. There were about sixty that they couldn't find. That was weird, all these invaders borrowing books from the Wirrawee Primary School library and returning them, like regular people.

It seemed in pretty good order now. I got a little thrill out of seeing my old friends, *The Magic Faraway Tree*, *Who Sank the Boat?*, *Tiger in the Bush*, *Charlotte's Web*,

Robinson Crusoe, *Where's Wally?*, *The Long Red Scarf* . . . I ran my finger along their spines, wondering why I hadn't shared more of them with Gavin. With each book came a film clip that ran in my mind: curled up in a cubby reading *Tiger in the Bush*, being in bed with Dad reading *The Magic Faraway Tree*, spilling orange juice on *The Long Red Scarf*.

"Now, what can I do for you, Ellie?" Mrs Rosedale said, and it was like a little slap, startling me back into the real world.

She led me into the side room. Before I could sit down she said, "I'm hoping you can give me a few tips on dealing with young Gavin."

I felt like I'd been given a quick elbow to the stomach. I'd been rather hoping that she would sit down, open the inner taps of wisdom that most adults seem to have, and pour out wonderful words of advice that would solve all my problems.

"Has he been a bit difficult?" I asked. I felt embarrassed, as though Gavin's behaviour was entirely my responsibility, so I should feel ashamed if he was not one of the best kids in the class.

She stretched her arms wide, rolled her eyes and laughed. "A bit difficult!" she agreed. "He's the original barrel of monkeys. Little bugger. We have a fight just about every day, but he still gets away with a lot, because with these big classes you can't keep an eye on half of what's going on."

She got up and opened a window, then, still standing beside it, took out a cigarette and lit it. "I can get away with this in here, just," she said with another laugh. I started to think that she was rather a nervous person.

"Ellie, the farm you live on, there wouldn't be any empty houses, would there? That you'd be interested in renting? Or my partner could do some work around the place in exchange for rent?"

I felt more and more dejected. I wanted to get this conversation back on track. It was like going to the station and expecting to catch the seven forty-five to Stratton, only to find yourself on the eighty-thirty to Cobbler's Bay.

"No, sorry, there's nothing like that," I said. It was awkward being put in this position, although it had happened a few times already, with the demand for housing, not to mention all the people who wanted a nice house in the country with fresh air and space. "Do you think Gavin's been getting worse?"

"Gavin? Well, possibly, a little, yes. He wasn't too great to begin with."

"Has he been violent?" I asked.

"Violent!" she said, puffing on her cigarette and pushing a strand of hair away from her eye. "God, every story he writes and every picture he draws. Mind you, there's a few of them who see life that way, which won't come as any surprise to you. But he is among the worst." She gave an exaggerated shudder. "If you had to read the number of gory stories I've marked since school started again . . . severed limbs and decapitated torsos and blood gushing like fountains. And some of the pictures are just collages of tanks and guns and body parts. Even the kids who didn't see much violence during the war have been infected by it."

"So what am I meant to do about Gavin?" I asked, feeling more helpless with every minute. "He seems to be acting a bit violently at times too."

I wasn't really being honest about him, but I didn't want to give him too bad a name.

She had that teacher suspicion thing though, where they can smell a copied essay or a cruel joke or a fake excuse from a kilometre away. She frowned at me through the cigarette smoke. "What's he done now?"

It was too early in the morning for me to avoid teachers' suspicious questions. And after all, I had come there for a bit of comfort and support. "Something to a cat," I stammered. "He was staying at Mark's, and they did something pretty horrible to a cat."

She pressed her lips together and looked away. "It might be time to do something about him," she said. "In the old days he would have been at the therapist's long ago, but the resources are few and far between at the moment. Still, I think he's about ready for some intervention. It's a scandal that there are no integration aides."

"I don't want to get him into trouble," I said. "I just want some ideas on how to handle him."

"Oh God, I've got every sympathy with you," she said. "And with him too for that matter. I haven't got much idea of what he went through in the war, but I know it was horrendous, and then there was the terrible thing out at your place . . ."

"The terrible thing"—seemed like that was its new name.

"Yeah, that came at the worst time," I agreed, and a moment later thought, "What a stupid comment." As if there's ever a best time.

Mrs Rosedale looked at the end of her cigarette. "You know, I've really got to give these up," she said. A whole lot of children's voices, laughing and squealing and chatter-ing, suddenly came through the other row of windows behind me. It sounded like a horde of wasps setting out for a day in the garden.

"You just have to try to ignore the bad behaviour and reinforce the good," Mrs Rosedale said. "When he does something good, give him lots of praise, and don't take any notice when he's been naughty. And I'll have a chat to Mrs Howell about him. That business of the cat sounds serious."

Walking back to the high school, I felt pretty miserable. It wasn't only that Mrs Rosedale had been no help, but there was the feeling that I might have made things worse. The last thing I wanted was a whole bunch of people who didn't know anything much about our situation to come poking around. I knew I wasn't doing a very good job with Gavin on my own, but I had the feeling that they might do worse.

CHAPTER 15

My first date with Jeremy was a wild and exotic experience. We didn't limo into Stratton for an expensive dinner and the movies, we didn't helicopter to New Zealand to spend the weekend with his father, we didn't camp on Taylor's Stitch and feast on lamb and wild mushrooms, we didn't even go to McDonald's.

We met under a tree at lunchtime, at the scoreboard end of the Wirrawee High School footy ground. I swapped him one of my curried lamb shanks for one of his cheese and Vegemite sandwiches. That's what you do when you like someone.

It wasn't a very good date, because I was depressed and irritated but trying to be bright and positive, not wanting Jeremy to see my worst side too early. But he seemed kind of distracted anyway. Neither of us even touched each other. It was hard to remember how warm and strong his hands had felt on my skin. Ten minutes before the bell we finally agreed to be honest and say what was bugging us, because by then it had become pretty obvious to each of us that the other one was pretty bugged.

Of course, as always, Jeremy, being the guy, got to go first. That increased my bugging just slightly, only by a couple of clicks, but I figured I'd be lucky to get two or three minutes by the time we'd sorted out his problems.

"It's this Liberation thing. It's all getting pretty crazy. I think what we did was worth doing, because we basically prevented major terrorism, and there's no way anyone official could have gone over the border and done it. But it's getting out of hand. Have you seen all the stuff in the papers?" His eyes were really beautiful, so full of life and intelligence.

I shook my head. "Haven't had time."

"Well, I read papers, and my father keeps me up to date. Every drunken lunatic who wants to be a hero is charging across the border and attacking people. It's still easy to get across, as you know better than anyone, and it'll be ages before they manage to put up decent fences and all the rest. They're talking about a DMZ, which could be quite wide, and filled with mines even —"

"What's a DMZ?" I interrupted. Jeremy had slightly curly hair and it was quite mussed up. I wanted to comb it into shape with my fingers.

"De-militarised zone," he said. "A neutral area, but no-one's allowed into it."

"Tell that to the kangaroos."

"Yeah, well, there won't be any of those if it's mined. Anyway, there were three guys from Stratton killed two nights ago when their car got shelled."

"On our side of the border?" His skin, when his shirt was open, looked brown and smooth.

"No, on their side. No-one even knows why they were over there, but there's a theory that they were just joyriding. They'd been drinking or smoking or both. And then last weekend there was a revenge attack at a truck stop near Cobblers Bay, with this bunch of anonymous people who sure looked like they were enemy soldiers and they acted like they were enemy soldiers except they weren't wearing uniforms, and they came out of the bush, killed six people, took their money and nicked off down the highway in a large new Merc."

"Yes, I heard about that one." I loved the pattern the sunlight and leaves made on his face. I shook my head, trying to concentrate on what he was saying.

"So my father's pushing pretty strongly for Liberation to do more, because they're organised and efficient, and he thinks that strength is good, weakness is bad, and history shows you have to fight stuff like the attack at Cobblers. He's not interested in the other stories, the ones about unprovoked attacks from our side. I keep telling him that history always repeats itself and history never repeats itself. Every situation—"

"Hey that's a paradox."

"Huh?"

"History always repeats itself and history never repeats itself. Paradox."

"Yeah, well every situation's different, even if it does have similarities to what's happened in the past. And then—"

"So every situation's the same and every situation's different? There's another one."

"Ellie, we don't have much time. I was going to say that it's complicated by the fact that he doesn't want me personally to get involved, which is really hypocritical of him, although he says it's not, it's just because I'm too young and inexperienced. But he knows that half the people in Liberation are young, and the ones who have experience train the ones who don't."

"What does the Scarlet Pimple think?" I asked, with a little smile just to show that if Jeremy was the Scarlet Pimple, I already knew, if that makes sense.

He laughed. "Huh. The Scarlet Pimpernel. Well, the Scarlet Pimple thinks that we should lie low for at least a week or two, to get a whiff of which way the wind is turning. But if something desperate comes up, something really important . . . And to make it more complicated, the whole thing scares the crap out of me. Like, it was a totally insane rush when we were out there, and even after we came back in a way, but there's also the total terror and the feeling that I aged about twenty years, and the fact that I couldn't stop choking for about a week afterwards."

"You hid that pretty well." Those two little ridges, from your nose to your mouth, I don't know if they've got a name, Jeremy's were a little longer and more prominent than most people's.

"Well, you do don't you? Why are you looking at me like that?"

"Oh, am I? Sorry."

"Anyway, it's time for you to spill your guts. There's only about two minutes left."

Yes, there was, just like I'd expected.

"Oh, it's just Gavin," I said lamely. "He's getting in more trouble than normal. He and his friend Mark did something pretty horrific the other day."

The bell rang. Jeremy started getting up, brushing bits of grass and leaves off him. "Yeah, I can imagine he'd be a bit of a problem," he said. "I don't know what you do with a kid like that."

Deep down I had known that Jeremy wasn't perfect, but

the only reason I'd known that was because no human being is perfect, and sometimes, especially when you meet someone new, you try to keep that in mind. But at least now I knew for sure that he wasn't perfect even if he was good looking. I tried not to grind my teeth as we walked back towards the lockers. Teeth grinding is so unattractive.

I tried again with Homer on the way home on the bus. He laughed when I told him that Gavin was being difficult. To be fair, I had made the same comment to him quite a few times before. I'm not saying that Gavin or Jeremy or Mrs Rosedale or anyone else was insensitive or uncaring. I think it was partly that people were so busy in their brave new worlds. Dealing with their own war scars, physical and mental, the injuries and the damage, was enough to keep everyone busy. And I guess I always understate things, so when I tried to tell people I was worried about Gavin, I didn't pitch it strongly enough.

When I mentioned something about the cat, Homer launched into a monologue about cow-tipping. This quickly became a conversation, because Sam Young got involved. Sam leant up from the seat in front of Homer, turned around, and they started comparing notes.

Cow-tipping is illegal, according to Shannon Young, who was sitting next to me. I suppose I should mention that cow-tipping is when you go up to a cow who's sound asleep in the paddock, give her a push in the right spot, and she just rolls over and lies on the ground, still asleep. It is pretty funny, because their legs stick out, but it's very bad for cows, although I'm not quite sure how. Probably bruises their meat for one thing, and even more probably gives them bad sleep patterns. I mean, how would you be if every time you went to sleep you did so with the fear that in the middle of the night some teenage idiot might sneak up to you and tip you over? Probably about the same as I felt every time I went to sleep since the war started, not sure whether some guy with a rifle might appear in the middle of the night and do something a lot worse than tipping me over.

Maybe that's why, when it came to cow-tipping, I took the side of the cow. Since the war anyway.

———

IT WAS TIME TO HAVE A SECOND ATTEMPT AT THE MOUN-tains. I was determined not to let them get the better of me. After all, what would they know? Just because they'd been around for thousands of years, just because they were made of rock, just because they covered thousands of k's, didn't mean that I, made of skin and bone and squishy internal bits like heart and liver, weighing as much as a fairly small boulder, but with a vast experience of life, couldn't conquer them. After all, I was a mountain girl. Just call me Maria.

This time I took Gavin, because I figured it would be harder for me to run away if he was there. And I thought it might be a good idea for us to have a break, spend an after-noon somewhere beautiful, even do a bit of bonding. A positive time, far away from Mark's place, and the poor dead cat.

Not that we actually needed bonding. Our relationship was good, despite all the frustrations and arguments. I could see how he still had big issues, was carrying a lot of baggage, was being inappropriate, etc, etc, but neither of us let that poison what we had. I knew he loved me, and if he didn't know that I loved him, then he couldn't tell the sun from the moon.

After the awful thing with the cat, and my visit to the school, he became painfully, painfully good. Not just doing his homework, but doing it conspicuously—coming and asking me for help every five minutes, and using some fake excuse to show me what he'd done, so I would realise how hard he was trying. Not only that, but doing all his chores like he loved them, going to bed without any fuss, getting up early in the morning, and being on time to the bus. I felt like gently pouring a cup of water over his head and saying, "Don't worry, just be yourself again, it's OK," but there were two reasons for me not to do that. One was I figured I might as well enjoy the peace while it lasted, and the other was my deep fear that maybe it wasn't OK.

Anyway, doing something reasonably normal seemed like a good idea. At first Gavin didn't want to go but he gradually changed his mind. We decided we'd make a picnic of it, and in the end we both got quite revved up by the whole thing. I'd made some relish the weekend before, using an old recipe of Mum's, with ginger plus the usual tomatoes and onions and vinegar. We had some cold roast lamb from Mrs Yannos, which she'd sent over on Thursday, so I made sandwiches out of that, with some lettuce from the supermarket. Sometimes I get sick of beef, but never lamb, and Gavin's totally carnivorous, so I knew we'd both be happy with that.

Climbing, climbing, climbing. There were a few steep bits that I really hated, but most of it was good, even when it was hard work. I stopped once to let Gavin catch up, but

I think he saw that as an insult, because he went on past me without a word, and from then on continued to lead.

Everything felt so familiar. The gum trees, the spur, the sky, and Gavin's stocky little body, head down, relentlessly ploughing forwards. I often felt grateful that we could walk through the bush in broad daylight again, and almost as often I wondered how we could have been so mobile at night. Of course, when the moon is good, you can go just about anywhere, but on those dark nights you can hold your own hand up in front of your face and say, "How many fingers?" and you don't have a clue.

As we got closer to the spot where I'd packed it in last time I wondered if Gavin would react. It must have held the same memories for him as it did for me. I fixed my gaze more and more steadily on the back of his neck, trying to concentrate on it. Not for the first time I appreciated the strength in him. I knew I was sweating more than the sun and the physical effort of climbing could explain. I just kept shoving one foot in front of the other. My heart was fluttering in my chest like the beating wings of a little bird that you find on the ground after a storm and hold in your cupped fist. Gavin didn't look left or right. I felt like he was towing me through the danger zone.

And suddenly, much faster than I would have expected, we were at the top. I broke into a huge smile and bopped him on the head. I felt like the mountains were mine again. I forgot about mangled cats and farm mortgages and war and put my head up and threw back my arms and drank in the sky instead. I ran in zigzags among the rocks and moss and tufty grass, then ran straight until I had almost lost sight of Gavin. Perhaps if Gavin had not been there I would never have come back. The sight of his sad little figure, watching me from the top of the track, didn't change my mood completely but it reminded me that I was still connected to the world. I couldn't fly. My wings were working well again but the anchors were holding fast.

I ran back and tackled him and we rolled down the hill a few metres, wrestling and laughing. I really had to fight to get the better of him these days. Just when I thought I'd pinned him he wriggled out and somehow got on top of me and sat on my head. I scrabbled my legs up under me and used my neck muscles to throw him off, then went after him again. I was on my hands and knees. He jumped up and ran straight backwards, with his arms out, like he was fending me off, still laughing, and he went straight over the edge like that, still laughing, still with his arms towards me.

Sickness ran through me. Every spot on my skin prickled, every hair on my head and neck and arms stood, and all the saliva in my mouth and throat dried. I tried to call as I ran forwards, and couldn't, then realised it was a waste of time anyway with Gavin being deaf. I saw the crumble of fresh dirt, the smear of it, where his shoes had scraped the edge, and only just stopped myself from following him over.

Instead I got down on my stomach and slid forwards and looked down. Jesus! What a place to pick. There weren't many sheer cliffs along here but this was as sheer as they got. I saw him straight away. He'd fallen, I don't know, twelve or fifteen metres. Somehow he'd been caught on a bump of earth and somehow he'd stuck there;

somehow it had held. I didn't know what damage he'd done himself but he was still alive. He was lying face down over this bump sticking out from the face of the cliff but it wasn't big enough to reach even halfway under his body, so he was tipping over it quite a bit. Like someone not lying properly on a sofa and about to roll onto the floor.

In Gavin's case the floor was a long way below. I don't know how far, whether it was sixty metres or eighty or a hundred. It didn't matter. It was enough.

His arms were moving as he tried to find some way to hang on to this bump of earth without disturbing it. Little showers of soil were falling from it, so it wasn't handling the weight very well. He had a bit of a grip with one hand on a root or something that was growing out on his left, but the other hand wasn't having much luck.

I stared down at him. I know my eyes must have been the size of DVDs. I could feel how big they were. He looked up at me suddenly. He stopped groping with his hand and gazed into my face. I saw the same determination he had always shown. He always wore it so proudly. Now I saw also his utter terror, the expression of someone who is about to die and knows it. I had one of those little insights you get sometimes, when you look at your friends and for a moment see them age fifty years. I saw Gavin age fifty years, then a hundred.

I tried to make my face mirror only the proud determination in his. My panic would do him no good. I tried to make my mind work. We had no rope, no mobile phone, no walkie-talkie, no helicopter. He was about to die and I would try to reach him and I would probably die in doing so. But at such a moment you have no doubt and almost no fear. Everything becomes completely and utterly focused on the moment. The weather, the view, the picnic, and beyond that, the farm, your friends, your school, your life, none of those have any priority any more. They have no existence.

I slid back a little, trying to think of tools, props, miracles. Nothing, nothing. My eye contact with Gavin, that extraordinary moment of contact and clarity, was over and my mind was starting to race again. I knew I had to start down that cliff in a millisecond and I wanted to do something before I went that would give me, us, some little chance, some tiny hope. I looked at our pack. Roast lamb sandwiches? Not much there. I had to be better prepared next time, except there wasn't going to be a next time. There weren't going to be any next times.

I looked around. Already I was backing towards the cliff, thinking I had to get going, I couldn't leave it any longer. Nothing but roast lamb sandwiches and a bit of salad in the packs, nothing but trees and rocks along Tailor's Stitch. We had brought nothing with us that I could use and the bush offered nothing either. That's the way of the bush.

I was at the edge of the cliff, not far from where Gavin had gone over. In a state of complete terror I eased myself over too. What did I know about rock climbing? I knew one thing about this climb. I had no real thought of saving him, of either of us coming out alive. I had some vague half formed idea that I would try to get to him to comfort him, to be with him, and that would be the end of the story. I glanced down. He was still there, thank God. Now he was starting to show his terror. He gazed at me. He'd realised, I think, that he couldn't move, couldn't cry out, couldn't beg, because it would take only a slight movement to collapse the clump of dirt that was holding him. In fact, as he stared at me he did shift a little, and I gasped as a cascade of dirt showered down from his feet. Soon the whole thing would give way. Even so he shifted again. I wondered if he was starting to cramp up.

I did know one thing about rock climbing, and one thing only. I couldn't remember who'd told me. A teacher at school, I thought. "Use the toes and fingertips." That was the whole thing. My entire knowledge summed up in five words. Oh yeah, and face into the cliff. More knowledge, more memory was coming back. Something about, "No matter what your instincts tell you, you've got to face into the cliff."

My instincts were telling me not to face into the cliff. They were telling me to go down with my back to it. My brain battled with my instincts. My brain said, "Someone somewhere has given you good advice. You must follow it." My instincts said, "You need to see where you are going. If you face out you'll be in charge of the situation. You'll control what happens. That's what you want, isn't it?"

It's all about control. It's always about control.

It took a lot of courage to turn my back on the world so I was facing into the rock. I don't think of myself as brave very often, but I suppose when you force your instincts to obey your brain it takes something, and you might as well call that courage.

I started down. One part of me was already out of control and that was my breathing. I hadn't noticed it but

175

suddenly I heard myself, heard frantic squeaking gasps. I tried to stop them. Breathe in, breathe out. I did that three times then forgot about it. There was too much else going on.

I found to my surprise that the toes and fingertips thing worked better than I'd expected. I pressed into the face of the rock with all the force I could, then decided I was overdoing it and eased off. The first part wasn't too bad, as it was still sloping, but I soon realised to my horror that it was getting sheer. I glanced across at Gavin again. He was watching every move I made. He never made a sound. They used to call deaf people deaf and dumb. I don't know about other deaf people but Gavin was as noisy as a lost cockatoo. He chattered away all day to himself, and when he was with me and people he trusted he tried really hard to talk properly. The only time he was quiet was when he was with strangers, and then he'd try to let me know with subtle gestures what he wanted.

He was quiet now. There was something odd about his sudden stillness. The rabbit in the spotlight thing maybe. For his sake I tried to concentrate on the climb. I had no hope for myself and perhaps I would have thrown my life away if it had been just me alone, having to climb down the cliff for some other reason. But I didn't want to, couldn't, abandon Gavin, not after what we'd been through together, not after all the other times he'd been abandoned.

With each foot, each hand, I searched for a little hole, a crack, a mound. It's amazing how the tiniest cranny can support a human body. I got my left fingers into a dent in a rock, my right into a crack that was full of sand and gravel. My left foot was resting on a small stone and my right toes were sticking into a curve where some stone showed through.

Then the little stone under my left foot went, and both my hands suddenly came out. My stomach lurched. I felt the blood leave my face. I grabbed at the cliff, at the same time trying to see something that could hold me. It was weird, my mind was still working, even in the middle of my panic. While my hands grabbed wildly they were also trying to grab carefully. I had a sudden dizzying glimpse of the ground a million miles below. I don't think I actually saw it, just saw it in my mind. My fingers found something, nothing really, just tiny indentations that would hold me for a few seconds if I was lucky. I kicked around with my loose foot trying to find something better, but not able to kick very hard, because I'd dislodge myself with my own action. Action would bring reaction, just like they say in Science.

I grabbed the cliff, sobbing with terror. I knew I was on the verge of death. Not for the first time, but usually the threat was from enemy soldiers with guns. Now it was down to me and nature, me and gravity. I tried to think of something, some thought to die with, something that would be worthy of death. I didn't want to die with my mind full of nothing, because that's what panic is, a whole lot of nothing going around and around at a very fast speed.

All the time while this was going on, another part of my mind, a reflex part I guess, kept making one hand grope for a better spot. Not with any hope, probably the same way a fox with a bullet through its chest tries to drag itself into the bushes, like you're suddenly going to lose interest and walk away and then it'll get better.

I found something that felt more secure, glanced at it, and thought it looked like nothing, just a slight swelling of the rock, but I trusted my fingers more than my eyes and dug my fingers into it and took a little pressure off my other hand. With the last shreds of my self-control I tried to make my body stop its trembling. I looked down quickly, not at the ground but searching for another hold. I thought if I could get myself moving maybe that would help me get calmer. It was that getting-back-on-the-horse-after-you-fall thing again.

Funny, I never thought for a moment of going back up. Instead I shifted down to another stone, still slow to learn that these soft little protruding stones were death traps. At least it fell immediately, doing me a favour, because I hadn't yet put any real weight on it. I hastily pulled my leg back up and tried to get it back to its previous position, but it was too late. I'd already lowered my centre of gravity too far. I had to find another foothold, and fast. I saw a button of rock away to the right and stretched across to it.

At some point I realised what was happening. All those stories on the news about drownings . . . so often it seemed like one person would get in trouble, be carried out to sea by the rip, and one or two or even three others would jump in to save him, men usually: father and uncles and brothers, who could not swim and knew that they could not swim, but in their hearts was another knowledge, that they could not stand and watch, they had to be with the person in the water and share whatever was coming to them.

I had to be with Gavin, or as close as I could get. I decided I could not take so long to move down towards him. If I did I would lose too much strength and energy and by the time I reached him I would have nothing left to offer. Already my arms and legs were vibrating with the nervous and physical energy I'd put out. I couldn't just go crazy and skedaddle across the cliff face. I'd fall to my death with the first false move. But I had to do better than this.

I tried so hard to get some control of my mind. I told myself that I had to become a skilled rock climber. I had to learn on the job. I tried to concentrate on technique. I had a vague memory of a moment with Jeremy, when he'd been talking about rugby and how he'd won some best-and-fairest awards, or man-of-the-match awards, whatever, and I asked him how, when he'd already told me that his main job was to pass the ball to other players, to be a link, and he said it was because of his tackling. This was an unusual conversation with Jeremy by the way, because if there's one thing he is, it's modest, but anyway, he managed to get across the idea that he was a pretty good tackler. And he said something about how he had been too scared to tackle properly when he first played rugby, so I asked him, "How did you get over that? How did you make yourself not scared?" And he said he would look at the player and think about how he was going to tackle him, what would be the best way to go about it, and somehow while he was doing that he didn't get frightened.

I said to him, "So you concentrate on technique?" and he said, "Yeah, I guess."

It was the struggle between the mind and the instincts again.

I didn't hang on the cliff for half an hour having a good think about that conversation with Jeremy. I thought about it for as much time as it took to write two words of it. But the little flicker of memory helped.

I got grim. I used my eyes with more concentration, more focus. I fixed on a crevice, a crack, about four metres to my right. If I could get there I could just about get to Gavin. What happened after that didn't bear thinking about so I didn't think about it. I knew now about the soft stones so I avoided those. I concentrated on technique, getting fingers and toes to grip little indentations and bumps. Funny how these tiny freckles, invisible normally, of no interest or importance to any human in the history of this mountain, were now major features for me. As big and important as mountains themselves.

My hands were getting tired and my fingers were forcing themselves into a more open position. Spreading, like I couldn't control them. Cramping, kind of. I had to keep moving. Halfway to the crevice I got in such a good position that for a moment I could give my left hand time off; my right hand and both my feet were secure, so I stretched my fingers and shook them, trying to make them work better. Even my mind took a few seconds off.

During the war there had been a time when I turned from Ellie into someone or something else. I guess the long and the short of it is that I became a soldier. At first I'd done a lot of blundering around, all the time in danger of being caught or killed or both. I'd thought I was being very professional and clever, but later, when I looked back on those months, I couldn't believe how we survived. Then one day I changed. I no longer had to think so much about what to do and how to do it. I became part of the environment, as much as a fox or a brown snake or a tawny frogmouth. But I was different to them. I became part of the environment of a war. After that I always moved quickly and quietly. From then on I was always aware— deeply aware—of every sound and smell and tiny movement. I didn't disturb anything, because I didn't want to leave any trace of where I'd been. I was cunning and scared and angry and determined and awake. It became second nature.

Sometimes younger kids say they wish they could have done what we did during the war, but with most of them I think, "You don't notice enough, you're so superaware of yourself you wouldn't notice a dozen blokes with rifles coming at you from fifty metres away, let alone a freshly disturbed bit of rotting wood on a track, or a cry of alarm from a magpie who's been distracted."

For me, the change happened quite suddenly, I think when we were escaping at maximum speed from the airport we'd trashed, somewhere just after that, when we abandoned the truck and took to the river.

On the cliff face I tried to get back into that way of being. I realised that it was the same as concentrating on technique in this way at least: you are no longer absorbed in yourself. You become part of a greater environment than your own mind and body. As well as thinking about each move and each step and working out how best to place each finger and toe and the whole of my body, I had to earn my right to be on this cliff by melting into it so that no-one would notice that I didn't belong. If someone was watching us through binoculars they'd be able to say to themselves, "There's a rock and there's a lizard and there's a tuft of grass and there's an ellie and there's another rock and there's a little blue wildflower . . ."

Still lodged into the crack, I considered the possibilities. I have to say there weren't many. I was so close to Gavin that if I stretched out my arm and he stretched out his I reckon there wouldn't have been a metre between us. But so what? The little mound he was caught on looked about half the size it had been when I started. Maybe that was the erosion caused by his weight, or maybe I'd had a false impression of it from the top, but I knew one thing—it couldn't support both of us. It wasn't going to support him much longer. The thin shower of soil continued steadily, sometimes just a few sandy particles, sometimes a serious trickle. It was like putting a plastic liner in a new dam and having a kangaroo puncture it with its feet when it wandered in for a drink. Only a few little holes, but that was a dam which would never hold water. Drip drip drip.

Gavin continued to be . . . to be what? I didn't know. In shock? Waiting bravely and calmly? Had he broken his back and was lying there wondering about the best model wheelchair for kids living on farms? Probably not. He was conscious and he seemed to see me, but as far as I could tell, he was making no movement. That was good, as long as he wasn't completely paralysed by his fear. His eyes were still fixed on me, though, and still following me, and I had the feeling that he hadn't taken them off me the whole time I'd been inching towards him.

I was fairly certain that if I got close enough it'd be just like those stories about people drowning. He'd reach out and grab me and not let go and like the mad drowning people who pull their rescuers under he'd pull me off the cliff and we'd fall together, fall forever, and hit the rocks below still locked onto each other.

Without any plan or a sane idea of what to do I spied out a route along the face that would take me below him. I didn't want to come in above him because if I fell I'd take him too and in the last few seconds of my life I didn't want that on my conscience. And I didn't want to come in beside him, for the reason I just said.

I did talk to him, meaningless babble like the songs you sing when you're guarding a mob of cattle at night, and of course he didn't hear any of it. But I thought it might calm him a little when he realised I was chatting away like I was on the school bus and sitting next to Homer and in a good mood. "Nice day for it . . . if by some miracle we survive this let's not do it again, OK . . . just stay right there my little thrill-seeking friend, don't be going anywhere now . . ."

My brief rest was over. I had a bit of strength back in my arms and legs, which had been the general idea of clinging there for those few moments, but my overall condition was weakening. In other words I was getting too tired. So I did a bit of manoeuvring and, with shaking legs, started going straight down the crack. It struck me suddenly that if and when we fell we would drop into Hell, the northern end of it where I'd never been, and how strange was that, to die in the place called Hell that had saved us so many times, that had been our refuge, but now in a final good joke was turning on us to claim the doomed souls that had never understood it properly. Clever Hell, such a smart trick to give comfort and help and then betray us. Much better than just killing us in the first place. How boring for the king of hell would that have been?

Trying to make like a spider, I inched across. I came in under Gavin like I'd wanted. That was good I suppose, except that it meant I'd committed myself to a plan that I really did have in my brain, in my subconscious anyway, but which seemed so stupid and impossible that I couldn't take it out and look at it, not even for a moment. But there was nothing else to do. Gavin shifted his head slightly and looked down at me. It was the first real movement I'd seen him make since I started. I was pretty sure that his stillness was more than caution: he was frozen by the knowledge that soon he would drop to an awful death.

I braced myself. I had a toe that felt fairly secure, on the bottom curve of a biggish boulder. Nothing else felt secure. My other toe was trying to worm into hardpacked dirt and my fingers were basically on sheer rock. But I would need those anyway, need my arms, so it didn't matter much. I spoke to Gavin calmly, knowing again that he couldn't hear but knowing there was a good chance that he would lip-read me.

"OK, Gav, just wriggle down here to me. I want you on my back."

CHAPTER 16

THERE, I'D SAID IT. SAID THE MAD THING. EVEN THE words brought me out in a sweat from every microscopic pore in my skin. You know how you squeeze a sponge and a drop of water appears at every point? Simultaneously? That's what happened to my body. It didn't worry me except that I knew my hands were suddenly slippery again, which wasn't good.

Technique. Concentrate on technique. Your balance, your angle to the cliff, the left toe that's trying to make a hole for itself. Try not to think about Gavin who actually twitched like he understood. At least half of you devoutly hopes he didn't understand. That way you could get out of this crazy offer.

He still hadn't moved but there was a different tension in him now. I kept drilling that left toe in. Then I looked up at Gavin again. I stared at him so hard I'm surprised I didn't bore holes in his face. But I had to know if he understood. And I thought he did. I said to him again, a little impatiently, "Come on, get on my shoulders."

I was scared that he would be too paralysed to do anything. If anything, it was the opposite. He made a sudden movement, as though he thought that all his problems were solved and all he had to do was step down to where I was and do the piggyback thing.

Immediately half the mound of dirt that supported him fell apart and soil showered over me. A bit got in my throat but I tried not to cough. A cough, a spasm, a hiccup, or worst of all a sneeze, any of those would be enough. Action and reaction.

With the mini-avalanche Gavin suddenly had no choice about whether to join me. He was about to fall. The big danger was that he would be so unable to move that he would leave everything to gravity. If he did, then we were both gone. He would knock me from my precarious spot and we would fall to the rocks. I felt my eyes dragging downwards, to look at those rocks, and it took all the strength I had to force them in the opposite direction. I wanted to see death but I mustn't let myself.

Gavin hovered over me but at the last moment some kind of desperate instinct cut in, and he did move voluntarily, well, a little bit at least. He swung a leg down to near my head, and then, as he started to slip, tried to get some control over the rest of his body. He scrabbled for handholds and footholds, with no real success, but the scrabbling for them meant that he stuck to the face of the cliff for a few seconds, instead of plummeting like a rock.

Those few seconds were just enough for him to reach me. I braced as I felt his swinging left foot touch my hair, then kick the side of my head on the way back.

A terrible silent wrestle followed. He continued to slide down, but now he used my body for his handholds and footholds. Although this was what I wanted, the struggle and the strain and the tension were almost impossible. I had known that he would wreck my balance, changing my centre of gravity, but I hadn't realised how severe it would be. He was so heavy! And he did cling to me like a drown-ing person.

For half a minute I fought with him, with the cliff, with death itself. But the main fight was with me, to find new strength, deeper strength, the physical strength to stay upright and to fuse my fingers and toes with the dirt and rock, and the mental strength to keep energy flowing to my body.

Within a second or two I realised that I couldn't fight Gavin, but that I couldn't help him either. I had to think of myself as made of wood or stone, a tree or old rock. I had to leave it to him to scramble all over me, dig into me, hang on to me. If he couldn't, that was his concern. If he failed, he fell. There was nothing I could do about that. I just had to concentrate on being solid, being strong.

We teetered outwards. There was a dreadful second when I lost three of my four points of contact with the cliff and we were about to drop. It was no use shouting at Gavin, but I shouted at him anyway, and I think he actu-ally felt the vibration of air around him, because he did calm down a little and get a better grip on me. He was still half strangling me, but as I recovered my balance, all I could do was wait and hope that he would work out how impossible the position was.

More seconds passed before he began to slowly, agonis-ingly, adjust himself. He needed to get a move on, because I couldn't hang on much longer. I simply didn't have the strength to stay there forever. No-one would. But he got his right arm from across my throat, which gave me a bodyful of fresh pure air again, and he got both legs around me, so that he was in a reasonable piggyback position, except for his left arm, which was around my stomach, and which meant that I was slewed to one side all the time.

But I knew I couldn't hope for anything better. And I sure as hell knew that I had to start going down, because I couldn't hang on any longer.

The first movement was painful in one way, because I was still shocked at the weight of him, and how much strength I needed. But it was good in another way, because I think both of us were relieved to be moving at all. That little sideways shuffle, where I managed to get both my hands and both my feet to a new position, thirty centimetres to my left, was like an action that ended a paralysis. I felt that he was slightly calmer, although his grip was still so intense that if we fell we would fall locked together and hit the ground like that. Well, we were pretty locked together in our lives now, and it seemed we would go into the next world the same way.

We began the grimmest journey of our lives. We'd been on some pretty grim ones, but this was the worst. Inch by inch, crevice by hole by tiny indentation, lump of rock by pimple of dirt by protruding root. Down a few inches at this point, but sideways for the next three moves. At one time I had to go back up about a metre, to get out of a dead end route, and I think those were the worst few minutes of all. I could almost feet Gavin's groan of disappointment and fear when I started climbing again.

He didn't actually make a sound during the whole time, but his grip never slackened. If anything it got tighter, although I wouldn't have thought that were possible. I began to wonder if, assuming we got to the ground, I'd ever be able to get him off me.

New muscles started to hurt. The backs of the knees, the arches of my feet, the joints of my shoulders. Sweat streaming down my face made my hair wet and dank. I couldn't see any more for the sweat that blotted my vision and stung my eyes. I refused to think of this ever ending because I was scared the knowledge would weaken me.

My left foot landed on something unexpected. I bounced my leg a little and realised it was wood; a branch or a root. It felt soft but I needed its help so much that I relaxed onto it. For a wonderful moment it took my weight. Then it broke.

We started sliding. Dust rose around me. Little landslides of gravel came with us. I grabbed madly with open palms and with fingertips. We passed the broken stick and I saw that it was an old root, quite rotten. Grab, grab, grab, there had to be something. My hands must be getting mangled but I didn't feel anything and didn't care. Grabbed at a protruding rock, caught onto it for a moment but couldn't hold it. At least it slowed me down. And a moment later I got my fingers into a split and held on.

I felt like an old snail. Do snails have a three-second memory? I had to forget the terror of the slide and just resume my journey. With the weight on my back. On and on, sobbing now, muscles locking up, slower and slower, can't go on, can't do it, it's too hard, just give up, fall away into freedom.

And then we were there. Even though I had longed for the moment when we would be three or four metres from the bottom and could separate and jump, it didn't work out that way. Gavin was still clinging so tightly that I couldn't risk jumping with him wrapped around me, so I had to grit my teeth and force my screaming muscles to move again. Until we were not much more than a metre from something that looked more like dirt than rock. And then I let go and dropped.

We hit the ground fairly hard and rolled a couple of times. There was quite a slope, and it wasn't until we were rolling that he started to release me. I shook him off and crawled away, then collapsed. I had no thoughts of triumph or success, no thoughts of anything really, only a complete and utter exhaustion, as though I could never move, never do anything again. Gavin crawled over to me and kind of slopped on top of me, and at some stage we both went to sleep, because when I woke up, the shadows had already reached us and it was getting cold.

My body ached like I'd been pounded with baseball bats by a gang of sumo wrestlers, but I knew no helicopter was going to pluck us out of there. If they hadn't come while we were on the cliff they weren't going to come now. I woke Gavin and we plodded our weary way back to the top, finding a kangaroo track that must have led to the creek we'd drunk from so often.

The day had started in one direction but gone in another and ended in a place we hadn't known about. So sore that I could barely put one foot in front of the other, I struggled home, wondering why (since the end of the war) the mountains seemed to be betraying me.

CHAPTER 17

TWO WEEKS LATER WE WERE IN THE CITY. IT'S ONE OF life's miracles . . . well actually, there are two miracles and they're closely connected. One is that you can move so quickly from environment to environment. One minute you're in the Sahara Desert; twelve hours later, with the help of a few helicopters or planes or something, you can be waist deep in snow in Alaska or strolling down the streets of Paris. Well, I think that's how it works anyway. Not having travelled further than New Zealand in my young life, I wouldn't know.

The second miracle is that you can adjust to it, cope with it. You'd think that the shock of the upheaval would be so overwhelming that you'd need to be put in bubble wrap for six months and fed through a tube. But no, the good old human organism is so resilient that it can bounce around from place to place with only a thirty-second adjustment. Most of the time anyway.

Actually, when I think some more about it, as I have done for about three hours since writing the last bit, I realise it's not that simple. You make the immediate practical adjustment, you don't wither up and die, you get on with it, but there are slow, long-term shifts needed, adjustments that happen at a much deeper level, and which maybe sometimes never happen. I guess this would be very unhealthy for the average human organism.

Anyway, how we got to the city is that after the dreadful, terrible time on the cliff, after we dragged ourselves home, after we drank a lot of hot sweet tea, after we huddled under a doona watching mindless television, after all that, at about nine o'clock, Gavin started to talk.

And oh boy, once he started, he wouldn't shut up.

I've always liked Gavin's voice. It's low and husky, and he pronounces some words, most words, slightly differently. Often he seems to clip off the ends or twist them slightly, which makes them kind of exotic. He talks quite a lot to me, although it took a long long time before we got to that kind of relationship. Like I said before, he only talks to people he trusts, which is probably quite sensible. So people who meet him for the first time, or who don't know him very well, assume he's the strong silent type. Strong, yes; silent, depends who he's with.

For the first time he told me his own stories. I remember writing quite recently about how stories give you an identity. In some ways they give you your life. You think you're a big lump of skin and bones and blood and organs and cells, and of course you are, but you're also a big lump of stories. You know those pictures they have in butchers' shops showing how sheep and cattle are divided into rump and blade and so on? They should have another one, in bedrooms maybe, showing humans divided into the stories of their early childhood, the stories of their primary school days, the stories of their birthdays and Christmases, the stories of their friendships, and so on.

If you know someone's stories, you know them. If you don't know their stories, you don't know them.

I hadn't really known any of Gavin's stories. In the early

days he'd told us how he'd lived with his mum and his little sister, and that his dad had been killed in an explosion at a factory. I think Gavin was only about three at the time. I always figured that this was why he attached himself so strongly to Homer and Lee, because they were like fathers to him. Bit young for it, but still.

Now he told me story after story, filling out the details of his life, so that I started to know him in a new way. I want to write it down, because like I said at the very beginning of this whole thing, when I sat by the creek in Hell with a pen and a bit of paper, writing stuff down is a way of recording it, but more importantly, making it important, giving it meaning, except most of the time I don't know what the meaning is. I just know that putting stuff on paper makes it solid somehow.

Gavin talked randomly and he told his stories in no particular order, but I think the general outline goes something like this: his dad was a boilermaker. I had to get him to write that down before I could work out what the word was, and as both of us were stiff and sore and tired and a bit dead mentally and physically it was quite a pain to have to go get pencil and paper, and then another pain to go get the dictionary. The dictionary said a boilermaker was someone who makes boilers. I don't know how many boilers the world needs, but probably quite a lot.

He worked either for the Army, or in a factory that supplied the Army. Gavin wanted to think that he was in the Army, but Gavin was Army mad, so he was a bit biased. I just couldn't imagine that the Army would have its own boilermakers, but maybe they do.

Anyway, the explosion killed four people. When Gavin tells a story he doesn't just tell it, he acts it. Even though he was so wrecked, he couldn't help himself. I wasn't very comfortable under the doona with his arms and legs flying in different directions though, so I cut the description a bit short.

He seemed amazed that I hadn't heard of the accident, but I couldn't remember anything. It was years ago, it was hundreds of k's from Wirrawee, and since then we'd had a full-scale war. Of course to Gavin it was the most important event of his life, but I would have been a little kid myself, with no interest in newspaper headlines or the evening news.

I couldn't quite figure out what sort of work his mum had done. He said she was an entertainer. At first I thought he was saying trainer but when I figured entertainer I immediately thought she might be a singer with five platinum records. But when I asked him what kind of entertaining he changed and said she wasn't an entertainer, just someone who looked after customers for a business in Marlon. Marlon's a pretty grotty area if you ask me, but Gavin's family lived in Mount Savage, which isn't any better . . . it matches its name.

After his dad died there was one of those epidemics of death that seem to happen to some people, including me, except that I'm talking about non-war staff, where a whole string of people die in quick succession. For Gavin it was two grandparents and his aunt and his rabbit. He didn't know what his grandparents died of: "They were sick," he said and shrugged. But his aunt committed suicide. He was more interested in talking about his rabbit. "Did he commit suicide too?" I asked, which was totally tasteless and unfunny except that he didn't notice me say it. I rather liked the idea of a rabbit locking itself in the bathroom and taking an overdose. He said he was really upset about his rabbit, and I believe it, but it made me wonder some more about the cat he had massacred. We still hadn't talked about the cat. It was too big a topic.

The rabbit's name was Rick. Rick the rabbit. My first reaction to any rabbit is to shoot it, so I'm not into giving them names. If we started giving names to our rabbits we'd have to employ someone to do it. Rick didn't seem much of a name to me but again Gavin didn't know how he got it. "My sister called it that," he said.

Gavin acted out the death of Rick, again with more energy than I could muster. I got the impression that Rick had eaten something wrong and died of stomach problems. It did occur to me, watching Gavin and listening to his stories, that there were gaps in him, and they were the gaps in his family . . . I don't know what the word is, mythology maybe? Just as each person is a big pile of accumulated stories, each family, and for that matter I suppose each culture, is the same. Maybe that's one of the problems for Aboriginal people, maybe so many of them were murdered that a lot of stories were lost and now there are too many gaps. Gavin seemed like he didn't have enough stories. I don't know how many stories each person should have but if you don't have enough, if you have blank spots instead of stories for part of your life, then that would be a pretty serious thing I think.

Gavin didn't know how his grandparents had died, didn't know what kind of work his mother did, didn't know how

Rick got his name, didn't know why his aunt committed suicide . . . I asked him how his parents met and he didn't know that either.

It soon became obvious that another bloke had moved in about a year before the war. His name was Ken. I'd never heard about this guy before. Gavin mentioned him once, accidentally, then again a few moments later, and looked mad at himself each time. Ken had done up a bike for Gavin and Ken had taken them to the beach for a weekend. Who was Ken?

"Just a man who lived with us."

"Where was he from?"

"I don't know."

"Were he and your mum like, thinking of getting married?"

"I don't know. He was stupid."

"You didn't like him?"

"No."

Gavin was starting to clam up. I didn't want that so I got off the subject of Ken. But it seemed like I was too late. Gavin had again turned into the stubborn self-contained little ball of silent grimness that I knew so well. After about ten minutes of saying nothing he got up and padded off down the hall towards his bedroom. I assumed that was it for the evening and he had shut down. Gavin has left the building. But to my surprise he came back a few minutes later, carrying something.

It was quite dark by then. I turned a light on, so he could see my mouth.

I recognised the envelope when I saw it. My mum wrote to the Red Cross after the war when we had been trying to find Gavin's mum and little sister. She wrote in Gavin's name, seeing it was his family. The answer, when it came, was pretty blunt. A couple of sentences describing what the Red Cross had been doing and where they'd gone for information, and then came the punchline. It was like a punch all right.

We're extremely sorry to tell you that our enquiries suggest that your mother, Mrs Fisher, was murdered in the first few hours of the war and no trace has been found of your sister, Rosie. Given the child's age and the chaotic and extremely dangerous situation at the time we are not optimistic about finding her . . .

Now Gavin seemed to think it was very important that I read the letter again. I couldn't work out why but I got it out of the envelope and opened it. And realised almost straight away that it was a different letter. I glanced at the date. This one had come quite recently, about a month ago. Funny, Gavin had never mentioned it to me.

I read it and my skin got that crawling prickling feeling I've had only a few times, for example when I'm looking at a large black automatic weapon that's pointing straight at me or staring down a cliff and seeing Gavin about to fall to his death. God, what was it about Gavin? Would I ever understand him? Did he have serious mental problems?

We are delighted to inform you that despite our fears for the safety of your sister and our doubts about finding her, we have been successful in locating her.

As you know, we rely upon people registering found children with us, but for various reasons many people do not do this. However, a letter received in this office recently started us on a new search for Rosie, and enquiries have established that she appears to be living at 87 Green Street, Marlon, with a family named Russell.

It appears that Rosie knew this family before the war, and they have been caring for her since they found her in a prison camp in the first few days of the war.

You would probably be aware that many unofficial living situations have developed as a result of the war, and many of these are not yet sanctioned or even recorded. We have referred Rosie's case to the Department of Child Relocation, but they have a large workload, and it may be some time before they can address her situation.

In the meantime, it was our impression that Rosie was as happy as could be expected, and that the Russells are taking good care of her.

Rosie was delighted to learn that you had survived the war, and she is looking forward to a reunion with you. Privacy legislation prevents us giving your contact details to the Russells but they have consented to your being informed of their address and telephone number.

I knew that if I let my face show my feelings, I would sit there gazing at Gavin like he was an alien or something out of a freak show so I tried not to frighten him off, but instead to look as though it was the most normal thing in the world for you to be uninterested when your missing sister is found after a year or so. He was watching my face pretty carefully though, and I'm not sure whether he was fooled.

So I said to him, "Do you want to go see her?" When he hesitated I decided I needed to be more positive, and hopefully that might transmit a little energy to him, so I changed it to, "This is fantastic. Let's go see her this weekend."

Well, he didn't say no. That's about all you can say for him. And that's why we were in the city, staying at Lee's and set for a reunion that I figured probably wasn't going to be as emotional as the ones on TV or in magazines. I even thought of going to the place myself first, to suss out what was happening, to set it up, but then thought that would be too sneaky, and not fair on Gavin.

Life at Lee's was pretty chaotic. What am I talking about, pretty? It was chaotic, and it wasn't pretty. I don't know how he put up with it, considering how precise and controlled he is about everything. I mean, the guy's a piano player, not a guitarist. He'd rather do chemistry than drama, rather play chess than Bullshit or Spoons, rather swim laps than run around the edge of the pool chucking people in and doing bombs. And here he is living in the middle of *Lord of the Flies*.

He was embarrassed about it, and kept giving me guilty little looks, as if to say sorry, and a couple of times he did actually say, "Sorry about the mess," "Sorry about the noise," "Sorry about the way they're carrying on." But he didn't seem very good at looking after the kids. Besides Pang there was Phillip, who was nine, Paul, who was seven, and Intira, who was four. Between them they could put together quite a party. Lee's method was to ignore them, then suddenly chuck a tantrum and rant and rave at them and hand out rules and punishments, which shut them up for a short time before the whole thing started again. I could see that he was going crazy with the strain of it, and I didn't blame him.

They only had a tiny apartment, which was all he could afford, seeing how most of his money was coming from government allowances.

The little guys accepted Gavin really well, especially Intira, the four year old, who immediately adopted him. It was pretty funny watching the effect on Gavin. At first he was uncomfortable and off balance, but she quickly softened him up, and within an hour he was starting to enjoy it but at the same time trying to preserve his Mr Tough Guy exterior. So he'd be on the floor, with her climbing all over him and pulling his hair, and he'd roll her around and tickle her, and then glance at me to see if I thought this was uncool. I had to work hard to not look in his direction, in the hope that he'd relax and get an idea of life in a real family.

I wondered if he'd be the same with his own sister as he was with Intira. He could have been doing this with Rosie.

Pang and I got dinner; Lee seemed incredibly relieved and grateful to be let off for once, and I didn't blame him. I could see that none of this came easy for him, but I admired him for sticking to it. I just hoped it didn't drive him straight to the loony bin. They were nice kids, but they were going a little stir-crazy, in an apartment the size of a double garage and with Lee not being very good at laying down rules and regulations.

But during dinner Intira was poking Paul, Paul was flicking food onto Pang's plate, Pang was telling them both to shut up, Paul knocked his glass of milk over, Intira decided she wanted to sit next to Gavin, Paul squeezed up next to Gavin just to make Intira feel bad, Intira screamed at Lee when he told her she couldn't move, and then she threw a piece of bread at Pang because she laughed . . . It was pretty much like that all the time, and the worst thing was that it didn't seem out of the ordinary for any of them. I had trouble believing the way Lee bumbled around the edges, so unlike the decisive, strong, calm and collected Lee that I'd known for a long time, and whom I'd gotten to know so well during the war.

I didn't intervene much, as although I was seeing Lee in a new light, I was pretty sure that some things were still the same, and one of those things was that Lee wouldn't like being shown up, or given any hints that I thought he was making a mess of it.

When the kids were in bed though, which took an exhausting forty-five minutes—and that was without baths—we sat down and had coffees at the kitchen table. It was funny, there was no hint of sex or relationship stuff in the air. There wasn't a good atmosphere for that kind of conversation after the noise and conflict of the kids. I was more than happy to avoid it anyway, given that my thoughts were about Jeremy these days, although every time I looked at Lee I couldn't help thinking how attractive he was.

"It must be pretty tough living with them all the time," I said, hoping this wouldn't put him into defensive mode.

"Tell me about it," he grunted, with his nose buried in the coffee.

"How do you get any work done?"

"I don't. Well, a little bit, after they go to bed, but I don't have much energy after putting up with them all night."

"It seems kind of weird to see you in a car park fighting enemy soldiers one day and then the next day you're fighting with Phillip over who does the washing-up."

He looked up and grinned. I was relieved to see that he hadn't lost his sense of humour. "I'd rather be doing stuff with Liberation than trying to get them to shut up and stop fighting for five minutes."

"What's happening with Liberation? Are there any missions coming up? Has there been any more fallout over our last effort? Jeremy gave me a bit of an update the other day."

Woops, there it was, I'd said the magic word, after I'd tried so hard to avoid it. Two minutes into the conversation and already Jeremy was there. But Lee didn't seem to notice.

"You have no idea," he said.

"What's that supposed to mean?"

"No idea how nasty they were. What they were planning."

"So no-one's blaming us?"

"It did get a bit sensitive," he admitted. "There were some heavy vibes about shooting up so many people in a public place. Seems like they'd have been a lot happier if we'd done it in the bush with no witnesses."

"That's quite chilling. Makes us sound like serial killers."

"We've killed a lot of people between us, Ellie."

I scratched the coffee mug with my finger. "I can't think about it but sometimes I have to. I got so sick of the smell of blood. I still haven't gotten over that smell."

"Well, most of the people we killed were soldiers, if not all of them, but you know what puzzles me? When they say on the news that there's been a bomb blast or something, they say, 'Dozens of people were killed, including some innocent civilians.' Now what does that mean? That all soldiers are guilty, so it doesn't matter if you kill them? That all civilians are innocent? What, do they run a check on each person's life and then decide if he should have been allowed to live? How many of those innocent civilians were, like, drug dealers or rapists or people who don't look after their pets properly? I guess if you or I were killed in a random bomb blast at a bus stop they'd say we were innocent civilians, but I don't feel too innocent these days."

I loved and needed these conversations and Lee was very good at them, but I also needed some good advice. I'd told him on the phone why we were coming to the city, but I'd only given him an outline, so now I told him the full story, including the cat. All his tolerance and wisdom immediately deserted him.

"God, that little toad, that little toad sucker. What the hell is he playing at? Honestly, Ellie, that kid doesn't know when he's well off. Put him in a postbag and pack him off to . . . I don't know . . ."

"Paraguay? The Philippines? Is this tongue-twister time?"

"Yeah, any of those'll do nicely. Patagonia."

"Parramatta."

I soon realised what was happening. Lee was like the others, so caught up with his own troubles, looking after the kids and trying to study, that he didn't have time for my problems with Gavin. It was disappointing. I could see how fair that was, but sometimes fairness doesn't count when you want help from a friend. Although we kept talking about Gavin, it was one of those awful conversations where you suddenly realise you're sounding like your parents. "These little kids, they're so cheeky, they orta show more respect . . ."

Not that my parents ever talked like that, but my grandmother did, using slightly different words. She'd never have said "orta."

CHAPTER 18

I COULD HARDLY EAT BREAKFAST FOR THE NERVOUSNESS I felt about this reunion between Gavin and his sister. In a way it wasn't my business but of course it was too. Not long ago I'd told Gavin he was my brother, but I hadn't known then that I was about to join an extended family.

When I thought about it I realised that a lot of my nervousness was to do with wanting him to handle the situation the right way. It's hard to describe how this works but I knew I'd be upset if Gavin screwed up. I'd felt the same when I watched him at the school athletics: I didn't want him to come last because I figured he'd feel bad. When he was with other kids, if he did anything that was uncool that had them frowning and turning away, I wanted to run over and say to him, "No, not like that, that's not how you do it," and to say to the other kids, "Hey, he's OK, you just misunderstood, he is cool really, really he is."

I had the horrible feeling that he was going to say the wrong thing to his little sister, or the people who were looking after her, and that because of this he would miss out on a whole series of future possibilities.

If I was stressed, Gavin was a disaster zone. Not in a million years would he admit to being nervous but you didn't have to be a psychologist to figure it out. You don't have to be a weatherman to know which way the wind blows. Gavin wouldn't get dressed, said something evil to Intira that had her screaming and running to Lee, broke a cereal bowl and wouldn't eat breakfast anyway, then told me I was a stupid bitch when I did the "Enough already, quit it or I'll take you to the zoo and feed you to meerkats."

Rather than have one or both of us explode, I got him out of the apartment and told him we'd walk to Marlon. He didn't seem to mind that. We left so early that we could have walked backwards and still been on time, but at least he was not in a confined space. Even so, he didn't get any better. It was weird, I couldn't help feeling that there was something else going on, something more than his natural nerves at this big change in his life. I started trying to guess what it might be but my imagination couldn't grip onto much. I thought maybe he was worried I'd leave him there, that once he was with Rosie and the Russells I'd nick off to the nearest bus stop and go bush. I hoped he didn't have such a bad opinion of me, but he was an insecure kid. The thing was though, that even if he did think that, it still didn't explain the way he was carrying on. To be honest, it was like I didn't matter much to him that morning. His mind was on something else, something more than a reunion. I couldn't for the life of me imagine what it might be.

If I had known what it was I would have grabbed him then and there and run hard in the opposite direction.

Unfortunately I'd put the pressure on him to make this trip and he'd given in to the pressure. It would have been better if he'd resisted a bit more, even though I wouldn't have thanked him for it at the time.

It was easy enough to get to Marlon, you just follow Fiddleback Road. It goes forever. And Gavin was confident that once we got to Marlon he knew how to find Green Street. Besides, we could always ask. But navigation was never an issue. The first clue I got that we were getting close was the North Marlon Tyre Service, followed by Marlon North Dry Cleaning, North Marlon Pizza and North Marlon Car Wash. We still had nearly forty-five minutes to go, so that was fine.

As we got into Marlon proper, Gavin nudged me to cross the road, into a big park. He said it was a short cut, and I don't know, maybe he felt safer in a park. It was closer to the kind of environment he was used to now. But it didn't stop him looking around even more, getting jumpier, and infecting me with his nervousness.

If it hadn't been for that, I would have enjoyed the walk. Marlon didn't look nearly as bad as I remembered it, and the park was seriously nice. There was an old footy ground with a grandstand just like the one in Wirrawee, but not the kind of grandstand you see in the city any more. Then we went up a bank of fairly wet earth and down into a huge flat area where people were exercising their dogs. It was quite cool: the owners hung around in groups talking, or sat on the grass reading, or lay back and looked at the clouds while the dogs partied. There must have been twenty dogs, ranging from a thing the size of a Shetland pony to a couple of large rats. Beyond that were two footy ovals, both with kids getting ready for games, and a paved tennis court and an old toilet block. Beyond that was a bunch of trees and a fountain, and then came the suburb of Marlon.

As we passed one of the football teams I got the first real clue that we were back in Gavin's home territory. A boy who was chasing a loose ball grabbed it to his chest as it bounced, and at exactly the same moment saw Gavin. He looked astonished, then said, "Hey, Gavin," in a completely normal voice, which sounded very calm compared to the expression on his face.

"Hi Lucas," Gavin grunted, looking a bit embarrassed, then said to me, "That's Lucas Bright." I think the last name was Bright. Anyway, the kid said to Gavin, "I thought you were . . ." and then paused and switched to something safer. "I haven't seen you since the war."

"Nah," said Gavin, "I've been staying with her." He nodded at me.

"Cool," said Lucas Bright. "Well, I gotta get back . . ." He nodded at the team.

"No worries," I said, and off went Lucas.

It was always hard to tell Gavin's feelings, and although he looked a bit red faced after the unexpected meeting, he also seemed pleased. I was hoping it would calm him down a bit as we went on through the trees towards the next street.

The Russells were two and a half blocks away. Once we'd left the park we got into a part of Marlon that was more the way I remembered it. Lots of shabby old houses, built right to the street, and lots of shabby new ones that didn't look very well built at all. Half-a-dozen dumped cars, or if they weren't dumped, they should have been. A couple of derelict houses, graffiti that wasn't even funny, just off, a school surrounded by a wire fence so high that it was more like a prison camp. And in the middle of this was Green Street.

If I'd suspected Gavin was frightened before, then I was

sure of it now. He grabbed my hand. Gavin holding my hand in public was about as common as dogs dancing with bunny rabbits. And the way he hung on to me, I'd be lucky if I still had a hand by tomorrow morning. I don't think there could have been any more blood in it, the way he was squeezing it. And his hand felt so sweaty. When we turned left into Green Street he looked so awful that I stopped and said, "Are you sure you want to do this? We can go home and think about it some more."

He just grabbed my other hand and said, "No, we got to get it over and done with," and let go again.

I shrugged and we kept walking. Counting down the numbers. 177, 157, 137. I could estimate where 87 would be. There was a row of houses that had little front gardens, some of which were pretty and filled with flowers and stuff, and others which were filled with weeds. Number 87 had to be in the middle of that stretch.

There was no-one out in front, at least that's what I first thought. As we passed the place next door I could see that the Russells had a really nice garden, with some fuchsias and two miniature trees that looked like they might have apples or pears in summer, and a brick path leading from the front gate to the veranda. The house wasn't the greatest though. The window frames hadn't been painted for a long time and were getting a bit rotten, and it was a long time since the gutter on the roof had held any water. Maybe they didn't have much money.

The front gate was open, which I hoped was done deliberately, to invite Gavin in, but then my heart gave a great flip as I realised that the front door was open as well, and above it was a big sign on white paper, done in a child's clumsy printing, with lots of hearts and stars and smiley faces, and the words *Welcome Back Gavin*.

I felt my nerves fade and a glow spread from my body to my face. I know a huge smile was forming. I hurried forward, clutching Gavin, almost dragging him with me.

I was expecting to see a little girl pop out, followed by her foster parents I guess, so all my concentration was on the doorway. The dark movement from the front corner of the house took me by surprise. A thought started to form in my head, "Oh, they're coming around the side," but then I realised there was no access at the sides of the house, and that someone must have been standing there in the shadows. I glanced across and saw a man. Gavin had already seen him.

I can remember the next few seconds as though they took a minute and a half. As I noticed the man, Gavin's face was already turning towards me and his mouth opening. The man, who was a weaselly-looking guy wearing a tracksuit, probably thirty-five or so, said, "Hello Gavin." Gavin wouldn't have heard this, or rather seen it. I saw Gavin's mouth open, and it was weird, I almost read the word before my ears heard it. It was like my eyes sent the word to my brain before my ears did.

It figures. I guess the speed of light is faster than the speed of sound.

He said only one word. "Run."

He let go my hand and took off, back through the gate and turning right, down Green Street, the way we'd come. I took off after him, and the man took off after both of us.

I did half shut the gate as I went. I tried to shut it completely but it didn't catch, and bounced back, which, as I could see looking around, slowed the guy by a couple of seconds. Boy, did we need those couple of seconds. I didn't know if he had a weapon or not, but there had been something menacing about him even before Gavin spoke. Now his eyes were narrowed and he had a look of total determination. I didn't think he had Gavin's best interests at heart. I stopped looking at him and raced on, swinging right after Gavin, along the street we'd taken just a few minutes before.

As I ran, the question pounded in my head: "What the hell is happening?"

Gavin was ahead of me by thirty or forty metres. He was flying. All that pent-up emotion which had grown in him day by day, hour by hour, minute by minute, as I first pressed him to come to the city, and as we got closer and closer to Rosie, had now translated into energy. I was struggling, trying to get my second wind. I took a quick glance behind again and realised the guy was gaining. I didn't really need to look: the pounding of his footsteps could have told me that.

I wondered what would happen if and when he caught up with me. Would he overtake me and keep going after Gavin? It was like his life depended on catching Gavin. What if he was seriously out to hurt Gavin? Sure seemed that way. Maybe I was just a nuisance in the equation. On the other hand, if he was going to hurt Gavin, then what would he do about me?

There didn't seem to be witnesses to this so far. I hadn't seen anyone appear in the corridor of the house during the couple of seconds that we'd been inside their front garden. And the streets of Marlon were quiet.

I guess it was Gavin's recent lifestyle that convinced him to head for the bush. The only bush available of course was the park. If he'd thought about it, he would have been safest in a crowded place. A shopping centre would have been ideal. Or, if he was so determined to go to the park, a dive straight into the middle of a football match would have been just as good. But during the war Gavin had learnt to go for cover, to get away from people, to avoid trouble, to hide. And since the war he'd learnt to trust the outdoors, and he'd developed a confidence in himself when he was in the open. So he wasn't thinking shopping centres or football teams.

We sprinted two and a half blocks. That is a long long way. Crossing one street Gavin nearly got hit by a taxi. The guy swerved and hit the brakes, letting off enough smoke from the tyres to attract the CFA. At the next crossing I nearly belted straight into a woman on a bicycle. She had to swerve and brake pretty fast too. The way she abused me! I didn't even look around.

I did think though, as I raced on, that there was one positive about these near misses. At least there were now two witnesses to our mad sprint. I don't know if they saw the guy chasing us, but if we both got murdered, then the taxi driver and the cyclist could give evidence at the inquest. Maybe then they'd start checking to see why we were running.

It wasn't a very comforting thought. I decided I'd better concentrate on getting away from the weaselly guy.

Ahead of me, Gavin belted across the road next to the park. He was still running strongly, driven by demons that

I didn't know about. But he was pretty fit. This road was wide and looked like it would normally be very busy, but there wasn't a car to be seen. I didn't dare look around again, but I knew the guy was even closer to me, probably within ten metres. Gavin was no more than twenty-five metres ahead, so we had gained on him, probably because we were both bigger and stronger and took longer strides. But the way the guy was panting, I'd say he was feeling the strain, and the way my chest and legs felt, I was definitely feeling the strain, and I thought Gavin would be reaching his limit too.

I was praying for him to head left, towards the football games, but he headed right, into the trees.

Of course it was nothing like the bush. These were nice old trees, elms and oaks and things like that, not a lot of leaves on them at this time of the year, but big thick trunks. Gavin ran straight down a paved path, then veered off across the lawn. He was heading for the thickest clump of trees, but I couldn't see how this was a good plan. Wherever he hid, the guy only had to look behind a maximum of a dozen trees to find him. It was a pretty short-sighted strategy.

I glanced back again at the man. He still had that look of absolute determination, his face focused on one thing only. And he must have been fitter than I thought, fitter than his panting had suggested. He looked full of running. Ahead, Gavin had disappeared. He'd chosen one of those trees and was behind it right now.

I swerved left, ducked behind a tree, then used it as cover to get behind the next one. This was like a childhood game of hide'n'seek, except it was no game. I'd seen expressions like this guy's before. To me it meant only one thing. He wanted to do grievous bodily harm.

He came after me. He skidded around the tree I'd just left, and when he saw I wasn't there came straight for the tree I'd chosen. Watching with the corner of my eye, I saw that one thing had changed. He was now carrying a knife. The blade must have been twenty centimetres long, if not thirty. That is a knife.

I broke cover and bolted across another path, swerved behind a gum tree, and zigzagged around a couple more trees, getting a glimpse of him at one stage. But he didn't see me. I was now behind one of the English trees, a thin young one. I took the risk of going back across the path again, hoping to find Gavin. Now the man saw me. So much for all that zigzagging. I'd wasted my advantage. I headed back towards the first couple of trees, but as I did I saw Gavin. The man must have flushed him out because Gavin was now running like crazy down the second path.

The man was following Gavin. I set out on a different route, to meet Gavin at the fountain. I don't think the guy saw me at any stage. He'd somehow hidden the knife again. I don't know how he did that, unless it was one of those trick knives that retract into the shaft. I guess he could have shoved it into his tracksuit pocket, but he'd want to be careful. He was gaining on Gavin. Gavin reached the fountain about three seconds before me, chucked a right, and went down another path, then immediately charged off to the left. I followed him. I'd say the guy was about three seconds behind.

Gavin had disappeared again, behind one of the trees. I

chose a tree at random, knowing the guy was too close and he'd see me for sure. But I was close to my limit and couldn't do much else. I did at least choose the widest tree I could find, a big pine.

We started another one of those childhood games, except that I don't think this one has a name, just me circling the trunk, and him doing the same, me trying not to meet, him trying very hard to get closely acquainted. It was bluff and double bluff. Rock scissors paper, trying to anticipate what your opponent will do. I edged around to my right, then looked back and realised he was following. I went faster, and nearly ran into him as he came the other way. He had the knife again, but instead of stabbing with it, he tried to grab me with his free hand while pulling back the hand with the knife, so that he'd get velocity. I pulled my hand away, shrank back, then ran to the next tree, round the other side of it. The game continued. This tree was much thinner, so there wasn't much room for bluffing and counterbluffing. It was just me spinning around the tree, trying to keep away from his hands. Then, as he changed direction again, I jumped back and raced to another tree. All the time I was thinking that someone would come along, see what was happening, intervene, save us. This seemed like the quietest park I'd ever been in.

Suddenly, like a wild little creature from the forest, Gavin raced up, kicked for the man's balls, missed, but by a miracle got the knife instead. It spun through the air and bounced on the paved path. But it was too close to the guy for either of us to risk diving at it. Gavin had already taken off again so I followed him, the man losing a couple of seconds as he got his knife back.

I'd only looked into his face for a second, but I thought I would remember it forever. The heavy eyelids, the thin eyebrows, the sharp nose, the badly shaved chin, but above all, the expression of cold hatred or, even worse, of no feeling at all. The total focus on one objective, getting rid of two people, and the sense that, nothing else existed, everything else in the world could take care of itself until this mission was accomplished. He was the ugliest, most horrible human being I had ever seen, but I guess I was biased by the fact that he was trying to kill us. If he'd been collecting for the Salvos I might have felt differently. If he'd been bending over me in hospital administering life-saving antibiotics . . . but no, I felt sickened at the image. That wasn't in his face, kindness wasn't possible for him.

Yet we were in a dance. The sun suddenly spread light over the whole park and over the three of us. There was no real warmth in it, but it felt warmer than the shade we'd been in, the shade of the clouds. And I was plenty hot enough. So we kept dancing. Gavin ran across the stage, from tree to tree, but in the distance. I couldn't work out how he'd got so far ahead. But it looked like he was doubling back towards the road we'd crossed a few minutes before. I hoped so. Any place where we could find humans was OK with me. His instincts, to run and hide, to be furtive, were not working well for us.

Like I said, the sun was out, but we were dancing in the dark. Except that the darkness was the mystery of what was happening now, and what would happen in the future. Who was this man? Why was he doing this? Would we still be alive in one minute, in five minutes, in a couple of hours? The questions were in my head instinctively as I ran through the trees, even though I had no time to formulate them, and certainly no time to think of answers.

I set out after Gavin. He was the leader of this dance. I had a sudden wave of fury that he was deaf. If he'd had hearing, this whole thing could have been resolved ten minutes ago. I would have shouted to him, "Go to the footballers!" But he hadn't figured that out, and because he was deaf he couldn't hear it from me. All I could do was chase him, and at the same time try to keep myself alive.

The man chased Gavin too. I'm not sure if that was a logical thing to do, because I was closer. If he was going to kill Gavin, then the smart thing would be to kill me as well, and it didn't really matter who he got first. But logic had gone out the window. I guess his primary target had always been Gavin. His focus was still on him, and he was gradually adjusting to my being in the picture.

So we both chased the little lonely lost boy. He reached the end of the park and turned left along the footpath for about fifty metres, while I prayed that he would keep going into a more public area, or that a whole crowd of people would suddenly emerge so he could run right into the middle of them. Where was everybody? It was a Saturday morning for God's sake! I guess they were shopping or at sport or sleeping in. They were probably the three choices for the teenagers. Plus it wasn't a very nice day, so that probably kept people away.

To my horror Gavin did what I suppose he could be counted upon to do: the worst thing possible. He turned left again and raced into the thickest patch of trees, the wildest and most remote corner of the park.

By then, the man was ahead of me. We had hit the footpath at different angles, and his had been better than mine, so if I had run the adjacent and the opposite, he had run the hypotenuse. Life's just all triangles. His route brought him out about ten metres ahead of me, onto the concrete. Suddenly I was in the weird position of chasing the guy with the knife, not knowing what I would do if I caught him. I probably would have caught him too. But I didn't dare to. I'm fairly strong, but I didn't think I was strong enough for him. If I tackled him from behind, I might bring him down. He might knock himself out on the footpath. But there was no guarantee of that. He could just as easily roll over on top of me and stab me to death. He could hear me coming, turn, and let me run onto the knife. Even as we ran, I was terrified that he would turn suddenly and I would be onto the knife before I could stop myself. The gap wasn't really as close as that. But if he turned and came at me, it would be a close thing. I would have to go left or right, or turn around, and in doing any of those things I would lose a split second, and he would be so close then that I wouldn't have put a dollar on my own chances.

But he didn't turn around. He wanted Gavin.

The cruellest thing of all happened then. A car came along the road. I thought it was unlucky that there was only one. He was going the same way we were, and I didn't hear him until he was fairly close. By then we were near the point where Gavin had plunged off the path. I had a terrible choice. Should I swerve onto the road and force the car to stop? If I did, by the time the driver got out and I explained what was happening, the man with the knife would have plenty of time to run into the trees, find Gavin, and kill him while I was still out on the road talking.

I could wave my hand to stop the car and at the same time keep running. Or I could ignore the car and concentrate on the man and Gavin.

With only a second to choose I waved my hand and veered, so that I was running along the edge of the gutter, trying to get the best of both worlds.

The car drove right on past. I had a glimpse of the driver, and he was talking on his mobile phone. He didn't even see me.

The man with the knife chucked a hard left, and went into the trees. I had to follow. It was dense in there, pretty really, like a European forest, or so I'd imagine, never having been in one. It was very quiet. The ground was sodden with dead leaves, and I tried to see any possible Gavin tracks, where he might have left the little paved path and headed into the trees.

Again, I didn't know what to do. Should I follow the man? Or should I go off on a different tangent and look for Gavin myself, and gamble that I would find him before the man did? If I followed the man and he found Gavin, he could have killed Gavin by the time I caught up with them. One violent stab to the heart would be all it took. Even if I threw myself on them before he had stabbed, what guarantee did that give? What hope did I have of holding his arm, of wrestling with him, of overpowering him?

Yet it seemed impossibly cold and heartless to leave him and go in a different direction.

As I thought about this, the man did what I had feared while we were running along the street. He turned suddenly and came straight back at me, at full speed, with the knife held in front of him. He wanted to run me through. I had another perfect mental photograph of his face. His eyes were so narrow that they might as well have been closed. His top lip was drawn back from his teeth, which made his teeth look like fangs. I think he was totally focused on killing me, and no other thought was in his mind, except of course the other one that said, "Kill Gavin." I could sympathise with that as there were moments when I'd felt the same way, but this man was taking it too far.

I swerved left, leaving the path. Right away, though, my legs were slowed by wet leaves. There were lots of conifers in this part of the park, but a lot of deciduous trees too, and they had shed leaves big-time. I was panting like crazy by now, and thinking that surely Gavin, even Gavin, could hear my fear, and then I had a quick thought about his terror, the special fear that comes with silence. The feeling he must have, hiding behind a tree and not knowing whether the man might appear beside him with knife raised. For Gavin, there would be no warning. Unless he could smell the man. But surely if he was smelling anything right now it would be my fear. People say cattle and dogs can smell fear. Maybe Gavin could do the same. If so, the smell of me must be filling his nostrils and overpowering his sense of smell, because I was terrified. This whole thing was totally inexplicable to me, and I guess that added to the fear. "May fears always have names . . ." That's from a poem I once read. This fear had a name, it was "man trying to kill us with knife," but I needed more information. Who the hell was he? Had Gavin done something terrible to him? Surely not. I know I whinge about Gavin all the time, and it might give a false impression of him, because the truth is that he's a pretty sweet kid in many ways. He really loves animals, which made the whole thing with Mark's neighbours' cat so hard to understand, but he loves people too, only they don't always give him a chance to show it. If you saw the way he hangs around Homer, and his constant attempts to guess what Homer might want when he's doing any work at my place . . . he gets him tools and holds the other end of things and rides on the back of Homer's bike without a word of complaint (he hates riding on the back of my bike). If I cook something, all he wants is to take pieces outside to feed to Homer, even more than he wants to eat it himself. And of course he never gets any argument from Homer on that one.

No-one in his right mind would want to kill Gavin.

So, this guy wasn't in his right mind.

That face, the pure focus on killing, the light of murder shining from him, the devotion to putting a knife through me and then through Gavin: he had to be totally psycho.

I skidded around a bush and for a moment I was out of his sight. I thought of doing a quick zig but decided on a zag instead. God, it's awful when your entire existence depends on whether you zig or zag. I was half trying to avoid the man and half looking for Gavin. I saw the fountain, closer than I'd expected, and sprinted back towards it, I'm not sure why. It was like that was the centre of the park. I suppose you are automatically drawn to the centre of everything. And maybe Gavin would be drawn to it too.

I got to it and ran around the side. Circumnavigation. Christ there he was. In the middle of the bloody fountain! Trying to be a cherub. Well, he would have needed more than a harp and a pair of wings. It was a pretty impressive fountain, with some old guy, his arms and legs spread out, holding a sceptre or a spear or something. Gavin had wet legs up to his knees, and he was clinging to the old guy like he was clinging to life itself. It actually wasn't a bad hiding place because someone small like Gavin, so long as he saw the man coming, could clamber around from side to side and even wriggle down into a spot deep inside the arms where I think he would have been well and truly hidden. The trouble was that instead of choosing the safe option, Gavin had popped up and was waving to me. He got my attention but he also got the attention of the man with the knife.

Things happened kind of fast from then on. The man hesitated but he was obviously going to wade across the pool. Gavin turned around to look at him. I didn't think Gavin could get down from the fountain and run through the water with his little legs in time to get away from the man. So I used the statue for cover and started into the pool. Freezing cold it was too. I'm surprised it didn't turn me to stone like it had the statue. But I ploughed fast through the water. Jumping in that quickly had given me a lead over the man, although I didn't realise it until I saw him again. He had only just got in and I was nearly at the left leg. Then he saw me and that revved him up a bit. He started coming at me like a hippo in heat. Not that I've ever seen a hippo in heat but I've got an imagination. Gavin had gone up the statue instead of down. I wasn't sure about that. He was pinning a lot of faith in this statue. But I realised that it had possibilities. The guy could chase us all over the statue but if he had to hang on with one hand while he stabbed at us with the other, we might be able to get out of his reach. We just had to be careful not to get trapped at the ends of the arms. And sooner or later someone had to come along. Didn't they?

So I climbed too. But I was surprised at how difficult it was. Wet and slippery, green with slime and moss, and I guess a bit of pigeon poo too. It didn't compare to the cliff on Tailor's Stitch but I struggled to get a grip. I was just above the old man's rock knee when the guy with the knife lunged at me. He grabbed my ankle with a grip that clamped me straight to the spot. I kicked out and his grip slipped a little, so that he had my foot rather than my ankle. I kicked again and my wet shoe came off, taking his hand with it. I climbed then, climbed like a professional fountain climber, motivated by terror, and reached the chest in about two seconds flat. I probably set a record for statue climbing.

The guy wasn't far behind me though. Gavin manoeuvred himself around to the back where I couldn't see him but that was OK as I thought he was fairly safe there. I went higher, up to the neck and then onto the beard, and sat looking down at the guy. I thought I was in a good position. If he came up there I could kick out and knock the knife from his hand, if not dislodge him as well. I glanced at the pocked and lined face of the statue. His blind eyes stared out at the park, at the sky, at nothing. Yet I felt there was wisdom in those eyes. Maybe I could trust my life to him. I peered around the back and could just see Gavin's hand and a part of his arm. I looked down again and saw the man. He was going after Gavin, seemed like, edging around the front of the statue. He was like a blot on the huge old figure, like a moving cancer. I wondered how God could create people like Robyn and Fi and Lee and Homer, who were good people, always trying to do their best, and also create people like this, who wanted only to destroy. And he was dangerously close to doing that. I don't think Gavin realised how close he was, because as I glanced down again Gavin came into view, doing a traverse around the back of the statue until he was directly underneath me.

He looked up and saw me, and I waved to him to come up, and at the same time started going down to help him. I guess I distracted him for that moment and suddenly the man's hand came around the side of the fountain and grabbed Gavin's ankle in the same vice grip that I'd felt only a minute or two before. Gavin looked like he'd got 240 volts up his bum. He arched his back and nearly lost his grip. For a moment he did a different kind of dance to the earlier one through the park; this time he waved his arms and kicked out with his free leg and waggled his head frantically, trying to keep his balance. The guy started dragging at him. I couldn't even see the man, could only see his hand and most of his arm, but I could see the pressure mount as Gavin got drawn away. He wrapped both hands around a knobbly bit of the statue, a kind of tree stump that the giant was leaning against, and he hung on for dear life, literally.

By then I was nearly at his level, descending fast and furious. That practice on the cliff had definitely helped, although I almost slipped and crashed down at one point. Still, on the scale of things that had happened to me, I thought that rated pretty low. I was on a route that took me out of sight of Gavin, pretty much, because I wanted to get around the other side. But he grunted, "Help me, Ellie," in one of the clearest statements I'd ever heard him make. It was a grunt, but one that would have gladdened the heart of any Speech and Drama teacher. Then I heard him scream.

Funny, I thought I'd been going fast before that, but I'd been shuffling along at the pace of a ute with thirty bales of hay. I know that because when I accelerated I could feel the wind through my hair. Almost. I got around the side of that fountain and launched myself onto the guy with a burning ambition: "Kill him."

I think from my limited knowledge that when you fight someone who wants to kill you, you're at a bit of a disadvantage. His motivation is stronger than yours. He wants to save himself from being killed, plus he wants to kill you. You only want to save yourself. But that's not enough. He's got double the drive that you have. So you have to want to kill him too. Otherwise your energy won't be as good. It's horrible but it's true. So I developed in that instant, from nowhere except my war experience, a total focus on ending his life right there in the cold waters of the fountain.

He had stabbed Gavin in the leg, to make him let go of the knobbly bit he was hanging on to, and so the first thing I saw was blood down the man's arm and on the knife and dripping into the water. At the same time he had heard me coming so he was expecting me, and he let go of Gavin and turned to take care of me. At least I'd taken the heat off Gavin for a moment. Now all I had to do was to kill this person. Our pleasant Saturday morning stroll through the park, towards a meeting that should have been wonderful, had turned into this: me intent on an act of homicide, having no greater purpose in life than to kill another human being.

I threw myself on him with such force that I knocked him off the waist of the statue. That was good. He didn't belong there anyway. Neither did I maybe, but he definitely didn't. We rolled down into the water. I no longer felt the cold. Weird. It had no temperature at all. Perhaps he had already stabbed me and killed me and I just didn't know it yet. But if I were dead, my eyes were still working. I see therefore I am. I saw his arm lifting to bring the knife down into me. We had this much in common: we both wanted to be locked together, him so he could kill me, me so I could kill him. I decided attack was the best method of defence and launched myself up at his arm, as fast and hard as I could, but not as fast or hard as I would have liked, seeing he was trying to cling to me. I knocked his hand at the base, next to the wrist. He kept his grip on the knife. I really wanted him to lose that knife. But he was thrown off balance. He swung around sideways and had to change his position quickly to get his balance back. I drove in hard at him and he went down. The trouble was that I went down with him. We were well and truly in the water now. I still didn't feel any heat or coldness but I had a problem with the weight of the water. It slowed me down all the time.

I could see the knife and I had another dive at it but he twisted away and then stabbed up at me, a short sudden attack out of nothing and nowhere. It was clever of him because I had thought he was too off balance. I recoiled but he got me all right, to the left of my belly button. I saw a bit of blood appear, not much, and no pain, just a thudding sensation, like I'd been punched there, and not even very hard. But it was shocking, really shocking. I gasped for breath, then realised I had to focus on what I was doing, killing him. I couldn't allow other thoughts or feelings. I kicked at the knife, knowing I wouldn't connect but just to give him something to think about, and at the same time with my right hand punched in at his face. I didn't connect with either my foot or my hand but already I'd followed that up by diving in on top of him. Now I had some advantage. He was quite light and I'm heavy enough and he was under water. Water that had my blood trailing through it.

I might have knocked his head on the bottom of the pool. I wasn't sure about that. Not very hard anyway. Not as hard as I would have liked.

The knife arm was on its way around again, strong and vicious. I leant sideways to push it away and this time tried to bang his head on the bottom. It didn't work. I felt like the knife had made contact again, but I didn't know exactly where and I didn't know how far it had penetrated. I decided to strangle him and drown him at the same time. I got my hands around his throat and leant forward, pushing down on him to make sure he couldn't get up. Out of the corner of my eye I saw his arm lifting. I realised this wasn't going to work, that he would be able to stab me many times before I could drive the life out of his body.

Until the knife went flying. Its silver shape spun through the air like a metal boomerang. A boomerang that wouldn't be . . . yeah, well, the "delete cliché" button won't let me finish that sentence. But Gavin had arrived. The pocket commando, splattered with his own blood, had smashed the guys hand with something, I didn't know what, couldn't see, and now I was free to concentrate on killing him. God these words, they flow so easily out of my brain but I shut off, fiercely and totally, the awareness of what they mean, otherwise I could never write them. I used my weight on his body and my arms around his neck to stop him breathing ever again. He started to kick and convulse. The force of him was frightening and I didn't know if I'd be able to hold him down, although Gavin piled in on top of me then and the extra weight did help.

The man suddenly went limp and I almost relaxed but something told me it was a trick. He still felt too tense. I made my grip even stronger, which was easier now that he had stopped fighting. God it was awful. I feel sick as I remember his throat, his neck. There was bone in it, but mostly it felt like muscle, although I don't think that can be right. And I'm never going to ask a science teacher. He had quite a scrawny neck and the first part was just all fleshy, or rather like the wattles under a turkey neck. Then there was the part that felt like muscle and then the bone was way back there somewhere. That was the part I was trying to reach. I pressed even tighter, wanting to have nothing but bone in my hands. And yeah Homer, go ahead and laugh at that but I'm not changing it.

I was right about the bluffing because suddenly he came back to life again and now he was desperate. He went crazy on me, like a fighting fish. Or a crocodile. Don't know, haven't caught one of those lately. He even got his head out of the water for a moment, but I'm sure he didn't get any air as my grip was too strong. His face was horrible, grey, and his eyes were staring at me and for the first time they were wide open but he didn't see me or anything else.

I got him under again and this time he went limp for real. I could feel the difference right away. I still didn't let go. I figured if I did, his reflexes would take over and breathe for him. He'd come back to life. I didn't want that. Then the cop grabbed me from behind and pulled me away.

CHAPTER 19

SOMEONE HAD SEEN US AT LAST AND CALLED THE POLICE. The cop had to work hard to get my hands off the guy's throat though. I wanted to let go, in one part of my mind anyway, but I guess another part was pretty committed to killing him. The cop kept yelling, "Relax! Relax your hands!" at me but it's a paradox to yell "Relax" at someone. It wasn't till Gavin shook me and patted my hands that I finally disconnected. By then they'd half dragged me and the man out of the pool. I found myself stretched across the little wall around it. The stone was digging into my back. They dragged the guy a bit further, till he was on the footpath, on his back, and then they went to work on him. Boy did they work. They were efficient too. They'd obviously done it before. Like, a thousand times. One cop, the guy, was at his mouth pumping away into that through a little black plastic thing. The other, the woman, went for the ribs. I crawled further out of the pool, so I could get away from the uncomfortable wall. It had taken me that long to notice how uncomfortable it was. My senses were starting to work and I could hear two separate lots of sirens, coming from different directions. I half sat, half lay on the ground watching the cops trying to undo what I had done. It was strange, they were putting so much effort into it, and just a minute earlier I had been putting so much effort into killing him.

The guy suddenly convulsed and twisted to one side, away from me, thank God, and started vomiting. I could hear the kind of retching you get outside a Wirrawee B&S as early as nine p.m. By eleven o'clock you can hear it inside.

The cop doing the heart massage climbed off the guy, wiping her hands on her trousers and looking fairly disgusted. I decided I wouldn't become a police officer. The guy twisted over further onto his hands and knees, spewing out water and other stuff. In the distance I saw an ambulance officer, then another one, running towards us. I didn't know why they hadn't driven right up to the fountain. The police had, well nearly.

Then the cold hit me. Like a blizzard inside and out. I actually gave a half-scream with the impact of it. I was incurably cold. I would never get warm, could never get warm. I had iced up inside. And no-one cared. This was the worst cold of all. The cops were holding the guy on the ground, trying to get him into a better position. The ambulance officers were heading straight for him. I didn't exist. The guy who wanted to end my existence was the star of the show. Everything was for him.

Then Gavin, wet and slimy and dripping, wrapped himself around me and folded himself into me and we sat together and rocked and hugged and somehow warmed each other. Two colds make a warm sometimes. It's that old body heat. Works every time. I felt very tired and could have fallen asleep on the spot. An ambo finally came over to us. I hadn't seen her arrive. She was a blonde girl with so many curls I didn't know how her cap stayed on her head.

She asked us how we were and if we had any injuries. Well, she probably regretted asking that question.

Suddenly she called to her partner for back-up and a second later there was a stationwagon right at the fountain, with ambulance markings all over it and two more ambos who I hadn't seen before and a couple of stretchers on wheels and Gavin and I were covered by blankets. He was already in the back of an ambulance and I was being wheeled to it. I hadn't seen that ambulance either. I was confused that they had all got there in one second but I think I was getting a bit confused about everything. It's possible that I wasn't entirely conscious for a while there.

The blankets started to work and I felt that I could let go of the last of my coldness. I did so, gradually, and lay back and opened my eyes. The sky was grey but becoming blue in the distance. A grey-white cloud was just above us and if I craned my head I could see a bank of clouds behind me. I didn't know which way the weather was heading. Sometimes you do need a weatherman. I asked the blonde curly-haired ambo where the wind was from but she just smiled at me and said, "Now why would you want to know that?"

"Just a country girl I guess," I said.

"Well I don't think there is much wind at the moment," she said, and they started putting my stretcher up into the back of the ambulance.

"Are you going to use the siren?"

"Everyone always wants to know that," she said. "What do you think, Col, will we need the siren for these two?"

"Might give it a burl if we run into a bit of traffic," he said. "Don't want to be late for smoko, do we?"

"Gavin's deaf," I said, and closed my eyes.

"Oh is he?" I heard the blonde girl say. "Col, the little boy's deaf."

"Uh, that would explain it then," Col said. I didn't know what it explained but I guess they'd tried to have a conversation with Gavin.

"How is he?" I asked.

"We think you're both going to be fine." But I had the feeling they said that to everyone. Like what else are they going to say: "We expect you to be dead by the next intersection"?

The ambulance began to move and I opened my eyes again. She was sitting between Gavin and me so I figured Col was driving. She gave me another of her extremely nice smiles. "You've both got penetrating injuries but they don't look too bad. And you're both in shock."

"Is that all?" I yawned. I couldn't get used to this idea that when you were in the middle of a terrible fight the police arrived and fixed it up for you. And when you got injured, ambulances came and they wrapped you in blankets and took you to hospital. Where were they when the war was on?

The blonde girl said, "There might be an issue with that terrible water in the fountain getting into your wounds. I'm guessing the doctor'll have a look at that. It's not the healthiest place to take a bath when you've been stabbed!"

"No."

I reached for Gavin's hand but couldn't find it.

"What are you looking for?" the girl asked. Well, she wasn't really a girl of course.

"Gavin's hand," I said.

233

She connected us up. He immediately gave my hand a big squeeze which made my eyes water (a) because we were friends (b) because he was still alive and (c) because it made me think the ambo girl hadn't been lying to me and he probably was going to be all right.

I didn't think I could cope with any more deaths of anyone even remotely close to me. These days I was perfectly capable of sobbing over the death of a heifer or someone's pet guinea-pig, or a dead rabbit on the road.

OK, I'm lying about the rabbit.

At the hospital we weren't given nearly as much attention or treated like royalty the way the ambos had looked after us. A doctor checked us and sent us both to X-ray but she said our wounds weren't life-threatening. She did give us a blast of antibiotics in a big needle—well, she got a nurse to give us a blast of antibiotics in a big needle—and then we waited in a corridor for ages for the X-rays.

When we came out a cop was there, in uniform. He said he'd been sent to look after us. It didn't occur to me till we were back in the main Emergency section that he might have been sent to stop us escaping, until the nurse who was washing grazes on my arm with disinfectant said, "What have you two been up to?"

She asked in that quiet voice, the one that means, "Just between you and me."

Of course I had been busting to ask Gavin what the hell had been going on. I'd been wanting to ask him from the moment the whole thing started, but I'd had no hope. And even now it was impossible. In the corridor we'd been twenty metres apart and now he was on the opposite side of the room. What had we been up to? Just trying to save our lives from a complete maniac who wanted to kill us. Was that so bad? But it wasn't a random attack. The guy knew Gavin and wanted to take him out. He must have had some reason.

So all I could say was the old favourite: "I don't know."

Then she asked: "Are you in a gang?"

"What?"

I nearly choked on the word. I didn't know whether to laugh or cry or call for a psychiatrist. For her. That's when I realised the cop might be there to stop us tying our sheets together, end to end, and climbing out the window. Good grief! I didn't expect medals and the keys to the city. That was one of my dad's favourite sayings: "I'm not asking for a medal and the keys to the city but it would be nice to get a little cooperation once in a while."

I wasn't asking for a parade but it would have been nice for someone to say, "Hey girl, you saved a couple of lives today, even if one of them was your own."

"No, I'm not in a gang," I said.

Nothing much else happened for at least two hours. The cop made himself right at home and was soon getting coffees for himself and the nurses. I was "nil by mouth" so no food or drink for me. I dozed quite a bit, then they came and took the "nil by mouth" sign away and ten minutes later I got sandwiches and cordial. I suddenly realised how hungry I was and gobbled the whole lot, even if the sandwiches were mostly white bread with occasional traces of chicken and wisps of lettuce. And the cordial tasted like they'd held a glass of water in front of the cordial bottle for five seconds and then taken it away again. I like my cordial strong.

A different doctor arrived and started stitching me up. He was a chatty guy who looked like he came from India or Pakistan and who spoke in this nice musical voice. He said I was fine, the knife had missed my vital organs, I'd been very lucky, I could go home but I had to take antibiotics because they told him I'd been in water that was probably full of dangerous organisms.

He had me roll over and he put a couple of stitches in another wound. I knew something on my back hurt but didn't realise it was a second stab wound. I hadn't properly registered that the guy had stabbed me twice—I'd thought the pain was from another graze.

Gavin was a bit more complicated. While I lay there having a snooze no-one told me that he'd been wheeled away for an operation. I went into total panic when I heard a nurse say something about "the deaf boy who's gone to surgery," surprising myself by how hysterical I got. It's embarrassing, but they had to hold me down and then the nurse hit me with another needle and ten seconds later, out I went.

I woke up in a room with a painting of gum trees and a billabong, and there was Lee, sitting next to the bed. "Yikes, how long have I been here?" I asked him. Then I remembered about Gavin.

"It's about four o'clock, I think," he said, putting down a copy of the *Bulletin* that looked like it was years old. "And don't worry, Gavin's fine. He had some muscle damage and he'll be sore for a while and he's gonna need a bit of physio. That's the full story."

"Where is he?"

"Just along the corridor. He's in 2210 and this is 2220."

"Can I see him?"

"I don't know. Probably. They let me have a look at him but he was asleep. He had a general anaesthetic. But if you can persuade the nurses, you should be able to waddle along and say hello."

"What the hell happened? Who is the guy? What was it all about?"

Lee looked surprised. "I was going to ask you that. I don't know anything, and no-one'll tell me anything. When I got here they had a cop guarding you but he got a message about an hour ago to say that you probably weren't on the ten most wanted, so he packed up and left. That's how I got this magazine."

"I'm very happy for you."

"Yeah, except he's already done the crossword."

"How did you know we were here?"

"You put me down as next-of-kin."

"Oh did I? I don't remember that."

"So what did happen? I thought I was sending you off for a nice walk followed by a heart-warming reunion for Gavin. Next thing I know I get a message to say some guy tried to kill you both. Is this to do with Liberation? Or the war?"

"I don't think so." I shook my head, trying to work it out. My head was a bit fuzzy, because of the injection I suppose. "No, I'm sure it's nothing to do with that. The guy knew Gavin. He was waiting for him."

I slipped out of bed, determined to clear this up once and for all. Bugger Gavin having a general anaesthetic and being asleep. He could just wake up and tell me what on earth was going on.

I felt a bit woozy but not too bad. Lee grabbed me as I grabbed for the end of the bed but I was OK again a moment later. "Sheez, what was in that needle?" I said.

Off we set, down the corridor. A nurse was at the desk halfway between my room and Gavin's. She looked at me suspiciously. "Now where do you think you might be off to on this fine Saturday afternoon?"

I grinned at her. "I just want to see how my partner in crime's going."

"Oh do you now? Well you can turn around and go right back to bed. You had enough Midazolam for a small elephant, so you can wait a bit longer before you go serenading along the corridors."

"I only want to ask him a question," I begged.

"You know I read your book about the war," she said.

"Oh you did?" The first one had been published but the rest were home in a wardrobe. It hadn't sold enough to satisfy the publisher, so they wouldn't take the others. It seemed to me that quite a lot of people knew about the book but not so many had actually read it. Maybe it was the title. I thought *The War from Hell* was quite cute but I guess people who didn't know Tailor's Stitch and Hell didn't get the joke until they were reading the book, and it was a bit late by then.

I didn't care all that much. I just like writing stuff down. It's become a habit, and now I do it for my own sake, instead of trying to get it published.

"Never thought I'd meet you," the nurse said. "It wasn't a bad book. I made my boyfriend read it too. If it's one question, OK, but don't wake him up. If he's asleep just let him be."

I took a moment to realise she was giving me permission to talk to Gavin.

"OK, cool, thanks. And thanks for buying the book."

"I didn't buy it, I got it from the library."

"You should buy a copy," Lee said loyally.

She laughed. "Maybe I will now that I've met you. You're that boy whose family owned the restaurant, right?"

"Yeah, he's Lee," I called back over my shoulder. Like he couldn't speak for himself.

I was already halfway to Gavin's room. It would have been nice to sit down and have a long chat about literature but there were more important things to worry about.

Lee caught up with me as I got to the door. I sure was moving slowly. That drug was a ripper. Everything felt normal enough but it had taken me a long time to travel a short distance. Story of my life.

I felt a tremendous surf inside me when I looked at Gavin. I was getting used to this feeling. It happened every now and then. I could almost hear the waves pounding. It was the fear of his getting hurt, it was the desire to protect him, it was the not wanting to let him down, it was love. Or else it was just hormonal, maternal stuff, which probably amounts to the same thing.

He opened one eye and looked at me. Then he opened the other. He had that stern look he gets sometimes. We just gazed at each other. With Gavin you gotta read the signals. If you get them wrong, then wham, he'll smack you in the face and take off, he'll head for the hills. Not literally. Well, usually not literally.

OK, I got the message, this was not the time for stupid girly emotional stuff like, "Thank God you're all right," or,

"I thought I was going to die when I saw the guy grab you, I actually felt death break out inside me," or, "You mean more to me than any other human being in the whole world."

This was apparently not the time for any of that rubbish. No more hugs for the time being.

"Gavin, what the hell was that all about?"

"He's my stepdad."

I gasped, and so did Lee, behind me. I toddled in a bit further.

"So I can understand why anyone connected with you would want to kill you but was there any particular . . . ?"

He couldn't lip-read all that. Too drowsy and drugged up, like me. This was the drugged leading the drugged. He frowned and did what he normally does in those situations—guessed what I was asking. I knew that sequence of his facial expressions so well.

So he answered what he thought I was asking. And got it right, as he usually does.

"He murdered my mum."

EPILOGUE

Seemed like Gavin was the only witness. Like the Red Cross said: his mum had been murdered at the very start of the war. What they got wrong was the person or people who'd done it. They all assumed it was enemy soldiers. I don't know who found her body, maybe one of those work teams I'd had a few encounters with myself, the people who'd been drafted to go out into shops and houses to clean up after the invasion. Maybe enemy soldiers had found her body and given it to people in a prison camp to bury or cremate.

But from then on, everyone, right through to the Red Cross, had blamed the soldiers.

Only Gavin knew the truth. He had seen his mum struck down from behind as she loaded the car. Over the rest of the weekend he told me about it and enacted it, as he does. She had decided to get out of the relationship, to Gavin's relief. She'd taken Rosie to a friend's place, along with some suitcases, then come back to the flat to get another load. Gavin and she were carrying stuff down to the car and were in the garage when the man arrived home. He hit her with a car jack, then when she fell, hit her again and again. Then he locked Gavin in the apartment. When Gavin escaped, hours later, he ran straight into the invasion.

All this time Gavin had carried his secret knowledge, all this time the fear and sickness of it had churned away inside him. He didn't dare tell anyone. He didn't want to bring the man back. He didn't want an enquiry. Like they say, you're as sick as your secrets, and his secret was a pretty poisonous one.

Funny I thought, Gavin and I were both the O word, the word I hated and couldn't say, and even worse, three out of four of our parents had been murdered. It only occurred to me as I was writing this. What are the odds? I mean, you'd have to say we were unlucky.

We had the reunion, or at least I should say Gavin and Rosie did. It was a funny experience. She was a bright little kid, feisty as hell, with fire in her eyes. The Russells seemed really nice. They were so shocked by what had happened at their place the day before. They'd seen the guy around, everyone knew him, Ken Manning was his name. He worked at the bottle shop part-time, and hung around the TAB. He must have heard on the grapevine that Gavin was coming home. Everyone had thought Gavin was dead, so it would have been a shock to him.

Anyway, Rosie opened the door when we went back the next day. She yelled to her folks, "He's here." Then she just stood there and said, "Hi Gavin."

"Hi Rosie."

"Do you wanna come in?"

"OK."

"Well take your shoes off then, you got mud all over them."

It was like that for about half an hour. She bossed him around and he took it without a murmur. Maybe it was the effect of the anaesthetic still, or the painkillers, or simply the shock of yesterday. But I don't think so.

When Mrs Russell suggested Rosie show Gavin her room and her stuff she ignored her and when she suggested it a second time Rosie just said, "No way." But after a while they drifted into the back yard and next time I looked they were on the trampoline and they seemed to be really talking. Gavin was going through another of his famous performances and she was lying back and watching intently and laughing. I think he was showing off about what he'd done during the war, but I figured he was entitled to show off a bit. And isn't that what little sisters are for? I haven't been one and I haven't got one so I wouldn't know.

Mrs Russell and I agreed we'd take them somewhere together next time and maybe Rosie could come and stay on the farm when they got to know each other a bit again. I think she really meant it, and I did. I do. I want Gavin to have whatever can be salvaged out of life for him, and Rosie is, as far as I know, his only relative.

Back we went to Lee's. We had to stay in the city an extra day for Gavin to go to Outpatients at the hospital and for both of us to have more interviews with the police. We'd had a long one already, plus they'd rung up and I'd relayed a couple of questions to Gavin about where he'd lived before the war. They were going to go and do DNA stuff in the garage I think.

For dinner Lee gave us a special treat, KFC for the entree and Maccas cheeseburgers for the main course. I just looked at him. "And your parents ran a restaurant," I said.

He shrugged. "My dad liked McDonald's."

Honestly.

Then the phone rang. He answered it and after a while it occurred to me that he hadn't actually said anything.

He was listening though. A kind of tension came over the room and everyone stopped eating, even Intira. Pang made a face.

"What is it?" I asked her.

She shrugged, exactly the way Lee does. "Trouble," was all she would say.

Lee hung up. He looked at me. "That was the Scarlet Pimple," he said softly.

"And?" I felt the knot in my stomach suddenly get pulled so tight I could hardly breathe.

"There's a problem over the border that we could maybe help with."

"And?"

He did the shrug thing again and sat down, picking up the other half of his cheeseburger. "No hurry. It won't be till the night after next."

"So what is it?"

"Oh nothing, you wouldn't be interested. I know you don't want to do any of that stuff any more."

"Lee! Don't play those games with me."

"Oh, so you would be interested?"

"Are they going to buy me a new motorbike?"

"It's being delivered tomorrow."

"Seriously?"

"Absolutely. The Pimple said to tell you sorry it took so long. It's a Polaris."

"Wow." I beamed at Gavin. "We're getting a new quaddie."

Then I realised. I was just getting up to fetch a cloth to clean Intira. "Wait a minute. The new motorbike is for the mission isn't it? That's why they've suddenly supplied it. So we can use it to go out and put ourselves in mortal danger. That's no better than a bribe."

Shrug.

"So are you going?"

"Wouldn't mind. Haven't got much on this week."

"Honestly Lee. You're incurable." I shook my head.

"Well do you wanna come?"

I didn't like to ask him if Jeremy was going but I could bet he was. After all, I was fairly sure Jeremy was the Scarlet Pimple. "Will I get a free tank of petrol with the bike?"

"That might be possible."

"What would we have to do?"

Sometimes I think I'm the one who's incurable.

Ellie's story isn't over.
Here's a sneak peek at

Circle of Flight
The Ellie Chronicles #3

YOU COME UP the driveway. You're late, but you knew you were going to be. That's why you took the ute to school this morning. And told Gavin to catch the bus. He'll have been back for two hours now. On his own. But you're not stupid. And he's not stupid. You both know what to do. He's been good about it. He takes the precautions. When he gets off the bus he doesn't just jump on the new four-wheeler and herb straight on up to the homestead.

He knows. And so do you. You detour into the bush, find a spot where you've got a good view of the house. You take a look. You watch for hostile visitors, enemy soldiers, an ambush. Even if the house looks OK, you still take care. You approach from a different direction each time. You use your eyes. If it's Gavin, you can't use your ears. But you use something else, better still. Your instinct. Your sixth sense.

Gavin knows. He knows that if there's any sign of trouble, there's a bolthole the two of you have organised, down near the lagoon.

He knows that if you're there on your own you go out to feed the chooks and dogs, and check the stock, but you're careful about it. Change your pattern all the time. Never leave by the same door twice running. Lock the house behind you. Take the rifle.

And you do the same things yourself. Today for example, you don't go in the main gate. You use the bush gate into the Parklands paddock. You stop behind a couple of trees, get out and take a good look at the house from across the creek. You notice that everything looks fine. Washing on the line, Polaris in the machinery shed, axe stuck in the chopping block where you were splitting wood last night.

Marmie's still in her run. That's a bit unusual. Normally Gavin'd let her out. He loves that little dog.

Then you see it. One little thing is wrong. The front door's wide open. Your heart starts hammering. You get back in the ute. You take off with a clumsy foot dance involving the clutch and the accelerator. You come at the bridge at a bad angle. The bridge is just a couple of logs with planks laid across them, and no railing. You think for a moment that you're going to roll off it, onto the rocks, into the water. Now your stomach is lurching. But you make it across the bridge.

You forget about security. That bloody Gavin. If he's just been careless . . . but what are you thinking? You want him to have been careless. Careless leaves the other option a trillion k's behind. Oh Gavin, please be careless. You can have both the Kit-Kats after tea tonight if you've been careless.

You jam on the brakes and stop the ute right in front of the house. You throw open the car door and jump out. Not for the first time you run into a building that could be full of guns, with death waiting for you. You don't even think of that until you're crossing the threshold. It seems like an abstract thought, interesting to a scientist perhaps.

A few metres down the corridor you tread on something. In fact you nearly wrench your ankle. You look down. It's a spare magazine for a rifle. It looks to be full, loaded with bullets.

Now it's too late to do anything else, so you go on.

You already know what you're going to find. Underneath the fear and horror and panic there's a cold realisation, that Gavin's body will be somewhere in the house. You can picture what those bullets will have done to his little body. You've seen their effect on adult bodies, the men in the barracks, your mother in the kitchen. You go first to his bedroom. His school uniform is there. God, for once he actually changed out of his uniform when he got home. It's still on the floor, and the shirt's all scrunched up, but for Gavin that's what you expect. The rule is that he changes every afternoon, as soon as he gets home. He actually does it about once a week. His Redbacks aren't there, but he could have left them on the veranda, like he's meant to do but never does. There's no sign of a struggle, but most importantly, there's no sign of the horror that you know awaits you somewhere. The open front door and the magazine full of bullets have told you everything. You run back to the kitchen. Nothing there either, except memories, terrible vivid images.

You go to the TV room. And you see everything, as though you were there when it happened. The chair on its back. Gavin's favourite chair. The cushions scattered. The television with a hole smashed through it. Sharp glass fragments, milky white, everywhere. It'll take hours to vacuum every last piece. No Redbacks, but one of his ug boots, the short ones that come up just past the ankle, lying on the floor, between the sofa and the door.